Praise for

"Glen Cook single-handedly something a lot of people didn't notice, and maybe still don't. Reading his stuff is like reading Vietnam War fiction on Peyote."
—Steven Erikson, author of the Malazan Book of the Fallen series

"Over the past 25 years, Cook has carved out a place for himself among the preeminent fantasy writers of his generation. . . . His work is unrelentingly real, complex, and honest. The sense of place that permeates his narrative and characters gives his 'fantasies' more gravitas and grit than most fictions set in the here-and-now."
—*New York Times* bestselling author Jeff VanderMeer

"A master realist of the imagination."
—*Locus*

"Glen writes a mean book."
—Jim Butcher, author of The Dresden Files

"These books, like so many of Cook's series, are epic in scale but intimate in focus . . . Cook is a brilliant writer."
—*The Green Man Review*, on *A Fortress in Shadow*

"One of the defining fantasy series ever written. Glen Cook's writing is a great flood that washes fantasy tropes and cliché's away and in their place we are given three novels that make us reflect on what it means to be human. . . . On more than one occasion I found chills running down my spine. Words don't do these novels justice."
—*The Ostentatious Ogre* on *A Cruel Wind*

"Glen Cook is the author of some of my hands-down favorite books. I hold out his Black Company series as arguably the best military fantasy ever written. The early Garrett books set a standard for the blending of fantasy and hardboiled fiction."
—*Black Gate*

"One of Cook's strongest storytelling traits shines through, his ability to cast no judgment and show the opposing sides of a conflict with honesty, empathy, and resonance."
— *SFFWorld*, on *A Fortress in Shadow*

"Glen Cook is a rare beast of a writer — he can vacillate between military fantasy, space opera, epic fantasy, mystery, and science fantasy with great ease. His writing is often marked by a purity; that he is depicting life in its most real sense, from the thoughts in a character's mind to the wind rushing across his or her face."
— Rob H. Bedford, *sffworld.com*, on *Darkwar*

"Cook's talent for combining gritty realism and high fantasy provides a singular edge."
— *Library Journal*, on *Water Sleeps*

"Cook provides a rich world of assorted races, cultures, and religions; his characters combine the mythic or exotic with the realistic, engaging in absorbing alliances, enmities, and double-crosses."
— *Publishers Weekly*, on *Bleak Seasons*

"New and innovative. [Cook] blends the urban, intimate, slightly seedy tradition of sword & sorcery with the pastoral, epic, expansive tradition of heroic fantasy . . . this is the book that injected a shot of realism into the genre, and helped steer it on the course towards modern so-called "gritty" fantasy."
— *Strange Horizons*, on *Chronicles of the Black Company*

"Glen Cook changed the face of the fantasy genre forever . . . and for the better."
— *Fantasy Book Review*, on *The Black Company*

"There is a way to channel the frustrations of a people,
a way of creating work and concerted effort
for a common end — WAR!"
— from *Ritual War*, published 2008

Books by Glen Cook:

The Heirs of Babylon
The Swordbearer
A Matter of Time
The Dragon Never Sleeps
The Tower of Fear
Sung in Blood

Dread Empire

A Cruel Wind (Omnibus):
    A Shadow of All Night Falling
    October's Baby
    All Darkness Met
A Fortress in Shadow (Omnibus):
    The Fire in His Hands
    With Mercy Toward None
Wrath of Kings (Omnibus):
    Reap the East Wind
    An Ill Fate Marshalling
    A Path to Coldness of Heart
An Empire Unacquainted with
    Defeat

The Starfishers Trilogy (Omnibus):
    Shadowline
    Starfishers
    Stars' End

Passage at Arms

Darkwar

Doomstalker
Warlock
Ceremony

The Black Company

The Black Company
Shadows Linger
The White Rose
The Silver Spike
Shadow Games
Dreams of Steel
Bleak Seasons
She Is the Darkness
Water Sleeps
Soldiers Live
Port of Shadows

The Garrett Files

Sweet Silver Blues
Bitter Gold Hearts
Cold Copper Tears
Old Tin Sorrows
Dread Brass Shadows
Red Iron Nights
Deadly Quicksilver Lies
Petty Pewter Gods
Faded Steel Heat
Angry Lead Skies
Whispering Nickel Idols
Cruel Zinc Melodies
Gilded Latten Bones
Wicked Bronze Ambition

Instrumentalities of the Night

The Tyranny of the Night
Lord of the Silent Kingdom
Surrender to the Will of the Night
Working Gods' Mischief

THE HEIRS OF BABYLON

GLEN COOK

NIGHT SHADE BOOKS — NEW YORK

Night Shade books may be purchased in bulk at special discounts for sales promotion, corporate gifts, fund-raising, or educational purposes. Special editions can also be created to specifications. For details, contact the Special Sales Department, Night Shade Books, 307 West 36th Street, 11th Floor, New York, NY 10018 or info@skyhorsepublishing.com.

Night Shade Books® is a registered trademark of Skyhorse Publishing, Inc.®, a Delaware corporation.

Visit our website at www.nightshadebooks.com.

10 9 8 7 6 5 4 3 2 1

Library of Congress Cataloging-in-Publication Data

Names: Cook, Glen, author.
Title: The heirs of babylon / Glen Cook.
Description: First Night Shade Books edition. | New York : Night Shade Books, 2019.
Identifiers: LCCN 2018016046 | ISBN 9781597809627 (pbk. : alk. paper)
Subjects: | GSAFD: Fantasy fiction. | Science fiction.
Classification: LCC PS3553.O5536 H45 2019 | DDC 813/.54--dc23
LC record available at https://lccn.loc.gov/2018016046

Cover illustration by Raymond Swanland
Cover design by Claudia Noble

Printed in the United States of America

For Carol, new wife; for Mrs. Harmon,
my fourth-grade teacher (because we both turned
out better than that snotty kid expected);
and especially for the Kurt Rankes of every name
and color and time who followed a Cause
to an unremembered Armageddon—

—Peace

FOREWORD

So there I was ...

It was 1968. A fiercely significant year: the worst fighting in Viet Nam, serious social insanity going on here at home. But I missed all that. I was at work.

Yes. Work. 11 ½ hours a day, every day. I had three days off in '68: Easter, July 4th, and Christmas. I could have raked in triple time those three days if I'd wanted—because it was 1968 and my employer manufactured projectiles for the 105mm howitzer.

Mine was a killer job. I just had to answer the phone. If it rang, as it might do three, four, even five times in a week, I would grab a brush and a bucket of red paint and head for the factory floor. I would use the paint to mark up any steel billets too damaged to be forged. It might take a whole hour to do a thorough job. So, while I waited on the phone, I read. A lot. Some of that stuff was awful, but it had gotten published. I decided I could do better.

Backstory: I first wrote during a long illness while I was in seventh grade. A Civil War western story. An aliens intervene in Ramses II's war with the Hittites story. An Adam and Eve story. All long lost. During high school I did stories published in *Rose Leaves*, the school "literary journal." Also lost. In college, sometimes I wrote stories as a way of faking papers. That worked well.

My high school aptitude test said that I should become a writer or a librarian.

In 1963, headed for duty aboard *USS Moale* (the ship featured in *Babylon*), while in the Newport, Rhode Island Greyhound station awaiting a ride to the pier, I had my first encounter with modern fantasy. I picked up a copy of *Fantastic* magazine, which featured "Bazaar of the Bizarre" by Fritz Leiber. That showed me what I wanted to write in the far someday when I would have time for that.

Six years later, Fritz would be my instructor at the 1969 Clarion Writers' Workshop and, not long afterward, both my mentor and, for a month, my roommate.

So, back to the factory. 1968 saw my decision to write with intent to publish. 1969 saw me apply to and be stunned to be accepted at Clarion State. General Motors generously granted me a six-week educational leave that I spent in Paradise, learning from serious pros.

In addition to the instructors, Clarion chief Robin Scott Wilson invited in visiting lecturers from the editing and publishing world. One such was David Hartwell, at that time an intern just setting foot on the path to becoming a giant of editing. David would have some direct or indirect influence on the purchase and publication of almost all of my first few dozen books. At that Clarion, David responded favorably to a post-apocalyptic story of mine, suggesting that I try writing a novel based upon the premise. If I could manage that, I should send it to his attention at New American Library.

I wrote the book, entitled: *Fallen, Fallen is Babylon* (the second verse of a chapter in the biblical *Book of Revelation*). It was accepted, pending changes suitable to senior editor Ellen Asher. Ellen, like David, would have a sustained positive impact on my career for decades as editor of the Science Fiction Book Club. The most memorable change she asked for was a change of title to *The Heirs of Babylon*.

Babylon was my first published novel and my first translated novel, into Brazilian Portuguese. I've never seen a copy of that.

Babylon is dedicated to my fourth-grade teacher. Mrs. Harmon was, after my parents, one of the two most powerful influences on my early life, the other being town librarian Jennie Menkinnen. In an age when Asperger's hadn't yet been invented, Mrs. Harmon had the genius to take a kid who was always in trouble, but never understood why, and manage to channel his OCD and lack of impulse control into an engagement with literature that ameliorated the greater part of his disorder and made it possible for him to survive to produce a body of work despite himself.

So now that kid has become an old, old man, haunted by recollections of stupid, rotten, sometimes just plain foul things done in the long ago, but at least now aware of why; shining proud of his children and grandchildren; pleased that not only has he had a long career, but it would appear that he has been a significant influence on several important writers who came up after him.

I hope you will enjoy this first effort, or at least exercise patience with a young writer's foibles.

Glen Cook
St. Louis, MO
13 May 2018

THE HEIRS OF
BABYL⊙N

Fallen, fallen is Babylon the great!
It has become a dwelling place of demons,
a haunt of every foul spirit,
a haunt of every foul and hateful bird;
for all nations have drank the wine of her impure
    passion,
and the kings of the earth have committed
    fornication with her,
and the merchants of the earth have grown rich
    with the wealth of her wantonness.

— Revelation 18:2, 3

ONE

A restless couple sat on a blanket on a twisted, rusted girder, holding hands sadly, occasionally glancing toward the ancient ship at the pier in the distance, silent love islanded in a forest of broken steel madness. The girl moved nervously, stared through the bones of the shipyard, hating the ship that would take her Kurt away—*Jäger*, a gray steel dragon specially evolved for the dealing of death, crouched, waiting beside the *Hoch-und-Deutschmeister* pier. Her hand tightened on his. She lifted it, rubbed her cheek against his knuckles, kissed them, and moved closer. He slipped his arm around her, lightly. Hers passed around his waist. The cool, moist fingers of their free hands entwined in her lap.

They were Kurt and Karen Ranke, married eleven months, two weeks, and three days, and about to be

parted by the warship—perhaps permanently. Both were tall
and leanly muscular, blond, blue-eyed, almost stereotypically
Aryan, alike as brother and sister, yet related only through marriage. Their sadness was for the War, on again.

A snatch of song momentarily haunted the ruins to their left.
They turned. A hundred meters distant, beside the shallow, scum-
topped water-corpse of the Kiel Canal, sailors made their ways
toward the destroyer; men without attachments, accompanied by
no women. One sang a bawdy verse. The others laughed.

"Hans and his deck apes," Kurt murmured. "Almost happy
because we're pulling out."

Karen leaned her head against his shoulder, said nothing.
Through narrowed eyes she searched the torn iron fingers surrounding them. Kurt ignored the question, unspoken, in her
eyes. He understood the need to create more such ruin no better
than she.

A whistle shrieked at the pier, a foghorn bellowed—*Jäger*
testing.

The warship had come through sea trials well, like a
great-grandmother proving capable of the marathon. Her officers and men had once been delighted as children with a new
toy. But their joy was fading. The toy was ready for the War, for
the Last of All Battles, as the Political Office had it. A pale specter on a far horizon dampened all enthusiasms. The games were
over, and death lay in ambush on a distant sea.

Kurt knew Karen doubted the Political Office, and bore a
grudge against the destroyer. Already the two were responsible
for a dozen training separations. Her darkest fear, and his, was
that this one might be permanent.

Karen's fingers, teasing through his hair, quivered. He tried to ignore it. He was going to the War—she said to no purpose. He repeated her questions in his mind. The War had managed without him for centuries. Why must he go? He had been assigned a good position, and the same wanderlust which had led him to spend three years with the Danish fishing fleets demanded he not refuse it. More than once she had called him a willing victim of man's oldest madness. If gods there were, Ares was the most enduring.

A murmur of low voices came from the direction of the canal. Kurt stopped thinking of Karen long enough to glance at Chief Engineer Czyzewski and his group of Polish volunteers. Then came the sound of small bells ringing. *Jäger's* gunnery and fire control people were making a last check of the gunmounts. The main battery trained left and right. Flags rose to the starboard yardarm. "Half an hour," Kurt observed. Karen said nothing.

More clatter along the canal. They looked. The officers: Captain von Lappus; Commander Haber; Kurt's cousin, Lieutenant Lindemann; and Ensign Heiden, the Supply Officer. Other officers were already aboard—except one.

He walked alone, a hundred meters behind the others. Tall, thin, pale, with cold eyes that seemed to stare out of a private hell in a bony face with skin stretched taut, skull-like, beneath sand-colored hair, he wore a uniform unlike those of the others, neither naval, nor of the Baltic Littoral. This was black, silver-trimmed, bore death's-head insignia at the collars, grim imitations of an age long unremembered. A Political Officer.

"Beck," Kurt sighed, shivering.

Karen stirred nervously, kicking a mound of rubble. It collapsed with a tiny clatter.

Beck stopped, haunted eyes searching the steel boneyard. The strangeness of the man projected itself through the hundred meters of ruin. The couple shivered again. He studied them a moment, then walked on.

"That man . . ." Karen sighed with relief. "He makes me freeze up inside, like a snake. Be careful, Kurt. He's not old Karl."

Karl Wiedermann was Kiel's resident Political Officer. He projected the same coldness, had the haunted eyes at times, but did have a spark of humanness in him. He wore black and silver only on military holidays, and seldom invoked his power. Kurt had happy childhood memories of his little shop on Siegestrasse where he crafted fine furniture of imported Swedish oak. Old Karl was not a bad man—for a Political Officer.

Beck—Beck was no Kiel-born man. He had no ties with the Littoral. He was from High Command at Gibraltar, sent to Kiel to summon *Jäger* to the War. He appeared a fanatic, cold as the devil's heart. Perhaps, as Karen had once opined, there was an association. Kurt, however, suspected he was as human as anyone, with loves, hates, hopes, and fears. He could not credit pure evil, as many believed Beck to be. He had seen strange men and stranger behavior while with the Danish fishing fleets, and always, no matter how unusual, a man's actions had been explicable in terms of human needs.

Kurt's mind, unhampered because Karen was unusually silent, drifted off to his years with the fishing fleets. A great adventure they had been, until he came home and found Karen grown into a lovely woman. He had abandoned the sea to court her, had won her, and had let her talk him out of returning—until Commander Haber offered him the post of Leading Quartermaster aboard *Jäger* because of his experience.

More sailors passed in time. Many were accompanied by tearful wives and lovers and mothers. There were few men. Kurt watched his sister, Frieda, as she and her fiancé, Otto Kapp, passed, she clinging to his arm so tightly her knuckles were white. "We give so much to the War," Kurt murmured. Karen nodded. Their families had given for generations.

Their fathers had gone to the last Meeting, aboard *U-793*, a salvaged submarine, and had not come back—those who went to Meetings seldom returned. Three of their grandfathers had sailed on the cruiser *Grossdeutschland*, decades gone.

"Let's walk," said Karen, rising from the girder, tugging the blanket. While putting his cap on and hoisting his seabag to his shoulder, Kurt took a last fond, deep look at the ruin surrounding them.

This was his home, this brick, concrete, and steel desert that stretched a thousand kilometers to the east and south and west. Only the north, Scandinavia, had been spared the mighty bombs. The plagues had raged through, but the survivors were left with livable land, and, in time, had developed a loose-knit, quasi-medieval, viable culture. Yes, Kurt lived in the bones of a fallen Germany, but this was his home and he was loathe to depart, albeit he had been thinking much of Norway lately, especially the province of Telemark.

They walked beside the canal. Suddenly, Karen revealed her own Norwegian thoughts. "Kurt, I'm going to Telemark."

The seabag fell, from his shoulder, thumped on the earth. No words of rebuke could he find, though he opened his mouth to speak. With dreamlike slowness he turned and took her by the shoulders, held her at arm's length while staring into the bottomless blue of her eyes. They reflected the misery of the rusty wreckage around her, they reflected ruin she must escape—and a crystal tear. For a brief instant Kurt shared her soul's agony.

Somewhere a lonely seabird called, a stormcarl.

"To the colony," she said, her voice soft as meringue, yet with an edge of steel daring his reply. "I can't bear Kiel anymore, Kurt. Look!" She swept an arm around, all-inclusive. "The Fatherland. The best part. We're maggots feeding on its corpse. We steal from the dead, create nothing new, waste what little we have on this endless madness—I'll not damn our baby to it! Not just to give the Littoral another sailor to die at the next Meeting . . ."

There were gray clouds rising, shadows moving, and a wind come down from the north soughed among the girders. Perhaps a storm was brewing. Perhaps not. These could be omens.

"Baby?" Kurt exclaimed, still off balance from the shock of Norway.

"Yes, a baby."

"You're sure?"

She nodded.

"Why didn't you tell me?"

"Wouldn't've made any difference, would it?"

Guiltily, he avoided her angry eyes—because it was true. The War was first in his life, even before babies. "But Norway?"

"Too much? No. When Karl Wiedermann calls the refugees traitors, do you have to break your neck agreeing? No one called you a traitor when you went to Denmark. Must I love Germany less because I go to Norway? And why do I want to go? Because there's got to be something better than getting ready for the next battle—and I can't have it here. Only in Telemark. Yes, Telemark! Where the weird ones go, the dropouts, the pacifists, the turncoats, the ones who go where there're no Political Officers to make them think about killing.

"Go to your damned War! No, don't argue. You can't change my mind. When the shells fly there, wherever, remember me and tell yourself it's worth it."

He suspected this was a prepared speech, so readily did her words come. Usually, she was as lame-tongued as he. "But . . ." Exasperated, he ran a hand through his hair, forgetting the cap he wore. With a curse, he caught it centimeters above the earth. The accident sparked anger he channeled toward Karen. "Why'd you marry me if I'm such an idiot? Why not Hans?"

She smiled weakly. "Hans is a bigger idiot. He believes. You're stupid sometimes, Kurt, but I love you anyway." She slipped her arm around his waist and his anger began to fade. "Come on. Let's get you to your boat before Hans comes after you—or Beck."

They walked in silence until they reached the moldering concrete surface of the *Hoch-und-Deutschmeister* pier, where, with *Jäger's* bow looming above them and her decks ringing with the clatter of shoes, they joined Kurt's sister and her fiancé. They exchanged greetings, but Frieda began moving around nervously, always keeping Otto between herself and her brother. Kurt was startled and a little hurt—although she claimed Otto's enlisting was his fault, and was still angered by it—until he suddenly realized that Frieda had broken her promise to herself and had done what she had meant to avoid until marriage. He chuckled, not at all dismayed. Indeed, he was pleased for them.

Otto, too, seemed withdrawn, uncertain, no longer the warm companion of childhood, prior to the death of Kurt's mother, and before Kurt followed his cousin Gregor into the self-imposed exile of the fishing fleets. Three years' separation had seen them grow from boys into men, and apart. Common experience no longer tied them together. Both had striven for the old closeness after Kurt's return, but soon realized they were trying to catch the wind. It was gone, fading through their fingers like gossamer on an autumn breeze. The old, once thought eternal, binding magic had failed, and they could never go home. . . .

A shout broke Kurt's study. He looked up, saw sailors preparing to single up mooring lines. Otto and Frieda were growing increasingly uneasy. With Karen close, he started down the pier.

A dozen steps onward, Karen said, "Put your bag down." He did. "Kiss me." He did. "Miss me, Kurt. Miss me bad." She was fighting tears against his shoulder, and failing. "Be careful. Come back—please?" She kissed him again, much harder, one to remember. Above, a Boatswain's pipe shrieked. "Remember, I'll be in Telemark. I'll wait. You'd better hurry on."

He kissed her once more, glad she closed her eyes and missed his own tears. Then he shouldered his seabag and walked stiffly along the pier, falling into step beside Otto. Silently, momentarily, they shared, as long ago, their departure despair. Kurt did not look back until they reached the brow. Lord, he felt guilty.

"Come on, Kapp, Ranke, we can't hold movement for you," someone shouted from the quarterdeck.

Kurt looked, saw Hans Wiedermann, an old enemy. Karen had been his loss to Kurt and he had never forgiven, though he had restrained himself well. He could have gotten revenge through his father, Karl.

Then, as he climbed the brow, Kurt saw Beck watching from the fantail. Fighting disgust, he jerked his eyes back to Wiedermann. Hans had something of a similar aura, but much mellowed. He was no Political Officer himself, merely one's son. Yet some of the austere aloofness (monastic? Jesuistic?) had attached itself. Beneath black hair his face was pale, his eyes were icily blue, narrow — but crinkle lines lurked at their corners, and about his mouth. Hans sometimes laughed. Political Officers did not, except at wakes and executions.

A false, stereotypical notion, Kurt knew, yet one he thought uncomfortably close to the truth. He had strong, perhaps exaggerated opinions about Political Officers, but not much so. They *were* a cruel and mysterious tribe.

Wiedermann smiled as Kurt started aft, toward his compartment. "We'll have the same watch."

Kurt felt ice-fingers caress his spine. Nominally, he and Hans were of equal rank, the senior ratings in their departments, but Hans's was the senior rate, Boatswain over Quartermaster. Kurt silently blessed Hans for the warning. He would walk carefully for a while, hoping Hans would realize a ship had no room for strong animosities.

Soon, after stowing his gear, he went to the bridge, looked around. Sea Detail was set. Hans was present, as were Captain von Lappus, Commander Haber, and Mr. Lindemann, Captain, Executive Officer, and Officer of the Deck. Otto Kapp had the helm. Bearing takers were on the wings, the walkways outside the closed bridge or pilothouse. A messenger stood by, as did telephone talkers. A full complement, once the lee helmsman arrived.

Outside, on a very light breeze, a drizzle began falling from the gray sky, into the gray water. It was a dismal day for beginnings, though no one aboard, or on the pier, seemed to notice. There was dismay enough already.

Kurt stepped to the chart table, glanced at his charts, opened his logbook—a handbound collection of scraps garnered from the ends of the Littoral. After noting the watchstanders, he went to the starboard wing—he did not sense the rain—and waved to Karen. Peripherally, he saw Wiedermann frown. But the Executive Officer stood nearby, waving to his own wife, and Hans dared say nothing unkind. Kurt allowed himself the petty pleasure of a smirk. He blew a kiss.

Strange. He felt sorry for Hans, never to have had the love of a woman, neither mother nor wife. Nor had he ever had close male friends, throughout his younger years having been shunned because of his father's position. Always, he had interacted most with Kurt, because so many of their interests and goals had been similar. What had most recently flared in fistfights over Karen had begun at the age of six, in a dispute over a torn and ragged picture book, of ships, each had wanted to borrow from Kiel's tiny library....

"Cast off number four!" the Captain growled. Kurt started, glanced down. Two mooring lines were already in. He hurried inside to get it logged.

"Hard left rudder. Port engine back one-third." *Jäger* shivered as her port screw came to life, a proud old lady looking forward to another assignation with the sea. The sea, the sea, the beautiful, lonely, endless sea, Kurt's first love, which was leading him to forsake his second and true for its sad, empty, rippled bosom.... *Jäger's* stern slowly swung away from the pier.

"Cast off number one." Stay-at-homes scurried on the drizzled pier as the last mooring line was freed. The forecastle bustled as the Sea Detail hauled it in and stretched it for eventual drying. The proud old lady was on her way to her ancient lover, Neptune, Poseidon, Dagon, god of a thousand names, who dwelt where shattered towers lie. . . . "Fair Atlantis . . ."

"What?"

Kurt blushed when he saw Otto had overheard, embarrassed by having his daydreams aired like a lumber-room carpet. "Nothing." He turned to his chart table, leaving Kapp bewildered. Otto had grown into a hard, practical man who was often bewildered by Kurt's lack of change since childhood.

"All back one-third. Rudder 'midships."

Jäger backed down slowly till she reached the center of the fairway, then stopped and used her engines to swing her bow to the proper heading for leaving harbor. During a lull in engine orders and rudder changes, Kurt glanced up from his log. Karen and Frieda had become tiny figures waving pathetically, almost indistinguishable for rain, crowd, and distance. His throat tightened. He suddenly feared he would never see them again.

His eyes shifted to the city, ruin forever on, angles and planes and steel fingers clawing at the sky whence had fallen the ancient death. Time had worn the sharp edges, except around the shipyards where the corpses of tremendous cranes and mysterious machines lay like scattered, corroded, vanquished trolls. The neat little shops and houses fronting the harbor to the southeast were out of place and time. Indeed, here, Man was out of place and time, yet he refused to acknowledge his fall.

Still, Kurt told himself, this was the heart of his civilization. All Europe, he knew, lay wasted from Hamburg south. The descendants of Germans, Poles, Danes, Lithuanians, and Latvians lived in small, scattered settlements along the Littoral, the narrow remaining band of tillable coastal soil, scratching out a meager living. This new country had few cities: Kiel, Kolberg,

Gdynia, Danzig, a new port city fifty kilometers southwest of ancient Riga. Kiel was the largest, the capital, with a population approaching ten thousand.

Jäger gathered speed as she nosed down the channel toward the sea, until she was making fifteen knots. Soon she entered the passage between Langeland and Laaland, occasionally sounding her foghorn as warning to the Danish fishing boats. The sailing craft scuttled from her path. Wide-eyed men in foul-weather gear watched the iron lady pass—Kurt leaned against a bulkhead and stared back through diamond raindrops on porthole glass, filled with happy memories—and shook their heads. Another one off to the War.

"There, Gregor," Kurt cried, pointing. "*Dancer!*" Near at hand was his own boat. He saw curious faces he knew. But, when he turned to his cousin, his enthusiasm died. Once again he had forgotten and let familiarity carry him across the line between officer and crewman. Eyes turned his way, anticipating. Kurt turned back to the sea, but the fishing boat had now fallen far behind.

Much to his surprise, Kurt found the mess decks crowded when he went to supper. He had thought most everyone would be too queasy to eat. Perhaps they wanted to get a last fresh meal—without refrigeration, Jäger could store only imperishables. Kurt sighed. He should have come early, to petty officers' mess. He grabbed the seat of a man just finished, settled down to his rough meal.

Five minutes later, Otto slipped into the recently vacated seat opposite him, said, "Well, we're finally on the way. It doesn't seem real."

Kurt grunted an affirmative through a mouthful of strudel. Otto avoided his eyes.

"It's like I'll wake up any minute and find myself at home." Kapp nervously prodded his food with his fork. "Uh . . . about me and Frieda . . ."

Kurt swallowed, said, "She's your problem, not mine. You got troubles, settle them with her. She's a big girl now." He hoped Otto would understand that he was undismayed by the new deepness of Frieda's commitment.

Apparently, Otto did comprehend. The tension faded from his face. He smiled weakly. "Think we'll catch that pirate galleon this time?"

Kurt grinned broadly as he remembered raft-borne pirate chases on the ponds of the silted-up Kiel Canal. That had been his game, imagined into being after reading old books. Then as now, Otto had gone along because Kurt was his friend. Which thought killed Kurt's pleasure at the question. He should not have talked Otto into coming. Frieda was right in being angry with him.

"What we catch," said Hans Wiedermann, assuming the seat beside Otto (which, Kurt saw by looking around, was the only one available), "may be a Tartar, like *Hood* catching *Bismarck*."

Kapp displayed puzzlement. Hans would not expand his cryptic comment, apparently feeling ignorance was inexcusable. Otto looked to Ranke. "Old-time battleships," Kurt said. "An ancient war. *Hood* and *Prince of Wales* were after *Bismarck*. *Hood* went down almost as soon as the shooting started."

"History," Kapp snorted. "You two live in the past. What good is it? Reading books about old times won't put food in your stomach." He launched a set speech long familiar to Kurt, who suspected Otto's feelings were based in envy. He, like many Littoral children, had received only the rudiments of an education. He could read numbers and puzzle his way through the simplest primer, but all else was beyond him, which had to rankle when conversations went beyond his scope. And, if he were working with some machine and needed to know how to operate or repair it, he had to do so by trial and error or knowledge passed orally by someone more experienced.

Yet, despite no knowledge of theory, Otto was a first-rate mechanic. Often, when not on watch, he worked in one of the gunmounts, deftly maintaining hydraulics and electrical servos whose physics he comprehended not at all.

The whole of modern technology, Kurt supposed, was mirrored in Otto Kapp. Very few people knew *why* things worked any more, nor did they care. To bang on or fiddle with a machine until it worked was enough.

It had to collapse. To maintain a technological culture on hand-me-down skills was impractical . . . it had collapsed already, he decided. *Jäger* was an anomaly, one of the few functional machines left to the Littoral. The culture as a whole there operated at the level of the sixteenth or seventeenth century.

Kurt grew aware that Hans and Otto were engaged in a spirited argument over the value of studying history. Otto maintained that the past was dead and useless while Hans reiterated ancient notions of learning from others' mistakes. Said Otto, "Avoid past mistakes? Hans, that's stupid. If it's true, why're we here? This mistake's already two centuries old."

Otto was, probably, the most openly anti-War person Kurt knew — with the understandable exceptions of Karen and Frieda. "You think people're sensible. That's the silliest idea . . ."

Kapp stopped in mid-career. Kurt had kicked him beneath

the table. Beck had appeared. For reasons unknown, he was eating at crew's mess rather than in the wardroom. The mess decks were silent as scores of breaths were held. Everyone waited for Beck to choose a seat. The groans at Kurt's table were inaudible, but very real within, when the Political Officer selected the open place next to Kurt.

"Good evening, men," he said as he deposited his tray on the table, his voice sounding somehow distant and hollow. "Don't let me interrupt." He hazarded a smile which was more a grimace. Elsewhere, sailors resumed conversations, though in hushed, cautious tones.

"Perhaps you're right," said Hans, half turning to Otto. "Hitler invaded Russia knowing Napoleon had failed. Yet the first failure didn't automatically guarantee a second. All indications were for a swift German victory."

"Uhn?" Otto grunted. Kurt chuckled despite Beck's inhibiting presence. Otto had only the vaguest notion who Hitler had been, and undoubtedly had never heard of Bonaparte.

"History?" Beck asked, thin eyebrows rising. "An odd subject for seamen, though, perhaps, after living with the Wiedermanns, none too surprising in Hans. The Political Office has always been interested in history, especially unusual historical theories."

He looked them each in the eye, as if asking for such theories. No one spoke. Kurt was afraid to say anything lest Beck take offense. Otto was subtly insubordinate with a flash of expression, with a quirk of the lip. Even Hans, who had had to suffer Beck's presence in his home for a year, and should therefore have been inured, seemed to suffer dampened spirits. Beck, who, Kurt felt, had been making an honest attempt to communicate, soon withdrew into himself, ate mechanically, and became his normal cold, faraway self.

TWO

Sunset. *Jäger*, moving fast, was 250 kilometers north of Kiel, past most of the Danish islands. As day faded in orange and violet riot, she slowed for safety's sake. With no up-to-date charts by which to steam, she must navigate by notes Kurt and Lindemann had made while with the fishers. And those did little enough to help seamen traveling this modern strait by night. The bottom of the Kattegat had changed considerably during two centuries. Mudbanks had formed and moved. The tides and currents had shifted. And there were uncharted wrecks scattered everywhere. The Battle of the Kattegat had been a seafight to rival Lepanto in magnitude.

The Danes, and Swedish traders at times, marked obstructions with lanterns and buoys, and all navigators kept notes much as had Kurt. Lindemann had also made a comprehensive list of the lights and buoys of the Norwegian coast, where the Danes maintained salting stations and trading posts. He had had charge of one of these, serving vessels working the Norwegian Sea, for two years. Kurt regretted their paths had crossed so seldom those days, for, as with Otto, young memories of his cousin made him fond of the man. Too fond. Once again, Gregor had had to remind him to avoid over familiarity before the crew. Their relationship was rapidly growing distant and strained.

But the lights and buoys, at the mercy of foul weather and inattention, were untrustworthy. *Jäger* steamed slowly, with many lookouts.

The Year of Our Lord 2193, and *Jäger* was celebrating her 250th year. Like other ships which survived beyond their times, she was cranky. She could sail and fight, true, but with none of the vigor of her youth. Countless tens of thousands of sea miles had passed beneath her keel, dozens of battles had been fought about her, from Iwo Jima to Anambas.

Once, when she was young, she had been *U.S.S. Cowell*, and she bore the name fifty years, until Russians captured her aground in Cam Rahn Bay. Rechristened *Potemkin*, she served first in the Soviet, then in the Siberian Fleet, until Sakhalinski Zaliv. There the Australians hauled her shell-crippled body off the Sakhalin rocks and rebuilt her into *Swordfish*. Decades later, after expending all her fuel at Anambas, German sailors from *Grossdeutschland* took her in hand-to-hand fighting, and she became *Jäger*, the Hunter.

An old lady, she was proud and difficult, with her arthritis and failing organs, her bad eyes and deafening ears—but men would not let her retire. She must pass in line of battle. Her radars worked not at all, her sonar was sporadic, radio was out forever for lack of spares—although there were no technicians to make repairs, even had spares been available.

She was cranky that night, steaming the Kattegat with her sonar and fathometer down. At midnight, while slowly crossing a sea spotted with lights like low-hanging stars—lights of fishing boats or warnings on hazards—still sounding foghorn warnings, she was betrayed. A sleepy lookout missed the death of a star.

Kurt dreamed of Karen, and snored across memories of their courtship.

Once again he came from the harbor, from his boat, to see Frieda, and again she was gone. A neighbor told him she was out with Otto Kapp. So he washed his face and left his bag, walked up the street toward Otto's, mind on making two visits at once. And, while crossing the Brennerplatz, a hand caught his arm and a soft voice asked, "Kurt? Are you blind?"

How had he missed her? he asked himself, resplendent as she was in a bright peasant dress of her mother's weaving and her own sewing. "Karen. I'm sorry. I was daydreaming."

"You haven't changed." She smiled, meaning no criticism. "Will you come to dinner?"

"I'm on my way to Otto's, to see Frieda."

"They've borrowed a cart and gone for a picnic up the canal."

Ah, Kurt thought, the same Kiel. Everyone knows everyone's business. But Karen *had* changed. The rather lanky, budding teenager of three years earlier had become something of a willowy beauty. "All right. What time?"

"Now?"

He learned of her engagement to Hans Wiedermann during the meal. "You don't seem enthusiastic," he observed.

"Oh?" Her blond eyebrows rose questioningly.

"No. You made a face." And, to the side, Karen's mother made another. Kurt then remembered she had been planning for him and Karen since before they reached their teens.

"He's too much his father's son," Karen said, and closed the subject.

Two nights later, as he walked harborward from a third supper at Karen's, he met Hans. Hans had little to say, merely asked if Kurt knew of his engagement. At Kurt's affirmative reply, the smaller man started swinging. Strictly speaking, Hans won, for Kurt quickly withdrew.

Yet, when *Dancer's* fish were sold and she put to sea, Kurt was not aboard. He resisted pressure in his own way, taking his struggle to its goal, the battlefield of Karen's mind. Two weeks later, he and Karen married. As the priest asked, "Do you, Kurt Ranke—"

Metal screamed. *Jäger* staggered as her sonar dome was torn away. The *bhong-bhong-bhong* of the collision alarm reverberated through the ship. She caught again, aft, more seriously, bucked, shuddered as screw blades chewed at the obstruction.

Kurt bounced from his rack, hit another, crumpled on the cold steel deck. He woke during the fall, was out for a second after impact, then painfully regained consciousness. He struggled to a sitting position, groaned, grabbed his head. Then, with the suddenness of a startled cat, he scrambled from beneath a pair of descending feet. The compartment lights came on. Clutching one of the small overhead I-beams supporting the fantail weatherdeck, he stared down at his undershirt.

Redness. Warm wetness. He was dumbfounded. Oh. His nose was bleeding. He snapped the shirt up and pinched his nostrils. It quickly stopped.

The compartment grew crowded with sleepy, frightened sailors asking sleepy, frightened questions. A few panicked and scrambled up a ladder to the fantail. Here and there, unreasoning men scrounged through their lockers, seizing possessions to take when abandoning ship. The panic spread, feeding itself. Carried by it, Kurt climbed the ladder with his division. He wore a cap, but had forgotten his jumper and trousers.

Metal screamed again. *Jäger* groaned. Kurt tripped as he stepped through the hatch, but steadier men caught him. There was little fear on the fantail. It evaporated with freedom from tight, crowded living spaces, and as it became obvious the ship was not sinking.

"Thanks, Ott. What's happening?"

"Hit something," Kapp replied. "Now they're trying to back her off."

"Here now, make a hole!" someone shouted. Chief Engineer Czyzewski, in his underwear, leading a Damage Control party, pushed through the crowd. "You men move forward!" the Pole bellowed, shooing them like unruly chickens. The sailors retreated, clearing the fantail, staggering as the ship again lurched.

"Tell the bridge to stop engines!" Czyzewski thundered. "They'll rip the hull open!"

A man with head-surrounding sound-powered phones relayed the message. The boiling beneath the stern died.

Someone muttered, "We're taking water forward. The sonar dome's gone."

But, before the disclosure could incite new panic, the telephone talker shouted, "Mr. Czyzewski! Zlotopolski says he's got the patch on forward!"

"Tell him to get it welded."

"We moving?" someone asked.

Kurt sensed the slight change in the roll of the deck. *Jäger* was free, drifting.

"Well, Kurt," said another voice, "what happened with those notes you're so proud of? Looks like you sold us worthless paper."

Kurt gave Hans Wiedermann a poisonous stare. "It's more likely the deck ape at the helm screwed up, not knowing right from left when a steering order was given."

Hans laughed bitterly, teeth glistening whitely in the glare of newly rigged emergency lights.

Another engineering party arrived, driving the spectators farther forward. Kurt, Hans, and others who thought quickly enough scrambled up a ladder to front-row seats atop the aftmost gunmount. Difficult seats. Dead in the water, *Jäger* was unable to keep her bows to the swells. She slowly turned parallel to them and began rolling. The back and forth was hard on some stomachs.

"My, Hans," Kurt said maliciously, "you look green. How'll you feel when we hit real waves? Be like Mr. Obermeyer?"

Obermeyer was First Lieutenant, Hans's division officer, and had been confined by seasickness to quarters almost constantly since *Jäger* had cast off mooring lines at Kiel. Hans had been carrying the man's workload for him and, though he kept it well hidden, Kurt had begun to see in him a quiet bitterness at not having been given Obermeyer's billet in the first place. Hans, Kurt decided, was a greener-grass man, always disgruntled by not being one step beyond his attainments. In fact, he recalled, he had felt some of the same distress on discovering that Gregor, with less sea experience, had been chosen navigator over himself.

He decided the engineers would manage quite well without his kibitzing, so scrambled down from the gunmount and returned to his compartment, to his rack where, in sleep, the throbbing pain in his nose might gradually fade.

He had hardly fallen asleep when Hans shook his rack. "Out, smart boy. Mr. Lindemann wants you in the wardroom, with your charts."

Kurt opened one sleepy blue eye and stared, daring Hans to be lying. He was not. His sadistic little smile proved it. Kurt reached out and mussed his curly black hair. "Yes, dear."

The smile vanished. Hans lifted a fist waist-high, dropped it. "Five minutes. In the wardroom." He stalked away rigidly.

Sighing, Kurt rolled out and pulled on a dress uniform, considered shaving, decided against it—no time. After quickly combing his hair, he hurried forward to the charthouse and bridge.

He reached the wardroom a minute past his five, found Hans glumly waiting in the passage outside. Kurt studied his dark features closely. Nothing. He knocked on the wardroom door. It opened and he entered. Hans did not. Kurt felt mildly frightened on seeing he was the only enlisted man present.

Commander Haber met him a step inside. The Executive Officer's brownish-blond hair was disarrayed, his uniform was tacky. Unusual. He was fussy about his appearance. And he was more nervous than usual, Kurt saw. His thin hands quaked.

Beck was there, cold as ever and angry red. Had there been a scene?

"Come in, Ranke. Take the seat beside Mr. Lindemann. We've a few questions for you." Haber paused while Kurt seated himself. "To sum up, we've been discussing our loss of the port screw and sonar. The latter we can do without. It was touchy at best. The screw, though . . ."

"No hope, sir?" He felt pain each time he called Haber "sir." Haber was another old friend who had become distant since Kurt had joined *Jäger*'s crew. Once the man had been almost a second father, when courting his mother. Everyone seemed drifting away, leaving him out of their lives.

"None. Mr. Czyzewski says it's bent dangerously. We'll warp the drive shaft if it's used. It tangled with the masthead of a wreck. The light on the warning buoy had gone out."

"Now we've a decision to make, to go on or to turn back. If we do continue, we'll be crippled. If we return to Kiel for repairs, we may not reach Gibraltar in time for the Gathering. We'd like to go on, if possible."

Haber paused briefly, touched the thin line of his mustache with shaky fingers while glancing toward Beck, watchful in a corner. Kurt had the feeling Haber's last words were for Beck alone, that Beck was the only man there who actually *wanted* to go on. "You're here, Ranke, because you know Danish waters better than anyone else. How likely *is* it that we'll encounter more of this sort of trouble?"

Beck turned his cold eyes on Kurt. Kurt understood why Haber was nervous and vague. The Political Officer hovered over the meeting like an eager hangman.

"Sir," Kurt replied, trying to ignore Haber's neck-scratching and Beck's stare, "it shouldn't be difficult, barring the steering problem. Wrecks in the Kattegat aren't all that common—"

"You have a chart of the Kattegat," Beck interrupted. "The obstructions were marked, and you were to instruct the watchstanders. What happened?"

Fright. Trying to blame someone? Kurt glanced at Gregor. Lindemann thoughtfully stared into nothingness, apparently unworried. Kurt realized the meeting was all for Beck's benefit.

They were much of the same appearance, Kurt and Gregor, tall, blue-eyed, fair, though Gregor's hair was a shade darker than Kurt's golden blond. They might have been taken for brothers in another age, but not in the present. The people of the Baltic Littoral all looked very much alike. They were descendants of a genetic type immune to a hideous weapon used early in the War, a virus which destroyed Caucasian chromosomal structures. Current physical differences were due almost entirely to environment. Von Lappus was fat because he ate too much. Haber was thin, small, and nervous because, as a child, he had been trapped in a collapsing building and had suffered prolonged starvation before being rescued. Of all those aboard only Hans and Beck were of truly different types, and for the same reason: they were from Gibraltar, where different weapons had been used.

Lindemann said, "Explain it, Kurt."

Kurt opened his portfolio and took out the chart Beck had mentioned. He spread it on the table, looked at the Political Officer. "Sir, this isn't a chart. It's a pre-War map of Denmark, southern Sweden, and southern Norway. It shows political features, not the sea bottom. Even if it was a chart, it'd be too small a scale. We should have the largest-scale charts possible when sailing close waters. But all we've got are old political maps, two ancient British charts of Scapa Flow, and the anchor chart for Gibraltar you gave me. I begged for better charts, but the Council planners . . ."

Von Lappus snorted porcinely, shifted his bulk, opened his small blue eyes, fixed Kurt with his stare. "We've already heard it from Mr. Lindemann. We don't have time for repeats just now."

The von Lappus twins, Sepp and Wilhelm, had been features of Kiel life for as long as Kurt could remember. Wilhelm was mayor, which was tantamount to being governor (or president, or king, or whatever) of the entire Littoral, and Sepp was commander of the military, such as it was. And, so Kurt remembered, the twins had always been fat and old. The only change in them was their common, increasing baldness.

Kurt hurriedly continued, "The best charts we have were captured with the ship at Anambas, of Australian and Indonesian waters. They're only forty years old. Yes, we can go on. The Kattegat and Skagerrak are safe enough, with care. Only the Channel should be dangerous. But I couldn't guarantee there'll be no more accidents. . . ."

"Ranke," said Haber, shaking his head, "we all know the navigational situation is critical. You'll just have to make do till we join the Gathering. The High Command'll take care of us from there."

Kurt forebore telling Haber what he thought of High Command at that moment. The Beck look of icewater and doom was standard, but the man had a knack for making it seem personal.

The Captain shifted again, nodded to Haber, who said, "All right, Ranke, that'll be all. You said about what we expected. Oh, don't bother the charts. We'll want them later."

Kurt returned the portfolio to the table, looked at Gregor. He took a keyring from his pocket. "Sir?"

"I'll take care of it."

Kurt dropped the keys on the portfolio, quickly left, sighing once through the door.

Hans was still standing outside. His presence surprised Kurt. Also, his apparent friendliness as he asked, "What'd they decide?"

Kurt studied his face. Hans seemed frightened. "Nothing yet. But I'll be surprised if we go home."

"Oh."

Kurt was two steps past the Boatswain. The dull, flat, disappointed reply so astonished him that he turned back. "I thought you'd be happy, Hans."

"Kurt, there's gung-ho, and there's gung-ho," Hans muttered, staring at the deck. Shadows veiled his expression. "There's the kind you put on in Kiel because your father's a Political Officer, and there's the kind you feel inside. There's the kind that makes you march on Victory Day, and the kind that makes you want to run for Telemark . . . oh!"

Wiedermann apparently realized he was speaking dangerously. His eyes widened slightly—hard to see them in the dark—and he backed a step away. Then he whirled and hurried forward, to the head of a ladder which led down to his compartment. Kurt shrugged and started aft. Though he had been given a powerful weapon, he soon forgot. He was not one to carry damning tales.

"Go away, dammit!" Kurt growled. It seemed he had just gone to sleep, yet here was the messenger, telling him to relieve the watch. And he would not go away. "Dammit again!"

Kurt sat up, bumping his head against the rack above. Its occupant growled and rolled over. Kurt dropped to the deck, grimacing as cold steel met his feet. He yanked his work uniform off a hook nearby, donned it, then went up a ladder to the head, to shave. Minutes later he passed through red battle-light-interrupted darkness, to the mess decks for a quick cup of ersatz coffee before going to the bridge.

Jäger was underway, moving slowly, as he had known since awakening. She was rolling heavily, steaming parallel to the swells. What direction was she running? North, into the Skagerrak? Or south, toward Kiel? For one unpatriotic moment, he hoped they were sailing home—but, when he looked over the helmsman's shoulder, that hope died. Course, 000°. He fought disappointment as he relieved his predecessor, Paul Milch.

Hans arrived, relieved the Boatswain of the watch. He too glanced at the steering compass and frowned. Curious, Kurt watched others of the oncoming watch. Otto showed the same momentary unhappiness, though Gregor, when he arrived to assume his duties as Officer of the Deck, merely shrugged. Of course, he had known already.

Man after man, each reacted the same, with disappointment quickly hidden. It made Kurt wonder. Just one day earlier many of these men had been eager to sail. Now they wanted to go home. The adventure was no adventure at all, once begun. But turning back could not be. No one dared risk the wrath of the High Command, for High Command was a jealous god, believed capable of anything—including the destruction of an uncooperative member state.

Kurt could see, in the battle-light-reddened faces of the watch, dread of High Command replacing patriotism and adventure as the forces behind *Jäger*'s sailing. He wondered if the mood was similar aboard all ships bound for the Gathering. Would they go just for fear's sake? Or because they felt there was some purpose in the War?

He wanted to talk to someone, to discover others' feelings, yet, as he looked around at men who were his closest friends, he realized they would not share. Time and circumstance had rendered null their closeness. He seized a cable overhead as the deck sank away, then rose shivering beneath him, listened to the sighs of the wind, to the *crump* of the seas hitting the bow — all the sounds of loneliness on a gray and forgotten sea.

He wondered if this unhappy small sample of the crew were truly representative of the ship's mood. His thoughts wandered to the engine rooms, the ammunition ready rooms, Combat Information Center. Would disappointment also haunt those places when men learned *Jäger* was going on? What of the officers? The Captain? Haber?

Why was *Jäger* sailing? Because of the High Command, that shadow organization at Gibraltar? No one really knew, except, perhaps, Beck, who had come from Gibraltar with platitudes, slogans, sentences with no meaning. Kill the enemy. Destroy. Why? According to Beck, to end the rampant savagery of the East, to drive a shaft of liberty's light into the slaveholder's darkness of Australia.

Kurt reviewed the old catchwords, epithets, and emotion-laden arguments, and found no solace. Who cared? Who had ever seen an Australian, or been hurt by one? How could he hate someone he had never seen?

He drifted back to his tenth summer, the day his father had sailed to the War. Years of slow, difficult work with makeshift tools, and a hundred men, had been invested in *U-793* — and she had sailed out of history as finally as if she had never been. Her story, for the people of the Littoral, had ended the moment she crossed the horizon. Why?

Another year, another ship. Was *Jäger*'s story already done?

Was she a metal coffin staggering off in search of a watery grave-yard?

Gregor put a hand on Kurt's shoulder, startling him. "Got a posit?"

"Just an estimated." He tapped the chart at *Jäger*'s approximate position.

Gregor nodded. "Come left to two seven zero," he ordered.

After logging the course change, Kurt went to Hans and whispered, "You ought to change helmsmen once in a while." He nodded toward Otto. "Must be a job trying to balance the screw."

Hans grunted agreement, directed a man to spell Kapp.

"Kurt?"

"Sir?" He returned to the chart table. Gregor was examining the northern coast of Denmark.

"Do you remember any shoals along here?"

Kurt shuffled through his notes. There was little to be found or remembered. He shrugged. "None to bother us, that I know of. You?"

When Gregor shook his head, Kurt continued, "You could send a lookout to the masthead."

"Right. Boatswain!"

Kurt was at the psychrometer, working on a weather report, when Wiedermann returned. He grew aware of Hans's presence as he closed the little wooden box. "What?"

"Kurt . . . uh, would you forget last night? I mean . . . well, I guess I wasn't thinking right."

Kurt studied him closely. Hans shuffled nervously, eyes fixed on the deck. This was out of character. Although small, thin, and physically weak, Hans had always been aggressive. For reasons Kurt did not understand, Hans was forever trying to better him. They had come to blows several times, especially courting Karen. But there had always been an unspoken agreement. No outsiders in their conflicts. Neither had run to parents when little, neither carried tales to authority now — yet Hans appeared afraid Kurt would denounce him to Beck.

"Hans, I never heard a thing." Kurt pretended to examine the seas while noting the nearness of lookouts. "We'll stop in Norway to cut firewood, you know. Up the Otra River, they've decided. We'll be only a few days from the Telemark colony."

Wiedermann's eyes widened, then narrowed. He slowly shook his head.

Kurt leaned on the rail and stared toward Norway, said, "Know what bothers me, Hans? I don't think there's anybody, except Beck, who wants to go on. Even the officers. But we're going anyway, and I wonder why. I could ask Beck, maybe, but he'd give me the usual crap about Australia."

"Wonder if *he* believes it?"

"That's bothered me for a long time. How does High Command *know* the Australians will sail against us next summer?"

"We'll find out when we get to Gibraltar," Hans replied. "You know, Beck says every operable ship in the West will be there."

"They said the same thing when my father sailed."

"Well . . ."

"That was the Final Meeting, the Last Battle, the Victory, too. And then there was *Grossdeutschland* — isn't that a joke? She went to a Last Battle too."

"Maybe this time . . ."

"Maybe Karen was right. Maybe there's not supposed to be an end. Maybe, when we run out of steel ones, they'll have us build wooden ships and cast brass cannons, or something. . . ."

"That's a lot of 'maybes,' Kurt. What bothers me, despite my father's yak, is that I see no reason for this. Would the Australians notice the difference if we just stayed home?"

The sun was sneaking up on the eastern horizon, speckling the sky with small orange clouds. Kurt mumbled, "I try not to worry about it, but I have to. Karen's fault. She's going to Telemark."

Hans shook his head, startled disbelief on his face. "Hey!" he suddenly hissed. "Don't look, but snake-eye Beck's watching us. On the torpedo deck. Bet he's looking for a traitor to hang. Probably thinks we need an object lesson."

Kurt glanced that way quickly. Beck was indeed watching, and with the mesmeric predacity which had led men to call him "snake-eye." Kurt grumbled, "He'd better not make a habit of strolling the weatherdecks at night."

"Quartermaster!"

Kurt turned, saw Gregor at the door to the pilothouse. "Sir?"

"I need a course for Kristiansand, with a turn in fifteen minutes." As Kurt stepped through the door, Lindemann whispered, "Be careful, Kurt. Beck's traitor-hunting."

Kurt nodded as he bent over the chart table, pleased that his cousin had expressed concern.

THREE

"Sir, lookout reports lights ahead," said a phone talker.

Kurt leaned out the pilothouse door, had a hard time finding the lights. Although the sun had set, twilight still confused the eyes. He finally found them almost directly over the bow, in a flat triangle which rose and fell slowly — the horizon appeared in constant motion while *Jäger* seemed stable. Although he was certain he knew the lights, Kurt turned to his notes.

"Those are the Lillesand ranges, Kurt," Gregor said. "The legs of the triangle, extended seaward, mark safe channels into harbor."

"Thought so. What's there?"

"Salting station, trading post. Let's see, we're about fifty kilometers northeast of the Otra now. Give me a new course to Kristiansand."

"Two one zero."

Lindemann ordered the course changed, and the vessel slowed until she was just making steerage way. She dared not hazard the river until she had morning's light. "You know anything about shoals or wrecks there?" Lindemann asked. "Can't recall anything myself."

Kurt shook his head. "Not about the Otra. It's strictly a Norwegian river. Never been there."

"When's sunrise?"

Kurt glanced at a note left by Paul Milch of the previous watch. "Four forty-eight, sir. Milch thinks we'll have a flood tide."

"Thinks?" Gregor smashed fist into palm, grumbled, "I'm repeating myself, I know, but how the hell're we supposed to sail a ship without charts or tables?"

Kurt smiled. If nothing else, Gregor would share their professional problems. But with that thought he grew reminded of his alienation and the loneliness came crashing in. Things had been better with the Danes, professionally and personally. He had had tools and friends in plenty. Tools. Here his complaints were always answered with tales of famous navigators who had sailed on less than what *Jäger* had available. Fine, he thought. So Columbus steered by astrolabe and the wind behind his ear. He had known no better.

Such thoughts depressed him. He left the watch feeling low, and tossed for an hour before sleeping.

Two pasts haunted Kurt's dreams. Awake, he often daydreamed; sometimes dwelling in medieval glories, not at all aware the age had been as bitter as his own; sometimes in the middle decades of the twentieth century, just before the War, when all the machines and people had been alive, not just mysterious, rusted, fallen djinn, and bones found in ancient ruins. By night, his own past plagued him, his sorrows, errors, and triumphs. While *Jäger's* bridge watch trolled the Norwegian night for landmarks, Kurt's soul wandered to a day that had been a little of each.

At the Ranke home, a month after the wedding, he, Karen, and Frieda lingered over a late breakfast of salty pork. Kurt grew aware of Karen hopefully staring—he felt he should say something kind, yet he had arisen in a restless, impatient mood, and the meat *had* been overdone. . . .

"Well?"

"It's okay, I guess."

Hurt appeared on her face, quickly departed. Kurt opened his mouth to soothe her, but there was a call from another room.

"Kurt? Frieda? Karen?" A moment later, Heinrich Haber walked in. "Let myself in," he said. "Hope it's all right." Such liberties were common in Kiel.

Kurt's eyebrows rose. Haber wore strange clothing, yet familiar. Then he recognized it. It was a uniform such as his father had worn on going to sea in *U-793.*

"No!" Karen gasped. Kurt turned, found her pale, on the verge of tears. He was dumbfounded.

"Can we talk privately, Kurt?" Haber asked. His lean body seemed somehow fuller, more manly in the uniform. And his shakes, which were always with him, were much less pronounced.

"Of course." Kurt always had time for Haber, a man he and Frieda wished had successfully gotten their mother to remarry.

As they took seats in an upstairs room, by a window looking out on the harbor, Kurt discovered the reason for his morning's mood. He had a restless, urgent need to get aboard a ship and reclaim the feel of the sea.

"Briefly," said Haber, getting straight to the point, "I came to ask you to join *Jäger*'s crew."

"*Jäger?*"

"I keep forgetting you've been away, and too busy lately to notice what's happening. *Jäger*'s the old destroyer. High Command has ordered us to outfit and man her, and bring her to a Gathering next summer."

"Oh." He had heard something of it from Otto, had seen the High Command representative about the city, but had not been much concerned. "I don't think so. Karen wouldn't like it."

"None of our wives like it. But there's a job that has to be done. And I'm not asking you just to be a deckhand. Your Danish experience counts for more than that. Leading Quartermaster, top enlisted billet in Operations, is still open. You're the only qualified man in Kiel. Your cousin Gregor has agreed to be navigator. He's on his way home from Norway now."

"Why not a fisherman?"

"Can't find one interested."

"And why a Gathering?"

"The War again. High Command's discovered that the Australians are putting together a fleet to come against Europe, summer after next. This time we'll end it for good. We'll destroy all their ships, then go on and smash their ports and harbors so they can't ever try again."

Kurt frowned. He had been quite young and disinterested at the time of his father's departure, yet it seemed he had heard all this before, then. Yet, to go, to see places about which he could only dream here, to have a major ship beneath and about him ... His eyes sought the distant warship, at the *Hoch-und-Deutschmeister* pier, where she had been waiting all his life.

"Do you really believe that, Heinrich?" Kurt jerked around. Karen had come in quietly, unasked. "Or are you as cynical a liar as Beck? I hope, for your sake, that you've been honestly taken in."

"Karen!" Kurt was shocked. This was no way to speak to a close and long-time friend.

"Karen," said Haber, gently, "I do hope you'll not talk that way in public. Even a lazy old man like Karl Wiedermann would have to do something—especially with a ranking Political Officer here. Beck would probably gun you down with that ugly pistol he always carries."

"I don't care!" Kurt's wonder grew. This was the first time he had seen her angry—and he still had no slightest notion why. Surely, not because of his reaction to breakfast. "I want you to leave," she said. "We don't want your phony patriotism."

"Karen!"

"Oh, shut up, Kurt. You don't know what's going on. You'll let yourself get talked into something you'll regret."

He was angered by her implying he was incapable of rational decision. So, to prove something, he made an irrational one. "I'll go." He meant to say he would think about going, but it did not come out so, and, afterward, Karen forever turned deaf ears to his explanations.

"Kurt!" she wailed, "why? Haven't our families been hurt enough?"

Then the argument began, their first. As each angry word took birth and flew, Kurt grew more determined he would not let Karen think for him. He was by nature a drifter, a follower, easily manipulated, yet, when accused of it, became stubborn in proving to himself he was not—sometimes in support of the stupidest things. . . . He committed himself to *Jäger* so clumsily there was no way he could withdraw without tremendous loss of face. He won a sad victory over Karen, and slept that night alone.

"Ranke!" It seemed sleep had just come, but here was the messenger of the watch, shaking his rack, stirring him forth from the muzzy depths of memory. "Time to relieve the watch."

"Goddammit," he muttered, "I just got off."

"It's three-thirty," the messenger said defensively.

"I'm coming, I'm coming." Then he chuckled. The engineers were standing watch and watch, six hours on and six off. He consoled himself by thinking of those with a worse lot.

"Go on. Get out of here," he told the messenger. "I'm up."

"Just making sure." The man hurried off to his next victim.

The Norwegian coast was a vague black line when Kurt reached the bridge. He relieved Milch, made the log entries necessary for a new watch, then stepped outside to stare at the shadowed land. Hans joined him shortly.

"Think we could see the mountains from here?" he asked.

"No. Maybe when we get upriver."

"When're we going in?"

"When there's enough light." Kurt looked eastward, astern. The false dawn had begun painting the foaming wake. Then he saw Beck on the maindeck, amidships, near an open porthole. "Look. Beck. Hope he doesn't hang the cooks. They're bad, but they're all we've got."

Hans considered Beck at the galley, chuckled. "Pray it's Kellerman if he does." Kellerman was the officers' cook, unpopular, considered a lickspittle.

They moved forward where Beck could not see them. Musingly, Hans said, "It'd be a pity if something happened to him, wouldn't it? Suppose a tree fell on him? Anything could happen while we're cutting firewood."

Kurt frowned. There was something wrong about Hans, something different. He was altogether too friendly, and the way he was talking, too, was unlike the Hans Kurt thought he knew. . . .

"Captain's on the bridge!"

Kurt's train of thought died as he hurried into the pilothouse, to the chart table, where he waited until von Lappus had a question.

"Ranke, what do you know about this river?"

"Not a damned thing," Kurt replied, surprising himself. Now why had he said that? As an afterthought, "Sir." Then, "But we should have a flood tide."

The Captain grunted and walked away. He spoke with Gregor for a moment, assumed the conn, and turned the ship toward the river.

Jäger reached Kristiansand an hour after sunrise. The old town seemed a thriving village of perhaps a thousand souls, many of whom came out to watch the warship pass. The men of the Sea Detail, which had been set when Kristiansand was sighted, waved and shouted. Petty officers passed among the seamen, growling, toning them down. There would be no fraternizing with the Kristiansander girls anyway. Their fathers and husbands and brothers were already hustling them home. An ancient custom, Kurt thought.

Jäger crept up the Otra until, near noon, she dropped anchor off a good stand of timber. Kristiansand, forty kilometers downstream, was an attraction no more. Kurt was wolfing a delayed breakfast, wondering about the Norwegian way of life, when

Hans approached his table with his own morning meal. "You've got boat three," he said.

"What?"

"You're in charge of boat three, to get wood. You'll need a dozen Operations men for your working party. There'll be one from Engineering, two from Deck."

"What about Gunnery?"

"Somebody's worried about the natives. Why, I don't know."

"I don't feel like chopping wood."

"Who does? Want to trade boats?"

"Why?"

"Beck's going over in mine."

"No thanks. Why?"

"To watch for deserters, I guess. It's a golden opportunity, you have to admit. We're awful close to Telemark."

"Two days' walk," Kurt replied, revealing his recent thoughts.

Hans's eyes narrowed. "You taking off?"

"I thought about meeting Karen there. But I won't."

"Get your tools from the Boatswain's locker. Deckinger'll have them ready."

"All right." Kurt hurriedly finished his coffee and soggy roll. After returning his tray to the scullery, he went to Combat, where he collected a working party.

"Muster the working parties!" was soon piped. Kurt smiled, briefly wondered why Hans so enjoyed the public-address microphone — perhaps he achieved a surrogate feeling of power, of godhead. He reached boat three as Gregor arrived.

"Everyone here?" the Lieutenant asked.

Kurt ticked off names in his mind. "Where's Weber?"

"Here." The sonarman hurried up.

"All present, sir," said Kurt, saluting sloppily. *Jäger's* crew, often to Beck's dismay, demonstrated little interest in ceremony.

"Very well. Weber, Hippke, get the tools. The rest of you stand clear here." Men from the deck force lowered the boat, rigged a Jacob's ladder. "All right, get aboard," Lindemann directed when the tools arrived. "Ranke, you're coxswain."

"We may need shovels, sir," Kurt observed later, when they finally managed to get the boat to shore. The bank was a clifflet six feet tall.

"Mr. Czyzewski's ahead of you." Behind them, the engineers were loading their own boat. Shovels were among their tools. Kurt shrugged, made the boat's painter fast to a sapling, scrambled up the bank.

A hundred meters of gently rising green meadow lay between river and wood, richly strewn with petaled jewels. The grass was deep and comfortable. Several men were lying in it, talking. Kurt breathed deeply of the meadow's lush perfume.

"A nice place," Gregor observed. Indeed. Here there was no sign of man or his foibles.

"Yes, pretty," Kurt replied. "Except for that." He pointed at *Jäger*. The ship, beautiful as a panther is beautiful when moored at Kiel, was a canker here in the wilderness.

"Uhm," Lindemann grunted. "All right, stand by!" He went to meet Czyzewski, just coming ashore. They spoke for a moment, then Lindemann returned. "Kurt, start with a few of the bigger trees. He wants a raft to float the wood over."

Kurt nodded, passed the word. Soon sounds of axes, of spades at the bank, and, later, of sledges hitting wedges, splitting logs, racketed along the riverside. *Jäger* added the sounds of chipping hammers and an occasional shout as someone hailed a friend ashore. The work was hard, but the sailors enjoyed themselves. Chatter, snatches of song, high spirits filled the meadow.

But there was always an island of silence, always in motion, following Beck. The Political Officer prowled constantly, watching, listening. No one remained cheerful in his presence—Kurt wondered if the power-feeling this must give Beck, and the sense of alienation which would attend the silence, might not reinforce the man's cold aloofness and make him even more of what he was. Something was bothering Beck, he saw as he surreptitiously studied the man, though he felt it was not connected with alienation—in his own alienation from friends he thought should be closer, Kurt felt he could touch Beck's being at congruent points (and here he also achieved insight into Hans's growing friendliness, for he, Kurt, was the only person aboard with whom Hans had a standing relationship, albeit based in lengthy enmity). The Political Officer had come ashore accompanied by two armed men, whose weapons the crew were certain were for use against deserters. The guns, Kurt decided, were bad tactics on Beck's part. They undermined an already decaying morale. If flights to Telemark were what Beck feared, his mere presence ashore should have been ample deterrent.

Otto was one of Beck's riflemen. Kurt collared him while the Political Officer was at the nether end of the work area. "What's Beck up to, Ott? Why the guns?"

Kapp checked Beck's location, then said, "I think he's hoping somebody'll run. He wants to kill somebody. He doesn't say it right out, but you can feel it there, like a maggot in his soul. It's like he has to get somebody quick, before the thing in him turns and destroys him. Kurt, I've never met anyone like that. He's like . . . like a devil inside . . . an eater of souls. But he's human, too. It keeps trying to get out, tries to make contact, like this morning when we were getting ready to come over. Out of the blue he asked me about Frieda, and, before I knew it, he was telling me all about his wife at Gibraltar. A slut and a dragon, to hear him tell It. Cruel . . . oh-oh. Better move on. Pass the word to be careful."

Beck was looking their way, wearing a calculating expression. Otto departed, leaving Kurt with a hundred questions about Beck. Had his wife beaten him into his present distorted shape? Did he hate all humanity because of her, especially women? Certainly he had had nothing to do with them in Kiel, where liberties were a byword. Might he be a man who thought he was complete unto himself? Kurt pounced on the notion, remembering a similar person met aboard a Danish boat, a man much like Beck outwardly. And, as Otto had suggested about Beck, that fisherman had proved an emotional time bomb. A small incident — the tearing of a net, as Kurt remembered — had triggered him one day; he had gone berserk, and had distributed injuries liberally before being subdued.

He was jerked from his speculations by *Jäger's* screaming general alarm. Men ran for the boats. Kurt looked around confusedly. A hundred meters downstream, just watching, were a dozen shaggy men clad in the skins of equally shaggy animals. Norwegians of the semi-nomadic variety Kurt had often seen at the Danish trading posts, men who farmed the high valleys of the mountains and hunted, and, someday, might fall into the savage raiding habits of their ancestors a millennium gone. These men were armed, as their sort invariably were, but their bows were unstrung, slung over their shoulders. Why the panic? he wondered.

The alarm ceased. Bells rang in the ensuing stillness as *Jäger's* after gunmounts swung around toward the hunters—who settled on their hams in the grass, laconically observing the panic.

Mr. Czyzewski began shouting in mixed Polish and German, driving sailors back to work. Sheepishly, they returned to their tools. Beck and his riflemen hurried past Kurt, took up defensive positions between hunters and sailors. Kurt found this pleasing. Beck would be out of the way, unable to snoop.

Uneventful days passed. *Jäger* lost her trim, wolfish look. Stem to stern, rail to rail, from her lowest void to her highest deck, she was stacked with fuel to drive her the long three thousand kilometers to Gibraltar. She rode very low in the water and her center of gravity had risen—dangerously so if she was forced to face a storm—and still Mr. Czyzewski was uncertain the fuel was sufficient. He claimed the wood would burn too fast, loudly mourned the lack of coal.

Jäger had burned coal thus far—coal brought to Kiel from Sweden, in driblets over the years, as ballast in the sailing ships of Swedish traders—but the little store left was to be saved for combat, when the ship would need its greater efficiency.

Sailors were loading a last mountainous raft while Kurt wondered where it was to be stored. A shout came from downriver. He turned. The Norwegians were striking camp—why had they spent so many days just sitting and watching?—and all but one vanished into the wood. The remaining man unhurriedly approached, smiling. Beck and his riflemen rose, waited. The meeting took place fifteen meters from Kurt. All activity ceased along the riverbank.

"What's happening?"

Kurt jerked nervously, then laughed. "Got me, Hans. Maybe he's bringing the bill for the wood."

"Hey!" Hans stared at the approaching man. "Isn't that ... what's his name? Franck? Yes, Karl Franck."

Kurt squinted against the sunlight. "You're right. He disappeared about the time I went to sea, after those speeches. . . ."

"My father still complains about him, usually when he wants to make a moral point." Hans grinned. "Prime example of moral decay. Dad says that, with my attitude, I'm sure to end up like him."

"Wait!" Kurt said. "Looks like trouble."

Franck had stopped a few paces from Beck, surveyed his uniform with exaggerated loathing, said something softly. Kurt saw color creep up Beck's neck, heard him mutter. His two riflemen retreated.

"What's happening, Ott?" Kurt asked.

"Don't know. Franck said something about the High Command, then Beck told us to get the hell out." Kapp fell silent, turned all his attention to Beck and Franck. An argument had begun. Beck appeared to be growing angry, which surprised Kurt. He had never seen Beck get emotional. He thought of his time-bomb notion. Someone laughed. Beck jerked as if stung, turned, narrowed eyes searching, promising reprisal, seeing nothing but sober faces. Growing angrier, he turned back to Franck, growled something.

Now Franck laughed. He made a megaphone of his hands, shouted, "Hey, men, thought you might like to know that High Command and the War are—"

He was unable to finish. Beck broke. He jerked his pistol out and fired. *Jäger*'s crew, ashore and at her rails, watched in dumb surprise, as Franck jerked to the repeated impact of bullets. Beck emptied his weapon, continued insanely pulling the trigger.

Berserk, just like that sailor, Kurt thought. He forced his rising breakfast back with difficulty. Hans muttered, "Oh, Christ!" and lost his.

Otto, after a silent moment during which the shots seemed to echo on, gasped, "He's finally done it. He's killed somebody."

Beck stood staring down at the corpse, shaking, yet with a beatific glow about him—a look of almost orgasmic satisfaction.

Then arrows streaked from the forest. Beck screamed as one hit his leg, was silenced as a second transfixed his throat. He took two more in leg and shoulder as he fell.

"Let's get out of here!" a sailor shouted. Everyone unfroze. Men caromed into one another as they raced for the boats. Kurt, stunned, walked after them, unable to hurry. Otto, retaining some presence of mind, snapped off random rifle shots as he retreated at Kurt's side.

Jäger bellowed like an indignant dragon defending chicks. Three-inch shells racketed over low, with a sound like nothing Kurt had ever heard. 40mms added their smaller voices to the uproar. The little shells hummed like bumblebees in passing. There were rapid explosions in the woods. Kurt saw a large tree suffer a direct hit. Five feet of ancient trunk disintegrated. The rest fell slowly, with the stateliness of a wounded giant.

But there were no more arrows. The Norwegians (or, perhaps, Littoral refugees) seemed satisfied with Beck's death. This bothered Kurt as he waded through shallow water and clambered into his boat. Why Beck alone? And why had the Norwegians opened fire so quickly—as if waiting? What had Franck been trying to say? Why had Beck felt the need to silence him? So many questions.

He sat in the bow of the boat and stared toward the dead

men. They were the first he had seen fall to violence. He was sickened. Franck lay in a grotesque position, some bones bullet-broken. Beck lay on his back, staring at cottony cumulus with cold, unseeing eyes. Kurt was certain Franck had intentionally baited Beck into his attack, but without expecting such sudden reaction — and his miscalculation had been fatal. Why he thought this Kurt was not certain, though. Perhaps because the arrows had come so swiftly, imply the shooting was planned. But to what purpose? He shook his head and stared around.

In the next boat he saw Gregor, pale and stricken. From behind him came the sound of warning bells as *Jäger* brought more guns to bear. Cordite smells, sour, bitter, assailed his nostrils. He saw, on looking back, men at *Jäger*'s rails with rifles and machine-pistols. He looked back to the wood. A curl of smoke rose from a small fire started by an exploding shell. Shattered trees leaned drunkenly in one another's arms. Raw brown wounds, shell holes, scarred the meadow. It was all so savage, so quickly come and gone. The feast of blood, he thought, the curse of Cain. He was grateful when *Jäger*'s stern interrupted his view of the destruction.

Later, when his nerves had settled somewhat, Kurt eased through a hatch into the after fireroom, which had been secured since the damage to the port screw. Czyzewski had decided to use the space to store the last raftload of fuel, and Kurt's men were to help stow it because the gunnery people were all on station.

After having made certain his men were at their jobs and doing them, Kurt began prowling. The engineering spaces, with their webs of piping, of electrical cables, and with their huge, looming machinery, oil smells, odd catwalks, and such, had always intrigued him. He did not understand why a man would want to work down in the heat, stench, and filth of the place, though.

He climbed a ladder to a high catwalk, to examine a control board with a vast array of valves and meters. Most were meaningless, as the ship no longer burned fuel oil, but he enjoyed trying to puzzle out their ancient functions. A short, half-open doorway caught his attention. He knew there was a small room behind it, inside one of the blower shafts which brought outside air to the fireroom. He thought the room might be a good place to store wood, if not already filled. He went across and opened the door. Empty.

No, not quite. There was a damp, muddy uniform on the floor. He glanced at it, then examined the rest of the room. Perhaps by stacking the wood crosswise . . .

His eyes snapped back to the uniform. Pieces of river weed clung to it. Something was wrong. He frowned. Why was it hidden here, as if someone had changed in secret? Then he grunted as if hit. None of the men who had gotten wet this morning had as yet had time to change. And there were no weeds in the river near the loading place. The nearest were a few hundred meters downriver, near the Norwegian camp.

A picture popped into his mind, of a faceless man swimming ashore in the night, downstream, where the weeds grew, to see the Norwegians. Had someone recognized Franck and gone to see him, perhaps to arrange this morning's disaster? He squatted over the damp uniform, looking for the name tag inside the waistband — and grew even more puzzled.

LINDEMANN, G.A. it said. Gregor. And Gregor, if he remembered right, had once known Karl Franck well. Had they met last night? And then a new thought entered his mind. Had they been in contact while Gregor was stationed here in Norway? Indeed, just what had Gregor been doing in this country? He had run a salting station, he said, but would say little more. Kurt began to feel his cousin was deeper than he had suspected, and that something unusual was in the wind.

But why wouldn't Gregor share it with his own cousin? Once more he was on the outside.

FOUR

"You look like a regular snipe, Ranke," said Erich Hippke, Quartermaster with the watch after Kurt's, as Kurt climbed out of the fireroom. "You're wearing enough grease."

Kurt chuckled. "Watch your language, sailor. Nobody calls me engineer and lives. . . ."

A Boatswain's pipe, shrill, cut across their conversation. "Now holiday routine for all personnel not otherwise directed," Hans's voice boomed over the public-address system.

"Ha!" said Hippke. "The rack for me."

"Why? You've been aboard, loafing, the past three days."

"Carried too much firewood." Hippke leaned on the lifelines, looking aft at a Damage Control party. "What's Czyzewski up to?"

"Bringing the bad screw aboard —"

"Kurt!"

He looked up, at Hans on the level above. "What?"

"Meeting in the wardroom, after dinner. Mr. Lindemann wants you there."

"All right. Erich, let's wash up. I'm hungry."

"I'll pass. Smelt, ugh!"

"You'll love it someday."

All leading petty officers were at the meeting when it convened. Von Lappus expressed its purpose. "I want to know how we get out of here, now we've got our firewood."

Once he had uttered those cryptic words, the beefy man slid down in his chair, folded his hands across his chest, and appeared to fall asleep. Kurt wondered, for the thousandth time, why this particular man was in command. He never seemed to *do* anything.

Haber expanded the explanation. "We're now eight feet lower in the water and no longer able to turn the ship. And we can't back out on one screw. Suggestions?"

Time passed silently. No one asked why they had originally gotten in that position—the ship could not have backed upstream, either. No one, though, had thought of the problem until von Lappus had had men sound the river around the ship. Hurry had its price—in this case, time lost and labor expended.

Jäger had to be backed downstream until she reached a place where she might turn. But how? Finally, after a long silence, Hans nervously offered an idea. "Sirs, I read somewhere that, on sailing ships, when there was no wind, they sometimes moved a vessel by 'kedging' her."

"And what might that be?" Haber asked. He looked hungry—for knowledge.

"Well, a boat was put over to carry the anchor to the end of its chain and drop it. Then the ship was winched up to short stay."

"I don't see . . ." Haber broke off in mid-sentence. He did see.

But Hans explained anyway, for the others. "We could do it backward, alternating anchors, walking ourselves down."

"Damned slow," someone muttered.

"How much chain do we have?" Haber asked.

"Five shot on the port anchor, six on the starboard," Hans replied.

"What's that in meters?" someone asked.

Haber penciled figures on the tabletop. "Roughly—and this is real rough—a hundred forty-five on the port, a hundred seventy-five on the starboard."

"We'll be a long time getting out, then," Lindemann noted, frowning. With his features tight he no longer looked much like Kurt. Older. Much older.

Haber nodded. "Depends. Ranke, is there a place we can turn?"

"There's a wide place about three kilometers down. We'd have to sound first, though."

"What interests me," said von Lappus, coming to life and folding his hands before his mouth as if praying, "is how Wiedermann plans to lift his anchors off the bottom. Our boats would be swamped by their weight. May I suggest rafts? We've got one already. Wiedermann, build another. Well, gentlemen, I've declared holiday routine. We'd better take advantage of it. I'll want the crew at quarters before sunrise, fed and ready to work. Wiedermann, you and Ranke will forego your holiday. Gunnery Officer, issue the shore party sidearms."

Hans looked frightened. Kurt felt pique. He did not want to go to that place again.

"Oh, Ranke," said von Lappus as they rose, "take a shovel. Bury Beck and that other fellow." Even in his dismay, Kurt noticed that Beck was no longer Mr. Beck. "And see you recover his weapon."

"Yes sir." Greatly depressed, Kurt walked with Hans to the mess decks, for coffee. Afterward, he drew a shovel from the Boatswain's locker, joined Hans and his men in a boat, dully accepted the pistol the Boatswain offered him. He thrust it in his waistband, tried to forget it.

The meadow he found peaceful again, yet Kurt could not keep his hand from straying to the gun. He was frightened by this haunted place. A pair of ghosts seemed somewhere near, mocking. The shell holes in the turf and the shattered trees beckoned him, like the War itself, to his own private little unremembered Armageddon. He threw the shovel across his shoulder, bit his lower lip, and determinedly walked toward the bodies.

Flies buzzed in that part of the meadow. Franck had already begun to bloat in the hot Norwegian sun. As he paused by Beck, a small animal, lean and ratlike, scurried off through the morning's trampled grass. A lonely bird mourned in the woods. Tears welled in Kurt's eyes, his throat became tight and sore. Such peace and beauty this place had, and horror—like the world. He wanted to hurl his shovel and pistol from him and run shrieking into the wood, off to Telemark to wait for Karen. . . .

Sounds stopped him: Hans shouting at his men, axes striking trees, a groan.

"Hans," he called softly, "Hans. Hans!" This last was a scream. The shovel fell to his feet. His mouth hung open, no articulate sounds coming forth. Hans came running, accompanied by two men with weapons drawn.

"What?"

The words came, though forcing them was next to impossible. "He's alive. God, he's still alive!" He pointed, and, as he did so, another weak groan fled Beck's scabby lips. "He's been here all morning, and we never came to help. . . ."

"Fritz, Jupp, get Commander Haber." Hans's businesslike tone sent the seamen hurrying off. "Don't seem possible. Four arrows in him, one through the throat. He can't be alive."

He was silent a moment. Oarlocks squealed on the river behind them. Then, thoughtfully, Hans said, "He can't last much longer. Suppose he died before Haber got here?" He reached forward to cover Beck's mouth and nose with his hand.

Kurt slapped his arm aside. "No! I don't like what he is either, but . . . well, he's a human being." Was this the Hans who had thrown up this morning?

"He'd probably thank me, if he was conscious." Hans's eyes narrowed, his face grew ugly. "If he lives, he'll be a burden for months, delirious, unreasonable. . . ." He reached again.

Again Kurt forced the hand away, the while wondering what was wrong with Hans. Why murder a dying man? "If he has to die, let him go by himself."

"It'd be so easy, Kurt. Nobody'd ever know. . . ."

"Too late, Hans." Kurt nodded. Hans's men were coming to see what had happened. They could not be ordered away without questions being asked.

"Well, you want him to live, he's yours."

Kurt tore his eyes from Beck's contorted face, looked at Hans. The man was pale and shaking. Afraid? Of what?

Commander Haber, carrying the ship's medical kit, arrived shortly, accompanied by Lindemann. Kurt thought he saw momentary disappointment flash across Gregor's face. He frowned, turned to watch Haber.

Haber was *Jäger's* approximation of a doctor, though his skills were limited to knowledge crammed while the vessel was outfitting. His tools were limited, his anesthetics and antibiotics almost nil. He examined Beck quickly, said, "Looks hopeless. The arrows missed the major arteries, but he's still lost a lot of blood. It's a miracle he's alive."

"*Do* something!" Kurt pleaded, unable to comprehend the calmness about him. But, outwardly, he was as calm as the others. Only his words betrayed his emotions.

"Right. I'll need help. First I'll have to open his throat so it's certain he can breathe. Kurt, open my bag and . . ."

"Me, sir?"

"You. All right, just hand it to me."

Despite his other emotions, Kurt was sheepish because of his queasiness, grew guilty because of a momentary regret at not having let Hans have his way, thereby sparing himself this.

Haber's cautious, uncertain work went on for an hour. First he removed the arrows from Beck's legs and shoulder—he admitted fear of trying the shaft in the man's throat. But it came to that eventually, once the other wounds were cleaned, packed, and bandaged. The last arrow he carefully cut to either side of Beck's neck, then, with several men holding Beck firmly immobile, he drew the shaft with forceps. Luck attended him. It came free easily.

But, for a moment, Beck's weak, rasping, open-throated breathing ceased. With a frightful grimace, Haber bent to Beck's throat and forced his own breath into the man's lungs. The Political Officer soon resumed breathing. Haber finished his bandaging, wearily said, "That's that, and probably a waste of time.

A thousand-to-one he's dead by morning. But I had to try. He'll need a nurse. . . ."

"I think that's a job for Kurt," said Lindemann.

Kurt glanced at his cousin, was startled by the anger in Gregor's face. Lindemann seemed to be thinking, "You want him saved? Then you do it." Had he not been distracted, Kurt could have become very angry.

"Get that stretcher over here," Haber ordered men who had been standing by. "Wiedermann, will you *please* keep your men working? This isn't a show. That raft has to be finished before dark. Ranke, go back to the ship with Beck. I'll have someone take care of Franck."

Much later, having been relieved of his nursing duties—there were out-of-work sonarmen with nothing better to do, and Lindemann's pique had apparently faded—Kurt stood leaning on the port bridge rail, watching Hans's men as they put the finishing touches on their raft. Aft, the engineers were just swinging the ruined screw aboard. It hit the deck with a clatter. Two of the three blades were mangled almost beyond recognition. Briefly, he hoped the drive shaft had not been bent. Then he wondered why. Silly, worrying about it. It did not matter. There was no way to replace the screw.

A mound of earth headed by a cross now marked the place where Franck had fallen. Kurt looked away, not wanting to be reminded, went down to the maindeck. After collecting a sandwich from the galley, he wandered aft, watched the Damage Control party cleaning up, then went to bed. Soon his mind wandered into a trap of thoughts of Karen.

Although, from the day he agreed to join *Jäger*'s crew, their marriage had grown increasingly stormy—and the final week had been a bickering hell as she strove to overcome his stubborn determination — Kurt wished he were home and in her arms. He wished there were a little less of the mule in him, a little more of the horse. Why did he, these few times he actually took a stand, always pick a place in the wrong?

It was a moment of lucid, honest self-criticism stimulated by the morning's disaster and the hard realization that in days to come others would join Karl Franck in dole and foreign graves. Until today Death had always been a remote acquaintance, more often a visitor to others' lives than his own. But now, with fresh earth mounded in a meadow nearby, he knew that pale rider had promised him closer attention. And he was afraid, afraid of a thousand things, things not of the world beyond, but of this, all the grim milestones along the road to his own dread appointment, all the things he would lose if he went too young.

The greatest loss would be Karen and a child as yet unborn. Karen, who had a harpy's beak and talons one minute, who was his warm Juliet the next, who was his Ruth and his Delilah, his Lysistrata and Helen. He was an Odysseus bound for the arms of a Penelope through a thousand Homeric terrors, by an equally circuitous route (his mind wandered in a maze of ancient images, the Peloponnesian War, the thousand ships and Illium, the horse, those who fell, the small reasons why, and he wondered at the lack of change in Man over the millennia) — but Odysseus was a hero and inveterate cutthroat. Kurt could not picture himself the same, a bloodthirsty swashbuckler eager for perils and plights.

As Karen had said one day, three months past, when *Dancer* had again put in at Kiel and Kurt had dragged her down to meet his Danish friends, he was not the type. She had had a tongue of bitterness that day, was still plaguing him for having talked

Otto into going to the War. After a quick tour of the boat, she had said, "I can see why you felt at home. It's a lot like you, small, antiquated, with no real goals or purpose, and a rotten stench inside. Real heroic."

And he had thought, "This's the woman I love?" Naturally, he had grown angry, there had been a scene, and he had accused her of being a bigger bitch than her mother, which had led to one of those arguments about mothers-in-law.

Yet he missed her. The harsh times quickly lost their hurting edges and he yearned for good times better remembered, the hand-in-hand days, the arm-in-arm days. He wished he could have yielded, could have stayed.

At last, sleep came.

Kurt rose muttering when reveille sounded. He rushed through his shower, shave, and dressing, and was on his way to the mess decks in minutes, determined to get one good meal that day. It would be a long one, with dinner and supper served on station.

Dawn was but a hint of light in the east, over the shadowy bones of low mountains. The Captain had kept his promise of an early start. Already the rafts were being maneuvered into position. Tripods mounting blocks and tackle had been rigged aboard them. The starboard anchor chain began paying out as the sun first broke over the spine of the mountains. *Jäger* swung slightly when she neared its end, the current pushing her inshore just enough to make her officers nervous. Commander Haber, who had the conn, ordered the port anchor dropped. Once it was holding, he had the starboard winched in.

Slowly, slowly, alternating anchors, *Jäger* kedged downriver. A few hundred meters, a kilometer, two, and, toward sundown, three, into the wide place Kurt remembered. Before she ceased operations for the day, men put out in boats to take soundings. There was room to turn.

Kurt and Hans, with Haber and Lindemann, watched from the port wing as the deck force rigged the damaged propeller for use as a stern anchor, to hold the vessel while the current turned her end for end. On the forecastle, another party waited to up anchor. The sun had not yet risen. Wan light, filtered through clouds over the eastern mountains, barely illuminated the vessel, gray light on gray, with gray ashore—the perfect world for the warship. The propeller, attached to a heavy mooring line, splashed over the stern.

"Take in the bow anchor," Haber directed.

A Boatswain shouted, his words ripping the fabric of the quiet Norwegian morning. Men scurried around and disorganization resolved itself into disciplined cooperation. The hook was up in minutes, was seated and secured.

Haber called into the bridge, "Tell the engine room to stand by." Then, "Wiedermann, get your leadsmen in the chains." Hans hurried off.

Slowly, slowly, *Jäger* swung with the current. Tense minutes passed. Soon she was beam on to the flow, then past with sighs of relief.

The ship shuddered, heeled over a few degrees, moved a little, shuddered again. "Mudbank," Kurt said softly, hoping the bow would find nothing more solid.

The swing continued. Another shudder and heel, longer-lasting and accompanied by scraping, made men stagger. It seemed certain the ship would be caught. But the current worked, forced the bow on over the mudbank. *Jäger's* centerline was parallel to the flow a few minutes later.

"Whew!" Kurt whistled, mopping his forehead and leaning heavily on the rail. "Close, that."

"Cast off aft!" Haber ordered, shouting. Softer, "I sweated blood, there. The men who took soundings should've found that bank. . . ."

A man chopped through the mooring line. It whipped over the stern. *Jäger* jerked, drifted forward on the current. "Make four four turns for five knots!" Haber ordered.

Kurt hurried inside to log it. "Hans," he said as he wrote, "can you put men on the peloruses? I'll need bearings soon. And I'll need a recorder." He took his makeshift bearing book from the drawer beneath the chart table, surveyed bearings taken coming upriver. Steering by their reciprocals should take *Jäger* safely back to sea.

Hans shouted graphically at several men who were doing nothing, apparently unaware that nothing was what they were supposed to do until needed. He took the recorder's job himself. "We've got the weirdest ship in history," he said.

"What makes you think that?"

"Our officers. Can you imagine a more uncaptainly Captain?"

"He gets the job done."

"Can't argue that. Uh, bearing to ruined silo, one two zero. What about Haber? He looks like a rat. If he'd get rid of that mustache . . ."

"He's as loud as you are, anyway."

"Course, Quartermaster?" Haber demanded from the wing.

"You see?" He calculated quickly. "One eight three, sir. Come left to one seven six about five hundred meters down."

"Very well." Haber gave Lindemann the conn, left the bridge.

Hans leaned closer to Kurt, whispered, "Mr. Lindemann's

the only normal officer aboard. Take Mr. Obermeyer . . ." Just a hint of bitterness could be heard in his tone.

"You take him," Kurt chuckled. "I'll grant you, the Council made a mistake with him. Where is he? He should be on the forecastle with the Sea Detail."

"The ship's moving. That's all it takes. Maybe we should feel sorry for him, though. He really does get deathly sick. But, if I have to do his job, why don't I have his brass?" This was the first time Kurt had actually heard him express displeasure at not having won the First Lieutenant's appointment.

"Time to make that turn, sir," he reminded Gregor. "One seven six. You'd think he'd get used to it."

"No. What about Ensign Heiden?" Hans asked. "I heard he's queer. . . ."

"Hans, every man on this ship is queer as a cow with a peg-leg. Up here." He tapped his forehead. "Otherwise, we'd still be home. You've read as much history as me. Think of the officers they had in the olden days, especially the English."

Hans's eyes narrowed thoughtfully. "Nelson. Maybe it does take madmen."

Jäger reached the sea without difficulty. The Kristiansand girls were cheered again. Kurt sighed with relief as the town fell behind, as *Jäger* entered deep, reliable waters. He removed his cap and tossed it into an out-of-the-way corner of the chart table. "How come we always get the watch after Sea Detail?"

Hans chuckled and took the hint. Of Lindemann he asked, "Permission to secure Sea Detail, sir?" Then, "Hold it!" directed at several seamen about to leave the bridge. "Come here, Ernst." Pointing down, he said, "See those rust spots on the forecastle? I want them chipped and painted before dinner."

Kurt cluck-clucked as Ernst went away grumbling. "You're a slavedriver."

Hans laughed. "Take the paint away and there wouldn't be any ship." There was a grain of truth in his words. Only the most intense, loving maintenance kept *Jäger* from expiring.

"Quartermaster?"

"Sir?"

"Do you have a track for the Channel?"

"Yes sir. We should come right to two zero zero in a half hour."

"Inform me when it's time."

"Yes sir." Kurt gathered his weather logs and stepped outside to see which direction the swells were running. Hans followed.

"I was surprised," the Boatswain whispered. "Nobody jumped ship."

"Surprised me too," Kurt replied. He winced, still not wanting to remember Beck and Franck.

"I sort of figured you'd go, what with Karen on her way. You know, I've been wondering. Why was Beck the only one they shot?"

"I never seriously considered jumping ship," Kurt said truthfully, and asked himself why he had not. Karen was precious to him. "As for Beck, I think someone wanted to get rid of him."

He was about to tell Hans of his discovery in the after fireroom, but thought better of it. "I wouldn't much miss the man."

"Who would? But he refuses to die." For a moment Kurt was afraid he would bring up their brief conflict over Beck's life, but Hans let it drop. He and Kurt looked forward, silently watched *Jäger*'s bow rise and fall as she met the swells of the North Sea.

FIVE

J *äger* wallowed through moderate seas at an unchanging eight knots, all she could comfortably manage on one screw, though she was capable of twelve in a panic. There was ample time to reach Gibraltar. The Gathering would not sail eastward until mid-July.

The ruins of a city lay three kilometers off the port beam. Kurt studied an old map, guessed it to be Cherbourg. He felt a sadness. This was even more depressing than Kiel, because it was dead. He suspected the ruins would glow by night. Calais and Dover had been horrifying, like the impossible, wicked cities of the evil beings of old folk tales.

The crossing of the North Sea had been unmarked by significant event. High points had been a fog, a squall, and a few fishing boats seen in the Dogger Banks, all of which had run when they spotted *Jäger*'s gray wolf sihouette on their horizons. Kurt did not blame them for their reactions. The warship was a ghost from a bloody past, a death-specter, a haunt.

The passage through the English Channel, thus far, had been equally uneventful. There were dangers, but these they evaded by careful sailing. The old mudbanks, which had once plagued Romans, Norse raiders, and the Spanish Armada in its time, had returned. But someone, probably fishermen, had kindly marked the banks with lighted buoys. All in all, Kurt decided, Norway to Cherbourg was a dull four days' voyage.

He glanced at the map again, frowned. Like most *Jäger* carried, it was English-language. For the thousandth time, he wished he could learn the tongue. His work would be so much easier.

He wondered what had become of the Americans, who had built *Jäger* so long ago. Word-of-mouth history, rapidly becoming legend, had that whole nation burned in the nuclear exchange following the Battle of the Volga. Kurt tried to picture millions of square kilometers of radioactive wasteland, and could not. He had been to the border of the vast dead plain south of Hamburg, but that could not be believed either. It was too big. The entire concept of the War was too big to comprehend. He took binoculars from a locker, leaned on the rail. His eyes watered when he examined the magnified ruins.

He wondered why. Was it because of his father's stories? Old Kurt had been fond of things French and fairy-tale adventures based on the deeds of real people: Napoleon, Richelieu, Jeanne d'Arc, the Black Prince, Roland, and a hundred others, some not French at all. Old Kurt had not been concerned with accuracy. In his stories, pre-War times became a Hyperborean paradise where temporal realities meant nothing. Kurt chuckled, remembering a tale in which Wellington defeated Charlemagne at Avignon during the War of the Spanish Succession.

Twelve years had passed since *U-793*'s departure. Young Kurt had stopped missing his father long ago. He remembered the stories best, his father's tears the day the submarine sailed, and how, afterward, his mother had been seized by an endless grief. Life had become her personal Hell. He felt little sorrow at her passing, for death had been a blessing finally freeing her from sorrow.

"See anything?"

"What?" Startled, Kurt hastily glanced over his shoulder. Hans.

"See anything out there?"

"The hoofprints of Death."

"Poetry I get. Pale Rider home? Let me see."

Kurt gave him the glasses. Wiedermann stared at the ruin briefly, then swept the entire coast. "You're right. Nothing. Hard to believe so many people used to live there."

"Efficient killers, the old-timers. Imagine *Jäger* new, and she almost a toy to them."

"She's still an iron cobra," Hans replied. "Now who's poetic?"

"It's true. If nothing else, her fangs are functional. She'll be a tiger when we find the enemy—if we keep her afloat."

"The enemy. We've heard that all our lives. What enemy? I wonder if there'd be an enemy if we just stayed home."

Hans gave him a strange look, shrugged, said, "You've got me, Kurt," and returned the glasses. "Did you hear? Beck came out of coma this morning." He stepped inside the bridge. Kurt heard him growl at Otto for wandering off course.

Then he shuddered. He had spoken dangerous words. Sure as death, if Beck were healthy he would have heard. Such talk could have a man hanging from a yardarm, though Kurt could not understand why, logically. Emotionally, he knew, anything could have strong meaning.

His mind went howling off after the mystery of the Political Office. What was its purpose? Why were its people so strange? He believed men served and defended things, ideals, and rules, in which they had a vested interest. Given that assumption, Political Officers seemed still more mysterious—they appeared to react only when the War was questioned or damned. Why should they want it continued? How did they profit? There were just six Political Officers on lifetime assignment to the Littoral, and not a one got anything out of his job except a small local power. The pay was minimal. Hans's father, for instance, earned more making furniture.

Once he had asked Hans why his father was a Political Officer. Wiedermann had simply twirled a forefinger at his temple. He did not know either.

Crazy? Might be, although, officially, the Political Office was that arm of the High Command charged with ensuring that member states made maximum contributions to the War.

Which again led him to question the purpose of the War. Was it a vast plot to destroy? That seemed where everything was bound. Kurt found he liked the theory. Deliciously insane. Everything was.

Or was there really some foundation to the shadow-threat of Australia? Was it true that, ten thousand miles away, madmen were gathering hordes to enslave the world? He glanced aft, at the ruins of Cherbourg. Destroy the world? Someone had done a first-rate job already.

Then he considered his thoughts. He was thinking in terms

of conspiracies, a High Command conspiracy. He grew nervous. His thinking was as crazy as that of the old-timers, who had seen threats and enemies everywhere. The first step to madness . . . He laughed at himself. His tenseness eased.

"What?" Hans was back.

"Nothing. Just wondering what strange things might be hiding under cabbage leaves."

"Babies. But I like the home-brewing method better."

Kurt thought this was too near bringing up Karen's pregnancy. He and Hans were getting on remarkably well. No point in chafing old wounds.

Guilt knifed across his thoughts. Karen had been out of mind for several days. Bad. A husband should think of his wife often. Briefly, he wondered if she had begun her trip to Norway yet. Probably. It was easy enough. She could walk north through Jutland, take a fishing boat across the Skagerrak. It was done all the time. . . . He hurt. Homesickness was worse than seasickness, took longer to heal.

"Almost time for our reliefs," he said. "Think I'll work on my track for the Bay of Biscay."

"What's the hurry? You've got till tomorrow night."

"Maybe. But I want to be ready." The charts were the only excuse he could think of for going away.

Kurt's timing played him false. As he approached the chart table, Gregor whispered, "Beck wants to see you after watch." Intense bitterness momentarily marred his features.

Heart in throat when the watch was done, Kurt went down to officers' country. His hands were clammy and shook as if he suffered Haber's disorder. Why would Beck call for him? He had nothing to do with anything. . . .

Beck's "Come" when Kurt knocked was a ghost of the ghost his voice had always been. "Sir, you shouldn't be sitting up. . . ." Nor should he have been talking—though his speech was confined to a whisper—through such a savaged throat.

"You found me." It was an almost inaudible statement. "You kept me alive. I thank you. But why? I'd've thought you partial to those who prefer me dead."

"Sir?" As pretended disbelief Kurt's gasp rang entirely false. Certainly, Beck sensed it.

"I know more than you think. I knew Franck, or someone like him, would appear wherever we refueled. There were just three stopping places under consideration when we left Kiel, and they were sure to know them all." He coughed lightly. "I have my own sources, who predicted the attack. But Franck had done his homework too."

Beck's face turned sour. "He knew just the way to goad me. . . . There's a man in Personnel at Gibraltar who'll be sorry."

Silently, Kurt wondered where Beck was leading.

"Why did you save me, Ranke?"

"Sir?" He was still uncertain himself. "I don't know. You were hurt. It didn't matter who you were. . . ." He shut up.

Beck coughed again, said, "No need for fear. I want frank talk. Anyway, I've grown accustomed to dislike. So, you would've done it for anyone? It wasn't a matter of loyalty?" He seemed disappointed by Kurt's nod.

"Ranke, I've been watching you. Nothing personal, understand, but Leading Quartermaster's an important position. Your knowledge makes you essential to ship's operations. I've come to think you're a very well-educated, ignorant young man."

Kurt frowned.

"No insult intended. What I mean is, you've plenty of book learning, but aren't very world-wise. Will you keep confidential what's said here?"

Kurt nodded, though he could conceive of no secrets Beck would willingly impart.

"Good. Have you heard of an organization fighting High Command?"

Kurt honestly had not. He said as much.

"That's why I say you're not world-wise. There've been a lot of rumors about it lately. And the organization exists. It's very small, very secret, with an excellent espionage system in Gibraltar, the Littoral, and elsewhere. Rumor and subtle sabotage are its weapons. It's based in Norway, somewhere in Telemark . . ."

Kurt's startlement must have shown. Beck asked, "Ring a bell?"

"Just surprised me, sir. I know people who went to Telemark."

"Yes, don't you?" Beck's gaze was piercing. He coughed again, grimaced. "This organization's too small to hamper High Command, yet its very existence has created a policy crisis at Gibraltar. The Political Office in particular has split over what action to take. One party demands swift suppression. The other, for political reasons, wants to let it grow. The factions were near blows, last I heard. A power struggle was shaping up. . . ."

Kurt felt lost. He had never thought of the High Command in these lights, nor had he ever dreamed of an anti-War underground. Some odd events clicked into place, made sense.

"Well," said Beck, "your loyalty to your friends is stronger than to High Command, so it'd be futile for me to ask you to poke around after underground activity. Oh, yes, there's a small cell aboard. I'm even fairly certain of several identities. . . ."

Cold fear washed Kurt's soul like the sudden shock of thrown icewater. He, too, was sure of one man. Gregor. There could be no other explanation for the curiosity he had found in that blower room. Gregor, Gregor, he thought, what are you doing? He was hurt, hurt deeply because a man as close as his cousin, and a woman as close as Karen, had never had the trust to confide in him.

Sea waves washed the hull, which formed one wall of Beck's stateroom, with mesmeric regularity. How like this ship I am, Kurt thought. The waves of the world splash against me repeatedly, and all the waters of awareness that enter do so accidentally.

Beck! The Political Officer was suffering a coughing fit. Blood spume colored his lips. Kurt ran out, found Commander Haber. Before the night was done, Beck once again owed Kurt his life.

Jäger rounded Brittany next evening, following a track from Ile d'Ouessant to Cabo Ortegal. A bit over fifty hours' steaming if there was no trouble.

But trouble there was, a small storm which cost an hour, and a man overboard—perhaps with help.

It may have begun at supper, when *Jäger* was halfway across the bay. Kurt, Hans, Otto, and several others were sitting at a table in the mess decks, grumbling about the food, and about the rolling of the ship in the last breaths of the storm. Somehow, Beck's name arose.

"Me," Kapp growled, "I wish he'd bought it. Got no use for Political Officers."

His eyes were angry as he glanced at Hans. "Nor the War, nor High Command. Maybe *Jäger* ought to blast High Command. Makes more sense than sailing around the world for nothing. At least there'd be no more War."

Kurt was startled. He had suspected Otto's feelings, but not that they were this strong. The others seemed equally surprised, and uncertain if Kapp were joking.

Kurt worried. Frieda would never forgive him if anything happened to Otto. Frowning, he leaned closer, and, as he had thought several times during the meal, caught a whiff of alcohol. There had been a rumor about homemade vodka brewing in an unused fresh-water evaporator.

"Ott, take it easy," he whispered.

Kapp was drunker than Kurt thought. "Take it easy?" He staggered up, spilled his tray in the process. "Take it easy? How can I take it easy when you're hauling me off to get killed like a slaughter lamb? And for nothing. If there's an almighty War to fight, why doesn't High Command do the dying?"

Otto shouted, "How many of you want to go on? What's in this War for us? Where're we going? Why? Just because Beck told us to? Let's go home. If we have to, we should—"

"Ott!" Kurt snapped, cutting him off before he could damn himself with a proposal of mutiny. "Shut up!"

"You shut up, Kurt! Don't you want to see Karen again? Maybe you don't. Beck says there's a War, and you always let people run you. . . . What's the matter with all of you? You don't want this stupid trip. We'll all get killed if we go. Why don't we do something about it?"

He was hitting them hard, Kurt saw. They were thinking. Trouble would come soon, bad trouble. "Hans, Erich, Fritz, give me a hand," he whispered. They rose and a moment later were wrestling Otto forward, down to his compartment, with Kurt praying he had acted in time to keep Kapp's head out of a noose. Von Lappus and Haber seemed to have low opinions of Beck, but they would not refuse his orders in a mutiny case.

Otto passed out before they heaved him into his rack. They tied him in, returned to the mess decks. Kurt thought he had better warn his men off the Polish liquor, lest they wind up as Otto had, spouting nonsense which made all too much sense.

Silence reigned on the mess decks. Men stared into their food, thinking much what Otto had said aloud. The same thoughts were in Kurt's mind, which made him frightened and sad; frightened he would eventually follow Otto's lead, sad because he had not the courage.

After his watch—which was miserable because he spent it dwelling on Otto's words and the possibility of never seeing Karen again—Kurt went to his compartment determined to sleep. But his thoughts would not cease haunting him. He was hag-ridden. Never again to see Karen, to hold her. . . . After an hour's tossing, he gave up, decided to take a walk topside.

He found the last of the storm gone, so strolled along the starboard weatherdeck, watched the phosphorescent water rush past and the occasional flying fish flutter away from *Jäger*'s side. These small miracles he never tired of studying.

He climbed to the torpedo deck and took a seat astraddle the starboard tube, still watching the passing sea and the rolling stars above. The soft sigh of the water swirling past, the gentle *crump* of waves being broken under the bow, was restful, eased his tension. He gradually regained peace.

He had been sitting there nearly an hour, thinking, when he heard angry voices on the maindeck portside. The sounds of the wind in the rigging, and of the passing sea, muted those voices, making them unidentifiable, yet left the anger easily detectable. He rose and started over, curious. A scream.

Kurt ran, stopped at the port lifelines, looked down. Aft, a watertight door squeaked shut. Directly below, a hand clung to the lifelines while another tried for a grip. The man called for help, weakly. Kurt scrambled down the nearest ladder, shouting, "Man overboard! Man overboard! Port side!"

As his feet hit the maindeck, *Jäger* nosed into a heavy swell. He staggered, grabbed handholds welded to the bulkhead. The swell hastened along the sides of the ship, seized the man clinging to the lifelines. His hold broke. He shouted something as his hands fell out of sight. Kurt reached the lifelines just in time to see the terrified face of Otto Kapp disappearing in phosphorescent foam.

A shouted question came from the bridge. Kurt shouted back, without words. *Jäger* ceased shuddering as her engines were taken off the line, to keep the man overboard from being dismembered by the screw. She slowly swung to port, throwing her stern away from him. Von Lappus, like a roly-poly teddy bear, appeared in nightshirt and sleeping cap. No one had suspected—neither did anyone laugh. No one noticed.

The Captain rumbled, grumbled, asked pointed questions. Kurt was too distraught to answer coherently, certain this was all his fault. If only he hadn't talked Otto into coming. . . . Would Frieda ever forgive him?

But he never mentioned his suspicion that Otto had had help going over. Why? He did not know, though he asked himself repeatedly.

Von Lappus quickly stopped trying to get anything out of him. He took command of the vessel, and, after a Williamson turn failed to bring her back to Kapp, ordered a search pattern. Searchlights probed the night, pale fingers caressing silver wavecrests. The few starshells in the magazines were squandered, floated down the darkness like tiny, sputtering suns. But there was little hope of finding a man overboard at night when he had gone without a lifejacket and flares.

Yet they eventually found him, floating face down, arms widespread. Kurt had recovered enough to ask himself if drowned men float, and he seemed to be the only one who noticed the small bloodstain on Otto's jumper, in the back, about kidney-high.

There was nothing to be done for Kapp. Von Lappus said to leave him there, with a prayer. And, among his shipmates, there were thoughts of what he had had to say in the mess decks earlier.

Jäger resumed steaming. Kurt, knowing he would get no sleep, went to the charthouse where he and Gregor both did much of their work. He took a copy of the ship's muster from his files, studied it a moment, used a pencil to black out four names: his own, Beck's, von Lappus's, and Otto's. He told himself there would be a day when just one name remained. Then there would be a reckoning, both for Otto and for Frieda, widowed before marriage. For a few minutes there he was a grim young man his Karen would never have recognized.

SIX

Jäger reached Cabo Ortegal on track, two hours late. Kurt had by that time recovered somewhat from Otto's loss, although he was still withdrawn from ship's affairs. She turned and followed the Spanish coast, passing Coruña near midnight, Cabo Touriñan early the following morning, and, after turning south, reached Cape Finisterre at midmorning. There she hove to.

A ship was on the rocks there, another destroyer. She had not been aground long—her paint was fresh and her flags flew untattered by the wind—but she showed no signs of life.

Kurt, called to the bridge for consultation, studied her unfamiliar colors and frowned. He did not know her flag. She was of pre-War American construction, but otherwise a mystery.

Von Lappus said, "We'll send a boarding party. She may have gear we can use."

Commander Haber, speaking to a gaggle of officers, said, "Each of you pick two men from your department to look for salvage. First Lieutenant, put a boat in the water."

Gregor turned to Kurt. "Find Hippke. You two go over."

Kurt wanted to protest. He had no desire for a boat ride across choppy seas. He killed it unborn. He could cry for a week and still have to go — thus things worked in the Navy.

Soon the boarding party gathered. They climbed down to the whaleboat, took seats at the oars, rowed. Once started, Kurt found he was eager to go aboard and explore this strange vessel — until he actually set foot on her maindeck.

Bloated corpses were scattered there, bodies perhaps a week old, bodies invisible from *Jäger* because of the wreck's cant. Weapons covered with a patina of new rust lay among them. The dead aft were enlisted men. Forward they found two mutilated Political Officers, as well as officers and ratings.

Almost from the moment he stepped aboard, Kurt was certain of the cause of the mutiny. These men — one side — had wanted nothing to do with the War. Perhaps they had had their own Otto Kapp, one who had been successful in getting men to follow him. And, during the fighting, the ship had run aground. Or, perhaps, someone had run her on the rocks intentionally. He thought of Beck's astounding disclosures.

Gradually, during a cursory examination of the vessel, Kurt recovered from his initial shock. "Erich," he muttered, "let's get done and get out of here."

Hippke was as shocked, though, in his time, he had seen

some grim sights. He appeared not to have heard. Kurt took him by the arm.

They found more corpses inside the ship. Each compartment and passageway had its bloated tenant. "Let's find the charthouse," said Kurt, gagging in the interior fetor.

To reach their goal, they had to climb over a corpse with its legs tangled in a ladder. The man had been shot in the head repeatedly. In the closed, narrow space, the stench was overwhelming.

"It should be on this level," Kurt said. "It was on most American ships."

"Here, I think this's it. Wrong side, though."

Kurt studied the little plaque above the door. The few words on it made no sense, but they were the same as those over *Jäger's* charthouse door. "Open it."

"It's locked from inside."

Despite a sinking feeling, Kurt braced himself against the ladder and kicked. The door gave a little. Two more kicks broke the lock.

"Oh, Christ!" Hippke muttered, gagging.

A man lay on the deck inside. He had, apparently, been wounded in the fighting, had fled to a safe place, and had died there. The deck was covered with brown scales of dried blood.

"All right," Kurt growled, trying to control his stomach, "let's get him out." They grabbed the corpse's clothing, heaved it into the passageway, held their breaths against the sudden increase in stench.

The vessel shivered. A small shriek of protesting metal ran through her as she shifted on the rocks. Hippke looked ready to panic, which surprised Kurt, considering the man's past. He fought his own fear.

"Let's go through their stuff!" he snapped. "There'll be plenty of time to get off if she starts breaking up." He opened a drawer, wishing he were more confident of that. "Hey! Look here! Notebooks."

He had found a dozen of them. Paper! Invaluable paper. *Jäger*'s records were kept on scraps likely to crumble at any moment.

"Yeah?" Hippke replied, excited. He opened another drawer. "Look at this! Ballpoint pens. And they work." He tested one after another with the wonder of a child.

Like children in an attic they pawed through the endless treasures the charthouse offered: publications *Jäger* lacked, charts, instruments, more ballpoints, pencils, paper—a wealth of usable paper.

"Kurt," Erich said after a while, "it's like digging for treasure and finding it."

Kurt remembered other duties. "We'd better go send the word."

"Good idea. The sooner they start, the more they'll get off before she breaks up."

As if on cue, the ship shifted and groaned.

They scrambled up ladders to the signal bridge, too excited to be bothered by corpses. "See if the lights work," said Kurt. "I'll look for a set of flags."

A moment later, Hippke called, "No power."

"Didn't think there would be," Kurt replied, coming out of the signal shack with semaphore flags. "These'll do. See if Brecht's ready."

Erich looked through the ship's telescope. "He's waiting. Captain's with him."

"Von Lappus? On the signal bridge? How'd he haul himself up?"

"Got me. Brecht's seen us. He says he's ready."

Kurt sent for several minutes, finished, read the Captain's reply, said, "Erich, tell the others it's time to go. I'll be down in a minute."

He scrounged up a pillowcase and quickly filled it with plunder, hauled it to the quarterdeck. The others were waiting. He laughed. The whaleboat rode low in the water, piled with loot. Kurt tossed his atop the rest. A moment later they pushed off. There were soft curses as water washed over the gunwales.

"You men report to the mess decks," von Lappus ordered once the boat was hoisted aboard *Jäger*. "Wiedermann, post a man at each door. We're not to be bothered."

Kurt did as he was told, found the ship's officers already gathered on the mess decks.

"I imagine," said the Captain on arriving, "from all the excitement, that salvage will be worthwhile. What's she got? You, Zlotopolski."

One of Czyzewski's engineers replied, "There were stores of coal, grease, lubricating oil, and gasoline. The screws were both intact, and of the same type as our own."

Von Lappus caught the inference, said, "Chief Engineer, that'll be your most important task. Deckinger?"

Deckinger spoke briefly of paint, tools, line, and such, which were of interest to Deck. Kurt stopped listening, thought about von Lappus and Haber. They were changing. The Captain grew steadily sloppier. Rumor said he was eating poorly. Haber was growing increasingly nervous, and in dress was following the lead of von Lappus.

Gunnery's man spoke mostly of ammunition and small arms.

"Ranke?"

Kurt was jolted back to the discussion. "Sir, our gear is primitive compared to theirs. Their bridge, charthouse, and Combat were all well-equipped. There're supplies and charts we need desperately."

"Mr. Obermeyer, you're to salvage her," von Lappus told the continually seasick First Lieutenant. "I want all available boats in the water. We'll work around the clock till she's stripped."

Kurt went to the bridge that evening to distribute his loot. Hippke came up, still shaken. Could this be, Kurt wondered, the same Erich who claimed to have adventured all through the Littoral? Who, supposedly, had served in *Freikorps Flieder*, a vicious private army officially ignored because it performed a valuable service; to wit, it confined its predations to Russians, who, given a chance, did the same to the Littoral. Hippke claimed to have been present at some noteworthy massacres, yet the mess aboard the wreck had shattered him. He was not what he claimed, despite his excellent credentials.

Before Kurt could question Hippke, Erich said, "Beck wants you."

"Now?"

"In his stateroom."

Again with heart pounding, Kurt went down to that place of fear. As he entered, the Political Officer whispered, "I'm indebted to you again. You must be my guardian angel. What happened over there?"

Kurt lifted his eyebrows questioningly.

"The wreck. Nobody's seen fit to tell me anything. All I know is what I overhear of conversations in the passageway." Beck looked much better now, past his worst days. He would heal, though it would take a long time.

"Nothing. We just poked around."

"Don't be coy. What happened to her crew?" If anything, Beck's gaze was more cold and penetrating than when he had been well. His face was more skull-like.

Kurt shifted uneasily. "Mutiny, I think, sir. They were too busy fighting to work ship."

"Mutiny? I'd heard it, but not believed. . . . Why?"

"Sir, it looked like the crew didn't want to go to the War." Kurt's words were almost inaudible, so frightened was he. "They shot the officers and ratings, then tortured their Political Officers to death."

Beck looked both startled and afraid — the first time Kurt had seen him express the latter. Perhaps he knew of Otto and how near *Jäger* had come. "They killed each other off?"

"The boats were gone. Some got away."

Beck grunted. "Damn! Wish I could go look. I'll have to file a report. . . . This'll cause a stir, give the extermination faction a powerful argument in the dispute about the underground. Tortured, you say?"

He was quiet for a minute. Talking obviously pained him. Kurt waited nervously, hands cold and clammy, heart beating faster than ever. He wondered if he should have marked Beck's name off his suspect list — but no, Beck would have taken care of Otto legally, with a trial and execution.

"Does this give you any ideas about the situation here?" Beck finally asked. "A mutiny could go hard on you, you being a senior rating. Have you discovered anything I should know?" His pale face seemed eager, predatory.

More frightened than ever, Kurt shook his head while remembering a blower room, Otto's death, and Hippke's strange behavior. He wanted away from the Political Officer badly, yet could not walk out unbidden. And he did feel sorry for the man, alone there day after day now continual nursing was no longer a must. He stayed another hour, talking of mundane things—including the harridan wife Otto had once mentioned—always staying clear of troublesome topics. Kurt thought he might have liked the man, had his appearance been more pleasant and his power lessened.

Kurt had to return to the wreck three days later. He was in the charthouse filing salvaged charts, when Gregor leaned in the door, said, "Kurt, you'll have to go over again. I know you don't want to, but Beck insisted. He's making a report for High Command. He wants the ship's nationality, Captain's name, home port, things like that."

"But . . ."

"You'll have to go."

Knowing further protest was futile, Kurt got a jacket and cap, then caught the next boat.

He found the wreck's decks clean. "Deckinger," he asked as the junior Boatswain happened by, "where're the bodies?"

"Deep six. Couldn't work with them around. Gag a maggot."

"Yeah." Kurt walked forward, looking around. The progress amazed him. The ship had assumed a gaunt, skeletal look. Then he groaned as two cooks came from the galley with a stainless-steel sink, the bowl filled with a paint locker. Hans's voice, commanding, came from the firerooms. Above him and aft, there was a clatter and curse as a man dismantling a 40mm gun dropped a wrench. Forward, Boatswains grumbling like trolls raided a paint locker. Hans's voice, commanding, came from the torpedo deck. Kurt wound his way past piles of salvage to a ladder.

He made a cursory search of the bridge, found nothing. And the charthouse was clean. He saw nothing to indicate whence the ship had come, nor why, though that was obvious. She had been on her way to Gibraltar and the Gathering.

He sat in the charthouse and tried to think where the information might be hidden, stared at himself reflected badly in the dusty glass door of a bookshelf stripped days earlier. Where? Where?

He straightened suddenly, smashing fist into palm. It would be out in the open, simply overlooked. He rushed to the bridge and went to the chart table, stared at the chart pinned there. He pulled two tacks with his thumbnails, lifted the chart of the Spanish coast.

"Oh, you beautiful!" Beneath the chart was another, of a smaller scale, showing the coasts of Spain, France, and parts of England and the Low Countries, which told him very little except that the ship had come from the north, following a penciled track almost matching *Jäger*'s.

He flipped that chart up, studied the pilot chart beneath it. The entire track was there, beginning in Iceland. Iceland! Incredible. He popped the remaining two tacks, folded the charts, collected the Quartermaster's notebook from nearby, tucked everything inside his jumper, and caught the next boat returning to *Jäger*.

As he was leaving he watched Hans and his men lower a torpedo onto a float of rubber liferafts. He found their excitement difficult to believe.

"I found their charts and notebook," he told Gregor on arriving. "They'll tell Beck what he wants to know." He handed the material over, disappeared before he could be told to do something else.

Three days passed. Relentlessly, around the clock, the cannibalization continued. *Jäger* became as piled and ragged-looking as when she departed Norway. In a heroic battle with the sea, Czyzewski's engineers liberated a screw and floated it over on Hans's rafts. Commander Haber kept busy patching battered divers.

All the ammunition, all the fuel, all the stores were scavenged from the iron corpse. Everything portable was taken, whether *Jäger* had use for it or not. Work shifted to heavy machinery. Gun barrels were dismounted and floated over. Air-conditioning and refrigeration systems were stripped. An automatic dishwasher and electric potato peeler were rescued by happy cooks. Fire hoses, pipes and fittings, even a few watertight doors and hatches were taken. . . .

Then a black little storm blew up. Not a nasty storm, but one that looked threatening enough as it came whooping in out of the middle Atlantic. Von Lappus ordered *Jäger* out, away from the rocks.

And, when she returned, the wreck had broken up, so she turned south, resumed steaming for Gibraltar.

SEVEN

The harsh clangor of the general alarm woke Kurt earlier than customary. He froze for an instant, not believing. Not a drill! It couldn't be a drill. They were always announced beforehand. He heard the confused voices of others. The lights came on. He piled out of his rack, narrowly missed the man below. Trousers he jerked on hurriedly, feet he thrust into shoes, then he grabbed jumper and cap and ran for the bridge.

Training paid. Although this was *Jäger's* first true general quarters, her men were on station in minutes. Kurt felt relief as he ran, thankful others knew what they were doing. How many times had he cursed the endless drills? Bless von Lappus, the ship might be able to defend herself.

He hurtled through the pilothouse door, grabbed its

frame to avoid a collision with the Captain. After donning his jumper, he asked, "What's happening?"

Paul Milch said, "Lifejacket and helmet on the chart table." Pale, he then pointed out the starboard door. "Look!"

As he tucked the bottoms of his trousers into the tops of his socks, Kurt looked, gasped, "What the hell?"

Ships, on the horizon, seven or eight kilometers distant and closing. Black ribbons of smoke trailed from their stacks. Kurt seized a pair of binoculars.

"Christ! A carrier! And five . . . no, four destroyers. The other one might be a tanker."

"They show their colors yet?" someone asked.

"Don't see any," Kurt replied.

A telephone talker, repeating a request from Gun Control, asked, "Permission to free guns, sir?"

"Permission denied," von Lappus replied. "Those fellows are nervous too. Let's not start something."

"Ranke," Gregor shouted across the bridge, "get the signal books from the charthouse. Then get up to the signal bridge."

Kurt collected the books, donned his helmet and lifejacket, and went up. He found Brecht, the signalman, studying the approaching ships through the telescope.

"They sending?"

"Yeah. Light. But it's nonsense." He handed Kurt a copy of the incoming message.

"Certainly not German, but it looks like language." He glanced aft and up. "Break a new ensign. That one's too ragged. I'll run up the interrogative pennant. Maybe they'll get the idea." As the new ensign rose to the gaff, he bent on the interrogative pennant and hoisted it, then hurried to the telescope.

The six vessels had closed to four kilometers. Kurt had no trouble distinguishing their ensigns as they went up.

"What flag?" Hans shouted from the bridge.

Kurt found it in one of his books. "Argentina."

"What?"

"Argentina. Argentina. In South America."

Hans's head appeared over the edge of the signal bridge. "I know that. But I thought America got blasted."

"South America. The continent. Not the United States."

"If you say so." He went back down.

Kurt picked up *Jane's Fighting Ships*—1986, salvaged from the wreck at Finisterre. It was two centuries out of date and written in English, but he thumbed through anyway. He found Argentina and, as he had expected, learned nothing. The carrier was not the one listed. The destroyers were of the American *Fletcher* class, active in many smaller navies.

He again studied the ships through the telescope. They were a ragged lot, worse than *Jäger*. All wore unrepaired scars from old battles, scars no one had bothered trying to heal. Perhaps the Argentines did not care about the appearance of their future coffins. Perhaps the vessels need float only long enough to carry them to the dying place.

Kurt was dismayed by his own pessimism. Probably, as was the case with many of *Jäger*'s ills, the Argentines just had no way to make repairs. Still, the ships could have been kept neat and painted.

"They're making signals," said Brecht.

Kurt glanced up. "So read. I'll record." He took out pencil, paper, and a copy of ATP-1(a), tactical signals current for NATO at the beginning of the War. He wrote, searched the book, broke signals, shouted down to the bridge, encoded signals, and re-layed them to Brecht. There were thousands in the book. Communication was slow and difficult.

Hours later, stories had been exchanged. The Argentine ships, on their ways to the Gathering, had wandered slightly north of their course during the recent storm. Kurt wondered how High Command had sent its summons to the Americas, but remained too busy to speculate long. *Jäger* was invited to join the screen around the carrier, *Victoria*. He listened as the officers muttered among themselves, discussing it.

Von Lappus's voice rose above the others. "We need practice steaming in formation. We'll do it. What station, Ranke?"

"Station six, sir, at eighteen hundred meters."

"Circular screen?"

"Yes sir." Signal traffic having fallen off, Kurt climbed down to the open bridge. General quarters was secured.

"Just in time to change the watch," Hans grumbled.

Kurt laughed. "I told you we always get the shaft."

The formation lumbered south at a slow five knots, the best the stores ship could manage. The journey down the Portuguese coast to Spain again was uneventful until, four and a half days later, they reached Trafalgar.

During that time, with little else to do, Kurt concentrated on scratching names off his list of murder suspects. One way or another, he learned where men had been at the time of Kapp's death. By Trafalgar he had eliminated a hundred possibilities. But it was slow work. He had to be careful not to attract attention. And the task went slower and slower as evidence grew harder to find.

Then Trafalgar, site of Nelson's victory, that grim headland so important to Napoleon's fall. Kurt was one of two men aboard who knew the battle had been fought. To everyone else, this was just another milestone along the sea road to Gibraltar, and whatever lay beyond.

Idly, he wondered if *Jäger* and this Gathering would be remembered by even one man four centuries in the future, if anyone would then care. Trafalgar had shaped all subsequent European history — though *Jäger's* sailing could hardly be as significant — yet no one today remembered or was much interested. Only he and Hans, lonely men out of their times, put any value on that ancient battle. . . . A wave of sadness swept him. He did not want to go for nothing, to be quickly forgotten.

Trafalgar, the unremembered headland. Sad, Kurt thought, that so many should have died and had such little effect beyond their own time. A tear or two in Dover, a French woman weeping in Nice, and forgotten. Just another landmark on the seapath to an ocean of skulls. . . .

Until the carrier launched her aircraft. Then Trafalgar became memorable as the place where Germans first saw men take to the sky. The launch was almost laughable, certainly pitiful. There were just six planes, all sputtering, prop-driven monsters cobbled together from cannibalized parts, all as old and weary as the ship carrying them, and not a designed warplane in the lot.

The fourth plane dropped like a stone off the end of the flight deck. It hit water in a fine splash, disintegrated, and was plowed under by the carrier. Wreckage appeared in her boiling wake.

The other planes circled and climbed, coughing with a sort of half-life, got into a ragged formation, and staggered off toward Gibraltar. Drunkenly, Kurt thought, or like tired old men.

Jäger's crew watched from launch to departure, dazzled. They had heard stories, had seen wreckage, but flying men remained unreal as kobolds till seen.

The planes returned after dark. Kurt was off watch, but he had stayed up to see their recovery. Sitting alone on the signal bridge, he stared at the carrier's brilliantly lighted flight deck. One by one, the ancient aircraft dropped from the night and squealed to a halt.

The third down missed the arresting cables with her tail hook. Kurt expected another fall into the sea, but the pilot hit full throttle, roared off the angle deck, and came around again, successfully.

"Really something, isn't it?" someone asked. Kurt turned, nodding. Behind him was Erich Hippke, who had the watch.

"Right. Tremendous. Think what it was like in the old days, with the American supercarriers and jets. Instead of five grumbly old prop jobs, a hundred jets. What an uproar they must've made."

Hippke had an imagination as vivid as Kurt's. He expanded the picture. "Think what the Battle of the Kattegat must've been like. Hundreds of ships and thousands of planes." He shook his head slowly, impressed by such magnitude.

"Big. I was nine when my father first told me about the Battle of the Volga. I thought he was a liar when he said it lasted a year and eight million men were killed—there just couldn't've been that many people in the world."

"It's still hard to believe, Kurt. But I guess the bombs could do it. How many people in Germany then? A hundred million?"

"Uhm. About. And now there's a hundred thousand. Eight million men in one battle. That's more than there are in all Europe now, I guess. Maybe more'n the whole world."

"Efficient killers, eh?" Turning, suddenly intent, Hippke asked, "Kurt, why's it still going on? What're we fighting for?"

Kurt shrugged invisibly in the sudden darkness left when the carrier shut down her lights. "I could give you the Political Office line. It's the only one I know. Hell, I don't know why. Maybe nobody ever thought to stop. I don't think anybody knows any more, unless it's High Command. Maybe it goes along on its own inertia, and won't stop until there's nobody left."

Kurt suddenly shuddered. His talk was approaching treason. He glanced around quickly, but no one was near.

"Maybe Otto was right. Maybe staying home's the only way to stop it," said Hippke, speaking cautiously. "Lot of men been talking about what Otto said, Kurt. Lot of men think he was right. Lot of men beginning to think of doing something about it."

Kurt got the impression he was being felt out. He remembered his earlier suspicions about Hippke. He did not want to be maneuvered by any underground, no matter his sympathy for its aim. "Erich, if you hear a man talking, remind him of that wreck. Men got to thinking on that ship. None of them'll ever go home. And you be careful who you try to enlist. Remember Otto. He went overboard the same night he spoke out."

"What's the connection?"

"Otto was stabbed and pushed, maybe by someone who believes in the War. I don't know that for sure. Maybe someone had a grudge. You might find out which the hard way."

"You don't know who?"

"No. And don't spread that around. I don't want a witchhunt. I'm telling you so I don't have to fish *you* out of the pond some night."

"All right, I'll shut up. About everything."

"Good." But he was sure he detected insincerity in Erich's voice. If the man was the undergrounder Kurt suspected, he would simply be more cautious. "Think I'll go crap out."

Kurt went down ladders and walked aft slowly, second-guessing himself about telling Hippke of Otto's murder. He might not keep quiet. If the murderer discovered he was being sought . . .

That night *Jäger* passed through the straits and turned north. Gibraltar itself became visible at sunrise, rearing above the horizon like some tremendous, crouched prehistoric monster. Slowly, creepingly slow, it drew nearer.

Gibraltar, Kurt thought, the place of Gathering, headquarters of the High Command. Inside that mass of rock was the War Room, fabled, whence all orders came. Within that stone were the men and women who directed the War Effort—and the operations of the Political Office. Kurt, in his mind's eye, saw it as the heart of a vast, invisible web. There the black-and-silver spiders dwelt, weaving their complex, mysterious plots, catching "traitors" with their complex, savage snares.

"Good lord!" Hans muttered a while later. "Look at all the ships! Kurt, will you look at the ships?"

Kurt looked. Hans had a right to be excited. Even from several kilometers, a forest of masts could be seen to one side of the Rock. Dozens of ships.

Later, when they were closer, Kurt saw that the nearest were destroyers. Behind them, better protected, were larger vessels. Cruisers, he realized. And another carrier—no, two—behind the cruisers. And beyond those, auxiliaries: ammunition ships, stores ships, colliers, ancient merchantmen converted for war use. And still farther on, more destroyers.

"Oh, Kurt, come over here," Hans shouted across the bridge.

"See what's coming. Look! Coming around the Rock to meet us. Isn't she beautiful?"

A ship was steaming to meet them, a titan of a vessel.

"Battlewagon," Kurt murmured. "I thought they were all gone. What a monster!"

A monster indeed. A killer. If *Jäger* was an iron wolf, this, then, was Tyrannosaurus rex in case-hardened steel. Surely the Australians could have nothing like her. Surely her huge guns would rule the ocean.

"Look it up! Look it up!" Hans demanded.

Kurt got the copy of *Jane's*. He turned to *United States*, where he remembered having seen a similar ship. "Here it is, Hans." He handed the book over, tapping a picture.

"What does it say?"

"How would I know?"

Hans carried the book to the chart table and bent over it, as if trying to puzzle out the statistics beneath the photograph. His eyes grew big with wonder. "The Australians can't beat this! Wonder where they found her?" He bent over the book again, studying the text below the statistics. "What flag?"

Kurt took a look through binoculars. "High Command."

"Boatswain," said Lindemann, "set the Sea Detail. Kurt, get Beck's anchor chart."

As he was fixing the chart to the table, Kurt watched *Victoria* start into a channel between the anchored ships. Like a hen and chicks, he thought, or like duck and ducklings, with *Jäger* the ugly one coming along last.

There was thunder from the battleship—and distress on *Jäger's* bridge, confused questions. Kurt leaned out the door. The huge warship had hoisted an Argentine flag and was busily blasting the sky with a secondary mount. "Gun salute," he said, ashamed of his moment of fear.

"I'm glad they've got ammunition to waste," Hans growled. Kurt saw that he too had been frightened, and was irritated about it.

There was a pause in the firing after the twenty-first boom. The Argentine flag came down.

Kurt felt a surge of pride as the red, black, and yellow of the Littoral replaced the gold, blue, and white. The thunder resumed.

"This one's for us." He stepped out on the wing. Glancing down, he saw the Sea Detail waving their caps at the battleship. They were idiots, he thought. The jaws of a trap were closing, and they cheered. Green sea slipped past *Jäger*'s flanks. Every meter forward made turning back that much more impossible.

"Hey, Kurt, come over on this side and look." Hans tugged at his sleeve. He followed the smaller man through the bridge.

"Look," said Hans, pointing to the anchored ships. "Portugal." Several ships flew a red-and-green ensign. "And Spain." Three vessels bore the red-and-gold with the black eagle.

He pointed to other ships. "Nigeria, I think, and France . . ." He indicated flag after flag, babbling.

Kurt marveled too, for here were men of nations as fabulous as those of the Arabian Nights. *Jäger* eased into the channel between ships, her men exchanging shouted greetings with sailors of other lands. Hans grew more excited. "Look! Look, Kurt. Britain! . . ."

"Quartermaster!"

"Sir?"

"We'll tie up at buoy thirty-four. Find it on your chart."

"Yes sir." He went inside and did so, the while thinking that Gregor need not be so glum. He returned to the wing, told Hans, "We've a good position. Close in."

"You going over?"

Nothing could keep him from exploring this hub of history. "On the first boat."

EIGHT

"It's not really fair," Kurt told Hans while descending the accommodation ladder to the liberty boat.

"'Rank hath its privileges,'" Hans quoted. "One's liberty every day. Why feel guilty?"

"I don't. But it's not fair, not when the others only get to go every other day. . . ."

"It could be arranged. . . ."

"Never mind. Hello, Deckinger."

"I'll trade you, Ranke," said the coxswain.

"Forget it. I'm not that fair." He and Hans took seats and waited for the boat to fill. The sailors who followed them were all neatly trimmed and polished, their uniforms clean and starched. They would return appearing to have wrestled tigers.

"What'd you do yesterday?" Hans asked.

"Just wandered around. There's not much to do."

"There's a cathouse near the landing. . . ."

"Hippke told me about it. Eight women. He said he was in and out before he knew he'd unbuttoned his pants. I'd rather do it myself."

Hans chuckled. "Cheaper, anyway. Cost me three kilos of potatoes yesterday. And the price'll go up."

Kurt glanced down at the bag in Hans's lap. "So that's where they're going. Kellerman said they were disappearing fast."

"The women won't take Littoral money."

"What about the taverns?"

"Same thing. They trade liquor for stores, and probably sell the stores back to the ships, where they're stolen again. Somebody's getting rich."

The boat pushed off and quickly crossed the five hundred meters to the landing.

"I'll see you later, Kurt," said Hans as he hurried up the pier.

"Yeah." Kurt slowly walked into a waterfront street crowded with sailors from a dozen countries, speaking as many tongues. He felt lost and alone, more than ever before. It was a great black loneliness like he imagined that of space. There was no feeling of belonging, as aboard *Jäger*.

And there were so many Political Officers. Everywhere he looked, on every street corner, was a man in black and silver, watching, cold and deadly.

Jäger had suffered a plague of them after Beck had filed his report. In bands a dozen strong, they came to ask about events in Norway. Kurt feared shipboard resentment might flare into violence if the inquisitions did not stop.

Gibraltar seemed unchanged from the previous day. Kurt

suspected it never changed. He stopped a few meters from the head of the pier and considered courses of action. The line at the brothel was a block long, so that was out—even had he been interested. He shuddered deliciously, wondering what Karen would say if she heard he had visited such a place.

Stretching away to the right, up a steep street, was a line of small shops and taverns. The taverns, too, had lines before their doors.

Well, what else was there? He looked upward, at the mass of rock where High Command was hidden. It might be interesting to walk up and see the center of the spider-web. He started up the road.

He met a Political Officer on the way, near the entrance to the underground fortress. A very old man, and much more pleasant than any Political Officer he had ever encountered.

"Can't come in here, son," the old man told him as he approached a gate in the fence before the entrance.

"What? Why not?" Kurt eyed a negligently held submachine-gun.

"Security. Can't have just anybody walking in and out." The old man seemed accustomed to dealing with would-be visitors.

"Why not? I just want to look around. We're on the same side, aren't we?"

The old man smiled a warm, friendly smile, a sort rare in Political Officers. "Now I don't know that, do I? Far as I know, you could be the Grand Marshal of the Australian Empire."

"Oh. Guess you're right." But Kurt felt that was not the true reason for his being stopped. "Hey! How come you speak German?"

"Well, son, a man has this job, he's got to know about every language there is." He pointed toward the fleet with his gun barrel. "I seen you comin' up, and I said to myself, 'Walter, that boy looks like one of them Littoral fellows.' Remembered the uniform, see? They don't change much."

"Oh."

"Pretty bad down there, uh? Crowded till you can't hardly breathe, and lonely as sin, eh?" He had struck right to the heart of it. "Same thing, every Gatherin'. Boys come ashore thinkin' the Rock's goin' to be like home. And they're disappointed when they find out she isn't."

"Always the same?"

"Yep. Boy, I seen four—no, five, if you count one when I was four—Gatherin's. They're always the same, except they've gotten smaller. Reckon there can't be many more."

Kurt remembered Karen on their last morning together, speaking of future Meetings. And he had echoed the official line, fool that he was. Now he wisely asked no questions.

"Tell you what, boy. There's a friendly little place I go myself, when I'm looking for a little excitement—when my woman's not watching." He gave the location of a house not yet discovered by the fleet. "But you keep that under your hat, hear? Else there'll be a line second time you go."

"That doesn't really interest me. I've got a wife. . . ."

"Well, will you look here now? Just tryin' to help, son."

"Sure. Thanks anyway. You know, what I'd really like is to find someone who'd teach me English."

"Now what would you want to do that for?"

"I'm Leading Quartermaster on my ship. All my charts, and most of my publications, are American, Australian, or English. I can't do my job well because I don't know what they say."

"Well, let me see," said the old man, cradling his weapon in the crook of one arm, scratching his chin. A minute passed. "Don't know where you'd find anyone, offhand. Wait! There's an old coot that's got an antique shop down on the waterfront. Crippled fellow. Likes to play mental games. Might teach you, if you'll teach him. He's a strange one, though. Lives in the past. Been down there a few times myself, pickin' up odds and ends to decorate the apartment. He's got more old junk . . . well, you'll see."

"How do I get there?"

"Just go back the way you came. You can't miss the place if you're lookin'. Windows full of junk, right next to the Ship's Lantern."

"Thanks."

"Sure, boy, sure. Sorry I can't show you around. Been nice chattin'. Gets lonesome here, sometimes." They parted with smiles.

As he descended toward the waterfront, Kurt worried questions the old man had stimulated. What did the High Command have to hide? That talk of spies seemed somehow false. And the man had seemed *certain* there would be more Gatherings. How did he know?

Kurt paused, looked back up the slope. His eyes were caught by the forest of radio masts at the top of the Rock. Was that how they had summoned the ships from the Americas? It presupposed there were long-range radios in operation around the world. Could they communicate with the Australians?

There was a booming to seaward. Kurt looked out and saw the battleship saluting two incoming corvettes of Liberian flag. He surveyed the neat ranks of ships in the anchorage. Almost fifty warships were there, and as many auxiliaries. Where did they all come from, in this battered, dying world? And where did High Command get the food and ammunition they were being loaded with?

Well, no point bothering himself about High Command. No one would tell him anything. To the antique shop.

As the old man had said, the place was easy to find. It was sandwiched between a roaring tavern and a café exuding abominable odors. Pausing outside, Kurt studied the dusty window. Just within was a treasure trove of the garbage of history: old books, a Roman helmet green with age, a few bronze spearheads, a lantern off a sailing ship which should have gone to the tavern next door, relics of Moorish Spain, a trio of tattered flags, Royal, Falangist, and Republican, and faded photographs of the last king, Carlos, of Franco, of Charles de Gaulle, and of Adolf Hitler, though Kurt recognized only the last. And a hundred other things. European history exuded from the shop, like a barely perceptible odor. It drew Kurt. The past had always been his favorite escape. He slipped through the door, his entry jingling a bell overhead.

At first he thought he had entered an untenanted shop. Dust lay over everything, as if the place had not been cleaned in a decade. There was silence, gloom, and countless piles of ancient treasure.

Something moved with slow, shuffling steps in the shadows gathered at the back of the place. A little man, not quite a dwarf but bent to the size by a hunchback, came forward. He moved as if each tiny, shuffling step were an individual agony. He cocked his head to one side, looked Kurt up and down.

Kurt shivered, wondering if the man were a mutant. They

were rare at home now, but there had been a time when . . . But so what?

The cripple's mind seemed agile enough. After asking a question in English and getting no answer, he shuffled across the shop to a wall covered with bookshelves. With a whithered, clawlike left hand, he waved at them.

Carefully keeping his eyes off the bent figure and deformed hand, Kurt surveyed titles, shelf after shelf. Nothing. Then a word caught his eye. He blew dust off the book's spine.

Deutsches-Englisches Englisches-Deutsches Worterbuch

"This . . ."

The old man rose on tiptoes and peered at the title closely, claw hand slightly lifting his bifocals. "Ah . . ." He shifted his cane to his bad hand and used the good to take the book down. Painfully, he crossed the shop again, dropped the book on a small, dusty table, sat in a rickety chair, and motioned Kurt to draw up another. Kurt sat down opposite him.

The cripple drew the book to him, riffled through, occasionally paused to stare closely at something. When finished, he looked up and said, "*Mein Name* . . . Martin Fitzhugh."

"Kurt Ranke," Kurt replied.

"*Sie . . . wünschen?*"

Kurt puzzled that for nearly a minute. Then he took the book from the old man's hands and thumbed through, trying to find English words for what he wanted to say. "I . . . would . . . speak . . . English."

The old man shrugged, obviously uncertain what Kurt meant. He tried again. "I . . . desire . . . to learn . . . English."

"Ah." The old man nodded vigorously. Kurt saw he was delighted. Perhaps he needed company, this old one. The shop seemed incredibly lonely—yet homey. Kurt felt he could be happy in a place this rimed with history.

Languages are living organisms, in constant change. Rate of change is a function of the speed and universality of the communications system. The faster and more widespread the system, the slower is change. The German and English of 2193 were the results of two centuries of the word-of-mouth and hand-carried-letter systems. Learning the languages through the dictionary rapidly proved impossible. Kurt could read his language as it had been written before the War, but could not speak it so.

Fitzhugh tried a new tack, the ancient way. He pointed to the table. "Name, table."

Kurt frowned his lack of understanding. The old man pointed out English and German words in the dictionary, then smashed his good hand against the tabletop. "*Diese ist . . .* table!"

Kurt got it. Laughing, he slapped his chair and said, "*Stuhl!*"

"Chair," the old man countered.

Kurt tried to pronounce it. The old man chuckled at his mangled "ch" sound. Then, like a gleeful gnome, he slipped off his seat and hurried round the room, pointing, naming. "Book . . . sword . . . helmet . . . nail . . . floor . . . window . . . door . . ." And on and on and on.

Kurt followed, naming a list of his own. "*Pfeil . . . Buch . . . Schaufel . . . Mantel . . . Kanone . . .*" Cannon? It was a toy, but a real one poking its snout from a mound of junk would have been no surprise. The old man had everything.

The wonder of naming wore off quickly. Kurt and Fitzhugh

returned to the table and laboriously worked out a systematic way of learning.

He left at sunset, leaving a promise to return the following day. Although he was mentally exhausted, he carried the dictionary under his arm and was determined to study it that night.

Kurt decided he liked Fitzhugh—perhaps because of their common interest in the past. He certainly looked forward to seeing the man again.

"What's that?" Hans asked as he climbed into the boat.

"Dictionary. German-English."

"Why?"

"I want to read my charts."

"So what's to read? You've got conversion tables for feet and yards and fathoms and miles, don't you?"

"Come to the charthouse with me, after we eat. I'll show you what I mean." Then they chatted of other things while the boat approached the ship, chiefly of the bizarre entertainments Gibraltar offered. Kurt whispered the location of the house he had learned from the old Political Officer.

After supper they went to the charthouse. Kurt selected a chart at random. "All right, tell me what this means." His finger rested beside a purple circle containing a black dot and depending a purple diamond, beside which was: *R"6" Occ R 3sec.* "Or this." He indicated a purple circle over a tiny trapezoid which sprouted a vertical, asterisk-topped line. Beside it was: *BRIGHTON REEF Occ 4sec 13M DIA.*

"And this would make sense in English?" Hans asked, chuckling. "Doesn't look like sense in any language."

"If I could read English, I could look these things up in the books. I can barely tell what ocean we're in now."

"But there's no need to worry. We'll let the flag do the navigating."

"Maybe. But that's assuming we don't get separated."

Hans shook his head slowly, said, "All right. You want to waste time learning English, go ahead. Me, I'll keep the black market in business. Think I'll go to the bridge."

"I'm going down to the mess decks to study."

But he did not get much studying done. Someone had traded parts from the wreck for an ancient movie projector and a dozen reels of film, from cartoons to stags. Despite the exigencies of breaking film, a trick sprocket, and a hand-powered take-up reel, the crew watched movies—for the first time in their lives.

NINE

"Hey, Kurt," said Erich Hippke as he took a seat across from Kurt at the breakfast table, "you hear what Damage Control's doing this morning?"

Kurt swallowed a mouthful of ersatz coffee. "What?"

"They've got a floating drydock coming to lift us out of the water so they can mount that screw they took off the wreck. It's behind us now. What a brute!"

The ship shivered slightly.

"Sounds like they're getting started," said Hippke. "They were bringing the dock up when I came in."

"I saw it this morning, but I didn't know what it was. Finish eating. We'll go watch."

Hippke ate quietly for a few minutes, then, after glancing around, whispered, "Beck bothering you any?"

"No, why?"

"Well, he's been calling you down a lot. Almost every day." This was true. Again and again, Beck summoned Kurt to his stateroom, where they often talked at length. "What do you talk about?"

In this Kurt sensed a more than casual question. "Most anything," he replied. "A lot about his wife. He's a lonely man. Did you know she hasn't come to visit him, all the time we've been here? Just because she doesn't like ships? I'd call that flat cruelty. And he refuses to go to her in a wheelchair." Beck was able to leave his bed now, but was still without the use of his legs.

"He's a funny man," said Erich. "There was a machine-gunner in *Freikorps Flieder* a lot like him. He killed a hundred people during the Memel raid—just marched them into a trench and started shooting—and the next day didn't remember. . . ."

Kurt's eyes narrowed just the slightest. What was Hippke after now? This beginning story was another of his lies, of which he had told many lately. Details of the Memel thing were common knowledge throughout the Littoral, and the freecorps had not become involved until afterward. The killers had been White Russian bandits, and the people massacred Lithuanian citizens of the Littoral. Memel had been the last big raid of the Russian bandit brotherhoods, for the freecorps had overtaken them as they retreated burdened with plunder. . . . But no matter. Hippke was the problem, Hippke was the man who knew so little recent history that he confused the sides of a noteworthy disaster. Hippke was a liar obviously from somewhere afar . . . from where, and why? Kurt resolved to catch him off guard sometime with questions about Telemark.

Kurt shrugged, said, "Let's think about something a little more pleasant." The ship shivered again. "Finish your coffee. I want to see this drydock."

The floating dock was already moving in along the length of the destroyer, sides towering above *Jäger*'s deck. Seamen ran about checking the fenders, shouting at one another and the men on the dock, confusing everything.

"It's not long enough," Kurt noted. "What're they going to do?"

"Just lift the stern out. The bow doesn't matter."

"I guess not."

"Kurt?" Hans had appeared. "Beck wants you again." Kurt could almost believe, from the stress on the final word, that Hans was jealous.

His spirits sank. Though Beck no longer frightened him, he was in no mood for a visit. Beck would spend the morning chatting his loneliness away, and Kurt wanted to get ashore to show Fitzhugh how he had managed three full chapters in the dull, complex nineteenth-century novel he had borrowed for the night. But there were no excuses.

Beck was in a rare high good humor when Kurt arrived. "She's finally given in. Coming out this afternoon."

With a smile on and happiness in his face, Beck was not at all the grim "snake-eye" Kurt remembered from Kiel. He was quite human, even warm. And this, though Kurt should have grown accustomed to it, was a surprise—emotionally, he had long ago decided all Political Officers were reptiles within, and, each time his preconceptions were betrayed, he was startled.

More seriously, with the smile fading, Beck said, "Kurt, there'll be trouble soon."

Kurt's eyebrows rose questioningly.

"No, not here. At least, I see no signs. On another ship—because political handcuffs keep us from dealing with rebels...."

While Beck paused, Kurt examined his growing conviction that the man was of the extermination faction, and the fact that Beck saw only the logic in a political pogrom, not the inhumanity.

"Kurt, how would you like to join High Command? You've got the brains. I could even get you assigned to the Political Office."

Kurt was taken completely aback. Emotions ran riot behind his blank face. First, he was both dismayed and mildly pleased — dismayed because there was nothing he wanted less than this, pleased because, in his own way, Beck was telling him he was well liked, was offering Kurt's friendship what he felt was a great reward. Then Kurt felt sadness, sadness because this man was so lonely he imagined between them a greater friendship than could ever possibly exist. For all these reasons, Kurt could not refuse outright. He could not hurt the man, though he hated all that man represented.

"I thought you had to be born into it."

"Not always."

"I'll have to think. . . ."

"Of course. You've plenty of time. Just let me know before the Meeting."

Kurt felt relief. Plenty of time. From what he had heard, it might be a year before the fleet reached Australia.

The interview quickly ended. In his excitement over his wife's visit, Beck was eager to have him gone. And, of course, Kurt was eager to get to Fitzhugh's shop.

But Gregor, of whom he had seen so little these past three weeks, intercepted him in the passageway as he was departing. "Come to my room a minute," he said. Kurt recognized an order.

Gregor closed the door. "What're you and Beck up to?"

"Sir?"

"Don't 'sir' me here, Kurt. I'm Gregor, remember?"

Gregor, Kurt thought, a cousin I loved as a child, a mystery of a man, a friend who had become a stranger.

"What're you and Beck doing? Are you going over to the Political Office?"

"Gregor! No! We just talk, like anybody talks. Women, history, ships, weather, women. Sometimes we play chess. He's very good."

"Maybe it's all innocent, then. But you should stand clear of him more. You're picking up the smell. Some people think you're spying. . . ."

Kurt put a finger on something that had been making him uncomfortable for weeks. Men he thought were friends had been avoiding him. Not openly, of course, but just not appearing in parts of the ship he frequented—he'd been too immersed in his studies to notice earlier. It hurt.

"Paranoia!" he growled. "You, Hippke, and whoever else's in on your plot are as crazy as Beck."

Shadows surrounded Gregor, who stood near his bunk at the far wall. He jerked around and away with a startled exclamation—and Kurt gaped momentarily. For just yesterday there had been a furtive man in the shadows at the rear of Fitzhugh's shop, getting out of sight with sudden movement.

"Get out, Kurt! And whatever you've seen or heard, or think you've seen or heard or know, keep it to yourself." Gregor lifted a hand, hit himself in the forehead. "Ask Commander Haber to bring me some aspirin."

How sudden that was, Kurt thought, remembering that Gregor always suffered severe headaches in time of stress or fear.

Or had he been frightened already? Did he really think I'd betray him?

Kurt's anger would not fade. He could not resist a parting shot. "For God's sake, tell Hippke to stop making an ass of himself with those stories about the freecorps. He doesn't know a thing about them."

After speaking to Commander Haber, he went topside, looked aft. Damage Control was still working with the screw, but he had no time to watch. He had to get off the ship. The gray walls were closing in. . . .

Soon, dictionary under one arm, he entered Martin Fitzhugh's antique shop. "Hello, Kurt, hello," the old man said, almost dancing. It seemed he had not expected Kurt to return. It had been this way every morning, all through the weeks. Perhaps, Kurt thought, Martin had been abandoned before.

"Good morning, Martin," he replied, concentrating on his pronunciation. "To study?" Kurt's English was still very rough — it came to him much harder than had Danish — though he could manage ordinary conversations.

"Not today!" Toward the end of the first week, Fitzhugh had given up trying to make anything of German. Too hard to learn, he had said, with a comment about old dogs and new tricks. Kurt had laughed and told him he should try English.

"How was the book?" Fitzhugh asked.

"Not good, what I read. Why do we study not?"

"I want to go outside."

"Ah?"

They had become good friends over the weeks. Kurt had discovered, to his delight, that Fitzhugh was not at all self-conscious about his deformities — which relieved his own self-consciousness and made dealing with the man much easier. And they had common interests.

"Why not? Business is terrible, and I want to see the fleet before it leaves. That'll be soon now, I think."

"Why think you that?"

"Oh, I hear things here and there. I get around. And I know people from up there." He jerked his head toward the heights. His face expressed loathing. Kurt had been surprised when first he heard the old man express dislike for High Command, but no more. Gregor might have been here. Beck said there were spies on the Rock. Who less likely to be suspected than a crippled old shopkeeper?

"Among other things, boy, High Command's bothered by the restlessness aboard the ships. They've been squabbling over what to do about all the young men who can't see any reason to get killed in this thing, the ones talking about going home. Always been those at any Gathering, but not near so many as this time. Times are changing—even in the Political Office."

"I had not noticed," said Kurt.

"No, you wouldn't. Not on your ship. And High Command's covering it up. The real trouble's among the Spaniards and Portuguese—they're so close to home. If the fleet doesn't sail soon, there'll be a blowup—they know that up there. They don't know they're running late."

Kurt frowned, remembered Beck's words to the same subject. He did not like it—too unpleasant.

"Be a good lad and fetch my wheelchair from the back, will you? We'll go up and take a look at the fleet—if you don't mind pushing me, that is."

"I do not mind. But we cannot go up. Once I was warned already."

"You went to the wrong place. We'll go where they don't mind."

Kurt returned a moment later, pushing the wheelchair. Fitzhugh had donned a long, heavy coat in the meantime. "Get me that blanket there," he said, pointing while seating himself. Kurt tucked it in around the warped body, then wheeled Fitzhugh out the door, locked the shop, and asked, "Which way?"

"Left, and straight up the street to the end."

They wove through crowds of sailors from many nations. The crush had become oppressing. The Gathering had doubled in size.

An hour later, as they followed a path high up on the Rock, Fitzhugh pulled out an ancient pocket watch and said, "Hurry! We've got to go faster."

Mystified, Kurt went faster and hoped for an explanation. They reached a wide, flat place. "Stop here!" Fitzhugh ordered. "Turn me so I can see."

The fleet lay in panorama below them, rank on rank of battered ships. Kurt thought it a marvel that some had survived the trip to Gibraltar. As if reading his mind, Fitzhugh growled. "They're a sorry lot."

He stole a peek at his watch. "They get worse each Gathering. I expect this'll be the last made up of steam-powered ships. They may go back to wooden vessels, sails, and muzzle-loading cannon soon—unless something's done to stop it."

"What?"

"Watch the Spanish and Portuguese ships!" the old man snapped, pointing with his claw hand. Kurt stared down at the little covey of destroyers and corvettes.

"Here," said Fitzhugh. He pulled binoculars from beneath his blanket. "Look close. And give them back quick if anyone comes along."

Kurt stared through the glasses. Several minutes passed before he saw anything of note. "It appears that they are going to hang someone on one ship."

"Ah?"

"*Nein!* On each ship! Three men on one. *Liebe Gott!* They are Political Officers. . . ."

"Anything else?" As he asked, a faint *pop-pop-pop*ping of small-arms fire reached them. Smoke curled up from the stacks of the six vessels, grew rapidly heavier. Men appeared on forecastles, cast off mooring lines. Gun batteries tracked right and left. It looked well-planned and timed.

"They're going home," Fitzhugh said in early response to a question Kurt was about to ask.

"Will not the High Command object?"

"Undoubtedly. Look around the point. See what the battleship's doing."

Kurt turned. High Command sailors were running aboard the huge warship. "To action stations they are going."

"Looks like they'll have to shoot their way out."

"They will not escape," Kurt growled. He wished his English would give his emotions more freedom.

"Maybe, maybe not. You might be surprised. But, win or lose, they'll've set an example by trying—which is more than anyone's ever done. Gives an old man hopes of seeing the War die before he does. Word of this gets out, maybe nobody'll answer the call to the next Gathering."

"What is your part in this, Martin?" Kurt stared at the old

man, wondering, remembering the dark sailors who had come and gone from the antique shop during the past three weeks, the Gregor-man furtive in shadows. He had thought little of them until today. With pretended innocence, he asked, "Are you an Australian agent?"

Fitzhugh's eyes widened in surprise. Then he burst into laughter, almost toppled from his seat.

"What is funny?" Kurt demanded. He was growing annoyed.

"Boy, you wouldn't believe a word if I told you. You just watch what happens down there."

Kurt lifted the glasses. "You may tell me."

"No, I may not. Not just yet. Maybe later, after you've seen this. There's your friend, Beck—a problem. Tell you what. I'll explain if you still haven't figured it out by the time you get back from the Meeting."

So. Fitzhugh knew of Beck. Kurt had never mentioned the man. Now he was certain he had seen Gregor in the shop yesterday. "Tell me, Martin."

Fitzhugh shook his head slowly. "You just watch those ships. You'll see something I've prayed for all my life—the first loosening of High Command's grip."

"Why will not you tell me?"

"Time, and Beck. But I'll see that you know what's behind it all. Eventually. What's happening?"

"The ships are getting underway."

"Any others look like they might join in?"

"I do not see any. *Gott verdammte!*"

A tremendous roar passed overhead. A moment later, there were almost simultaneous booms from the anchorage and the Rock above.

"Holy Christ!" the old man bellowed, excitedly standing in his wheelchair. "They're doing it. They're really doing it! Again! Again! Get the antennas!" He shouted something more, but his words were lost as another salvo roared overhead.

Through the glasses, Kurt watched as all six vessels opened up with main and secondary batteries. Gibraltar shuddered as a ragged salvo exploded around the peak. A swarm of three-inchers racketed over and hit, too close for Kurt. "Martin! Out of here we must get."

"Why? They're not shooting at *us*. You look down there and let me know what's happening. Let me do the worrying."

The top of Gibraltar now received a steady pounding. Glancing upward, Kurt saw a salvo fall amidst the forest of radio masts.

"That'll clog the gears for a while!" Fitzhugh shouted.

Kurt turned back to the ships. They were leaving the anchorage in line astern, gathering speed rapidly. Around the point, the battleship was getting her anchor up. Her guns turned toward the rebels. Nine waterspouts rose a few hundred meters beyond the destroyer leading the line. A moment later, Kurt heard a rumble like that of distant thunder.

"Battleship opening up," said Fitzhugh. "She'll have a hard time using her main battery, this close in. Wish my eyes were better."

Kurt watched the lead ship shift her guns from Gibraltar to the battleship. Her automatic five-inchers, each capable of forty-five rounds per minute, snarled defiantly — like a house cat cornered by a tiger. Destroyer against battleship at half a kilometer was hardly a match, yet, as she began running an evasion course, the smaller ship shot everything she had. There was no missing.

Flashes of light, puffs of smoke, flying metal, engulfed the giant warship. Most of the shells did little real damage because they hit massive armor plating, but the superstructure suffered considerable ruin.

Then the battleship, like a sluggish giant, spoke again, with the mouths of dragons. The leading rebel stopped being. The other five ships hurried on, trailing the smoke of their muzzle blasts.

"Hit her fire control!" Fitzhugh shrieked. "Knock out her fire control!"

The destroyers and corvettes slipped past. The battleship tried to get up steam to chase them. Her guns continued thundering, but with less effect. Perhaps, as Fitzhugh demanded, her fire control had been destroyed and they were now being aimed by optical systems.

Kurt looked back at the rest of the fleet. There was fighting on one small ship near where the rebels had been moored, but, otherwise, nothing happening, except that decks were crowded with curious men, men who could see next to nothing. The firing was taking place around a corner of the Rock, out of sight of all but a very few ships—and the rebels were now making smoke to confuse the battleship's gunners.

"You'd better take me back down now," said Fitzhugh. "High Command'll order all liberties canceled soon. And I've got something to give you, something to explain everything."

Shaking, Kurt returned the man's binoculars, glanced at the three surviving ships fleeing to the southeast, then started down with the wheelchair.

They were halfway down when the guns fell silent. "Faster now," Fitzhugh commanded. "They'll soon start thinking, up in the War Room." Under his breath, he added, "I wonder if they'll make it?"

Crowds of mystified sailors milled in the waterfront streets. They asked one another wild questions, and gave the wildest answers: Australians had attacked, but been beaten off; an ammunition ship had blown up; the Rock's defensive guns were holding target practice.

"Some ships rebelled against High Command," said a sailor who seemed better informed than his fellows, in English, the most common tongue there. "They shot their way out, and now they're going home."

This rumormonger was different. Kurt saw it in his face—a face faintly familiar. Was he one who had come to visit Fitzhugh recently? Surely he was spreading the word intentionally. Kurt was certain he winked at Fitzhugh as he passed.

"Quick! Inside the shop!" the cripple ordered. Kurt saw he was staring down the street at a party of Political Officers working through the crowds, apparently searching for someone. Kurt hustled the old man into his shop.

"Lock the door again."

He did. "Can you not explain what is happening?" he pleaded.

"No time now, Kurt. But you can figure it out for yourself." He wheeled his chair over to the table where they had spent so many hours studying. A stack of books rested on it. "Take these. They're mostly novels, there to cover the important one, the one that'll help you understand."

Kurt surveyed the titles.

"Wrap them up." Fitzhugh offered him a large rag. "Good. Now get back to your ship while there's still enough confusion."

"Why? What is wrong?"

"Nothing—unless you're caught carrying that copy of *Ritual War*. That's a death penalty, son. Go along now, and beware of Marquis."

"Marquis?"

"Code name for a Political Officer, true name unknown, on your ship. Not Beck. His code's Charon."

"I will." Confused, yet impressed and frightened by the old man's urgency, Kurt said a hasty farewell, shook Fitzhugh's good hand, and hurried out.

He reached the pier as one of *Jäger*'s boats was about to leave. A shout held it long enough for him to pile into a seat next to a pale, frightened Hans Wiedermann.

"What's the matter, Hans?"

"I don't know. Political Officers came down from High Command and told everyone to go back to their ships. What've you got?"

"Huh?"

"What's in the package?"

"Oh. Some books I bought to study. English."

"Can I see?"

Kurt pulled several from the bundle and prayed his memory had not played him a trick. He remembered the dangerous one as being at the bottom. He handed three to Hans. The little Boatswain studied the dull covers, opened each, glanced at such illustrations as there were, and asked, "What are they?"

Kurt leaned over and looked. "The red one's a novel. *For Whom the Bell Tolls*. The green one's a geography book. The other one's another novel, *A Tale of Two Cities*."

"What else have you got? Anything with pictures?"

Kurt took the three books back and returned them to his

package. "No pictures. Just novels: *The Anger Men, The Guns of August, Andiron Blue.*"

Hans shrugged, leaned against the gunwale, closed his eyes, said, "I hope we leave soon. Just sitting here's driving me crazy."

"Ran out of potatoes, huh?"

"Didn't run out. If you'd wake up, you'd know von Lappus cut us off. Put an armed guard on the spud locker."

One of the few extant motorboats roared past, rocking the whaleboat with her wake. It sped toward the cluster of aircraft carriers. There were now six of the battered old queens anchored out, with perhaps a hundred makeshift planes between them. Not much of a strike force. Kurt wondered what the Australians had.

A bit later, as the whaleboat eased in to the foot of *Jäger*'s accommodation ladder, planes began leaving one of the carriers. Kurt at first found the launch surprising. Fuel was too precious to waste on training.

The planes circled up and headed in the direction the rebel ships had fled. So, Kurt thought, they had outrun the limping battleship.

"What's so interesting, Hans?"

"I've never seen planes like those. Where do you think they're going?"

Kurt shrugged, said, "Who knows? Why don't you ask High Command?"

Hans gave him a sharp look, then chuckled. "They never tell me anything. The other day I went up to look around. An old man with a machinegun ran me off without even telling me why."

Hans stepped onto the platform at the base of the accommodation ladder. Kurt was a step behind. He quickly evaded Hans, once aboard, and hurried to the charthouse. There he mixed his novels in with the navigational publications. The dangerous book with the title *The Beginnings of the Ritual War* he locked in the safe. There would be time to look at it later.

TEN

It was a terrible dream. He was in Norway, with Karen, running through the mountains of Telemark, fleeing, their limbs moving with dream-slowness, hand in hand, terror close behind them. Karen's hair floated behind her like wind-blown pennons of thread-of-gold, like hair teased out in underwater currents.

Wolf-howls, close. Behind them were black wolves with silver collars, with silver death's-head eyes, dark wolves, hungry wolves, drawing closer as their prey ran with floating steps. One gray wolf with little form and no head ran before the pack.

He did not understand. He asked Karen, "Why? Why?" He looked at her, and her young, fresh face changed, became that of his own mother buried these many years, corrupt. . . . He shrank away moaning.

She cackled madly and said, "Because."

There never was a better reason.

They fled the hungry wolves, knowing there was no escape. A malignant god would not permit it. He screamed as rank wolf-breath seared the back of his neck . . . and woke up shouting incoherently.

Then a hand covered his mouth and another seized his shoulder, held him down. "Take it easy, Kurt!" someone growled in his ear.

Kurt jerked free of the controlling grasp, eyes wide with terror. The man who had awakened him was a shadowy figure beside his rack. He shrank against the metal partition at the rear of his bunk, his mind painting the shadow-figure with the pale face, cold eyes, and dark uniform of a Political Officer.

"Kurt! Come on! Snap out of it!"

Recognition at last, and a vast feeling of relief. "Oh. Hans. I'm sorry. Nightmare."

Somewhere nearby, someone muttered sleepily, "For chrissakes-shaddup-willya?"

"My fault, maybe," Hans whispered. "Come on. Get up."

Still shaking, Kurt asked, "What's up?"

"I'm not sure. They woke me and told me to get you. Deckinger on the quarterdeck said a group came over from High Command."

Kurt sat up on the edge of his rack, rubbed his temples. "Feels like a hangover, I'm so fuzzy. But I didn't drink anything. What time is it?"

"About three."

"In the morning?"

"Come on. Will you hurry?"

Kurt dropped to the cold steel deck, slipped into the rumpled uniform he had worn the day before, and pulled his cap on over uncombed hair. "All right, let's go." They climbed the ladder to the lighted passageway above.

"You look like hell!" said Hans.

"Tough. That's what they get for hauling me out at this time of night."

"Hostile this morning, aren't you? Where're you going now?"

"Mess decks. I need some coffee." He was still a little fuzzy, and the adrenalin in his system did not help. Exasperated, Hans started to growl something. Kurt growled first. "You could use a cup too. They'll live without us for a couple minutes. Hell. Why don't we take a pot and cups down with us?"

"Good enough."

They went to the mess decks. Kurt drew the coffee while Hans found cups. Then they walked forward, to the wardroom.

"Ah!" said the Captain as they entered. Kurt immediately sensed the tension in the room. Von Lappus was putting on his jolly old Father Christmas act, but it was doing little to conceal the tired, put-upon bureaucrat he was. "You see the resourcefulness of our ratings?"

Kurt glanced at the man for whom the words were intended, a Political Officer at least eighty years old. The old man stared back, his gaze a sword of ice.

"Over here," said Commander Haber, indicating chairs at the end of the table. Kurt now counted five Political Officers, an unusually large gathering. He also noted, as he set the coffee pot on the table and took his seat, that they seemed ordered according to importance. The ancient on the right was obviously senior. Beck sat at his left, then the other three, all still in their teens, without the iciness of their elders (they seemed a little awed and frightened, as if in an unexpected situation), but trying to match it. A pity youth should be so warped. . . .

"Kurt Ranke," the Captain said, making the introductions, "Leading Quartermaster. Hans Wiedermann, Leading Boatswain."

He did not add that Hans was by now virtual master of Deck Department, that Mr. Obermeyer had been relieved of the First Lieutenant's duties because of his incompetence. Hans, Kurt felt, was now secretly bitter because no formal commission had come with the informal investiture of those duties. "Fill them in, Commander."

Haber coughed behind a shaky thin hand, said, "High Command has sent out an emergency directive. The fleet will get underway at dawn."

Hans's eyebrows rose. Kurt found he was not at all surprised. High Command would want the fleet too busy to think about yesterday. But Haber . . . The man's shakiness had increased to the point where he had difficulty holding a pen, and his uniform looked as though it had gone unchanged for days. The stresses must be overwhelming, Kurt thought.

"The three younger gentlemen," Haber continued, "will be working in Operations. They're to handle signal traffic between ships. . . ."

Cunning, Kurt thought. Rebellions would remain localized if the Political Office controlled communications. He wondered what else they were to do. A little spying?

Haber spoke on. "We've been given charts for the Mediterranean with our track laid out. Ranke, you're to get with Mr. Czyzewski and determine anticipated fuel consumption. We're lower than we should be. We may have to refuel underway. Make it during the stop at Malta, if you can. . . ."

Kurt stopped listening. He knew he could catch up later. Beck and the old Political Officer were more interesting. They were speaking English, softly, unaware they were being overheard.

"What's that dunderhead spouting off about?" the old one asked.

"Just explaining about pulling out," Beck replied.

"Light a fire under them, will you? Sooner we're done, the sooner I can get home and get some sleep. We wouldn't be here if someone had passed on fleet reports off those Spaniards."

"Or if the Milhouse faction hadn't gotten the upper hand," Beck whispered back. His throat still bothered him some.

"We need more people with common sense, and fewer idealists. If only that woman had seen what blocking the report would cost. She didn't want anyone hurt, she told the interrogators. And now we've got five hundred casualties aboard *Purpose*. Someone'll get hurt. Her. Milhouse's throwing her to the wolves."

"Trying to save his own hide, eh?"

"Indeed. But too late. *Purpose*'s half a wreck and the General Staff's asking how the Political Office let it happen. Heads will roll. Milhouse's whole lot, if we play it right."

Kurt fought to keep expressions from racing across his face. He was hearing the internal problems of the Political Office, at which Beck had hinted. The old man, he assumed, was a leader of that faction favoring extermination of the underground. He certainly seemed pleased that a less savage viewpoint had failed.

Kurt's ears almost pricked up. The subject had changed. He listened intently.

"Did Milhouse decide what to do about those pilots?" Beck asked.

"All the way to the opposite extreme. He's having them shot. Another mistake that'll help topple him. He lost six planes and sank only one ship, then talked too much—got angry—when the others came back. We'll soon have a new chief. Our own man."

"Yourself, sir?"

"Myself, Garfield, any of several others. Anybody, as long as there's a change in policy. The Office's falling apart under these idealists."

Beck shrugged. "If he won't die, and he won't step down?"

"I think, after yesterday, the General Staff will insist. They're interested in results, not methods, and the Milhouse system's a disaster. We'll be out of contact with Bermuda and Corregidor for at least six months, until they cobble together new radio masts. Oh, for God's sake man, will you shut that fellow up? I can't listen to these idiots all night." He rose.

Kurt kept his eyes carefully glued to Commander Haber, wondered who or what Bermuda and Corregidor were. People or places? Corregidor sounded vaguely familiar, though he could not place it. Had he read it somewhere?

He also wondered about the pilots. What had this Milhouse person let slip? Certainly something important, if he was willing to shoot trained flyers to keep it quiet. Kurt grew more and more curious—and suddenly wished he had avoided all this by going to Telemark with Karen.

"Ranke?"

He looked up hurriedly. "Sorry, sir. Sleepy."

Haber ignored the excuse. "You and Mr. Lindemann get

started. You'll have to be ready by sunrise." He glanced at the departing Political Officers, then at the clock on the bulkhead near the door. "That's not much time."

Kurt nodded and rose. He was glad to leave. More than enough questions were bothering him already. Gregor followed him from the wardroom.

"Now, Wiedermann, Deck has to . . ." Haber's voice faded behind them.

The door to the charthouse slammed shut. Gregor visibly relaxed. "I never thought there'd be a man creepier than Beck. But that old one . . ." He shook his head.

"Yes," Kurt replied. "So what're we supposed to do? I didn't understand all that about getting ready." More, he did not want to open the safe to get his gear. He was painfully aware of that dangerous book. . . .

"It was nothing." Gregor rubbed his temples, then rolled his head in a circle. "Just talk-talk so the Political Officers think we're doing something. We might as well crap out. I'll match you for the table."

"All right." Kurt took coins from a drawer, gave one to Gregor, flipped the other, held it against his wrist. Lindemann did the same, said, "Heads."

"Tails. You lose." Kurt crawled onto the table and stretched out on his back. He stared at the ceiling awhile, finally forced himself to ask, "Gregor, what'd you do in Norway?"

"Ran a salting station. You know the type." He sounded displeased.

"What else? How'd you get involved with Karl Franck and the Telemark people?"

"What're you talking about?"

"Gregor, Gregor, this's me, Kurt Ranke. Family. Do you have to lie to me?"

Lindemann seemed momentarily distressed. "Why do you spend so much time with Beck? Why're you withdrawn and un-committed? You take no stands."

This was Gregor's reasoning? Kurt thought a painful mo-ment. He did not like exposing his soul, putting his beliefs out as targets for any sharp-tongued marksman. "Beck's a man, whatever else. My conscience wouldn't let me shun him, or love him, to satisfy his or your politics." He paused for more than a minute then, carefully, formally ordering his next words. "I am tolerance, I am moderation, I am the cautious man who weighs rights and wrongs before jumping into causes. Here I see no causes with rights."

High-sounding stuff, he suspected, but when were moral is-sues depictably mundane? "There're more wrongs than rights in High Command, it's true, yet there's a right outweighing the others. High Command is a force binding the West, preventing the fall to bickering feudalism. . . ."

"An evil force!" Gregor's exclamation sounded fanatical.

"A force aimed in the wrong direction, but the one real power with a real means of dealing with real problems. From what I've learned of your party, it's bound down the bloody-damnation road of most fanatic revolutions."

"What?" Now he was growing irritated.

"The use of any means to an end is what I mean. You want High Command broken—even if the rest of the world has to tumble down with it. If you'd really known anything about High Command, you'd've realized you were better off as a force-in-being, ready to move in if they failed. You'd've known liberal forces were moving there, powers that may've favored your own objectives. Yesterday you killed them. You cunningly planned — your real enemies let you — and, as you thought you were winning physical and moral victories, you bought defeat. The liberals were discredited. The hard-liners take over tomorrow, or soon, with the avowed intention of exterminating you. And they'll probably manage. They know the places and names, and have their agents in havens like Telemark."

(Here Kurt experienced a moment of fear. What if High Command mounted an operation against Telemark? What would become of Karen?)

When Gregor gasped, Kurt rolled onto his side and looked down. His cousin, seated on the floor, was deathly pale, was beating his temples with his fists. Kurt had never seen him so bad.

"Was it a game, Gregor? If you thought so, open your eyes. You've lost a pawn already. How'll I tell Frieda about Otto?"

"I know!" It was almost a moan. "How do you know all this, Kurt? How do you *know*?"

"A mutual acquaintance, a crippled old weaver of webs, taught me English, which is the language of High Command. I eavesdropped on Beck and his superior, reasoned from what I already knew. *They* play no games, Gregor. It's a deadly-serious business for them, and they're watching you. You and Hippke. And your nemesis won't be Beck himself, but the one called Marquis, who might have killed Otto."

"Marquis, yes," Lindemann said softly. "Well, we have our unknown men, then, he his Marquis, me my Brindled Saxon."

"Brindled Saxon?"

Lindemann shrugged, forced a weak smile against the pain of his headache. "Do you talk this frankly with Beck?"

Kurt shook his head. "I talk to you now only because you're my cousin. I don't favor you. You've shut me out of your life, and I think it's just as well. All I really want is to be left in peace."

He rolled onto his back again, closed his eyes and swore he would hear nothing more. But Gregor remained silent. Kurt fell asleep with his brain re-echoing all the high wonderful phrases he had meant as much for himself as for Gregor.

A knock at the door, not much later, woke them. Both bounced up and tried to put on wakefulness. Kurt scattered papers on the chart table to give it a workaday appearance. "Who's there?" he asked.

"Executive Officer. You ready?"

"Yes sir."

"Get some breakfast. We'll be starting soon." Haber's feet clunked on the ladder outside as he climbed to the bridge.

"Get squared away while you're at it," Gregor said. Kurt's uniform was rumpled and his cheeks were covered with blond stubble. Lindemann avoided his eyes.

Kurt left when he heard the bridge door clang shut. He breakfasted, showered, shaved, got into a fresh uniform, and returned in time for Sea Detail, which was piped late. It need never have been. Beck, working on the signal bridge with his three young underlings, despite his incapacity, passed down the word that *Jäger* had to wait until all the vessels to seaward had gotten underway.

Von Lappus secured Sea Detail and ordered holiday routine. Kurt took the opportunity to go for a cup of coffee.

He had been sitting in the mess decks fifteen minutes, brooding about Karen, High Command, pilots to be shot, and what was the need of it all, when Erich arrived.

"Got a minute, Kurt?"

"Got all the time in the world, Erich. All the time in the world. Got a year till my dying."

"Hey! Why so glum?"

"Nothing, really. Just thinking about Karen."

"Oh. I didn't know her well. Pretty, though." He looked around. "What do you think of Beck now?"

Kurt shrugged.

"He's alive and looking for trouble," said Erich. "He might have more luck than before."

"Only good one's a dead one, eh?"

"You might say. I wanted to ask you what happened yesterday. You were over. What was the fuss?"

Kurt wondered how much he dared tell. Why not the truth? He would get it from Gregor anyway. "Some ships tried to go home."

"Sounds like a good idea." Hippke was elaborately unconcerned.

"High Command sank them."

Hippke's eyebrows rose, his face paled the slightest. "How'd it happen?"

Kurt described what he had seen from high on the Rock.

"Kurt, you ever feel High Command's evil? Like the Devil runs it, or something?" Hippke's voice was lower, cautious.

"I doubt it. Evil's a matter of viewpoint, of what side you're on. We're probably black-hearted villains to Australians."

"No. I mean . . . I guess so. High Command probably believes in what it's doing. But the world would be better off without it."

"Maybe, Erich. But the job's to stay alive. Dead men make no changes."

"You think there're changes needed?"

"Some. Maybe a new direction for High Command."

"A new direction? Sounds like a good slogan. Kurt, did you ever think about what *you* could do?"

In a rare flash of insight, Kurt saw what Erich was after, read his future words, and retorted, "There's no point trying to recruit me. I can't see anything your group has to offer."

This was true enough, yet Kurt was unable to analyze the emotions founding his statement. Fear for Karen was there, fear for himself, belief that High Command was the only stabilizing power in the West, knowledge of the corruptness of historical revolutions, a love for his country and peace which wanted no rebellious devastation there. Yes, the War needed ending, but not at the cost Gregor and Erich thought needed paying.

"Can it! Beck!"

Kurt looked up. Beck had come in, was surveying the mess hall. This was his first day afoot. He leaned on a table for support. The place grew silent. Only Beck could have had that effect.

The Political Officer walked the length of the mess decks, nodded to Kurt, and drew himself a cup of coffee. He took a seat to one side, alone.

The mess decks soon emptied themselves. Kurt departed, wondering what it was like to have people leave when one entered a room. Did it bother Beck? Did it give him a feeling of power? He had never probed the matter in his meetings with the man.

Outside, as they moved to a lazing place on the fantail, Erich asked, "How much longer do you think he'll last?"

"What?"

"Beck. How long before someone gets him?"

Kurt stopped. "Erich! Be careful what you say — and who you say it to. Beck's looking for an excuse to hang you. Be careful around those kids, too. They're not supposed to speak German, but don't bet on it. Not your life."

"I wasn't planning anything, Kurt. Just curious, that's all."

Hippke departed. Kurt strolled aft, leaned against the empty depth-charge rack. His head swirled with confused thoughts about Martin Fitzhugh, Beck and his old master, Gregor and Erich, and Karen. Karen. She often lurked on the borders of his mind. Had she reached Telemark? How was her pregnancy coming?

Sea Detail was piped again after dinner. In a better mental state than earlier, Kurt went to his station. The last ships to seaward were getting under way. *Jäger* soon cast off her mooring buoy, slowly turned toward the sea. Kurt's heart beat rapidly. This time a Meeting, not a Gathering, was her goal.

"She feels like a new ship," said Gregor, leaning on the chart table beside Kurt. He now seemed under no strain.

"Uhm. The new screw. The helmsmen'll be happy. I tried steering on the way down. That was work."

"Where's that station guide? Captain'll want it soon."

From the drawer beneath the table Kurt took a fleet-formation diagram High Command had sent days earlier. He and Gregor examined it for perhaps the twentieth time, making certain of *Jäger*'s station. "This should be Combat's problem," Kurt grumbled.

"So fix the radars, you don't want to do it," Gregor growled back. "Where's the stadimeter?"

"You figure it out yet?"

"I think so," Lindemann replied. "I've practiced enough. You try. Get me the distance to that collier. . . ."

The hours passed, the sun set, and ships still milled about, trying to find their stations. *Jäger* had assumed her own with little difficulty, but others ... well, some crews knew nothing about formations. All was confusion. *Jäger* had several near misses.

The fleet began moving eastward the following day, and spent the next ten sailing to Malta, where Italian ships were waiting.

On the fourth morning the barometer plummeted. By the end of the watch, *Jäger* was taking white water over her bow. Great spumes of foam heaved into the air as the shuddering vessel dug her nose into the seas. The howling wind grew steadily stronger. Rain fell in angry sheets.

The evening watch was worse. The wind blew a whole gale, force ten, and promised more. The waves ran as tall as *Jäger*'s bridge. She took green water over the bow. Her stern lifted clear as she crossed each wave, staggering while her propellers cut nothing but air. Little could be seen through the haze and driven spray. A small carrier on the starboard quarter took water on her flight deck. A corvette on the port beam disappeared at times, as if spending part of her life underwater. And the wind screamed.

Watertight doors and windows soon proved they were not. Smashing waves, driven by force-eleven winds, pushed fingers through the seals, gradually soaked interior decks and passageways. Salt encrusted the feet of equipment, though sailors labored to keep the water away.

The rolls were murderous, as much as sixty degrees, so far over the yards almost diddled the crests of waves. Men had to tie themselves into bed. There were injuries, bruises, a broken arm, and a fatality when a man fell from a catwalk in the forward fireroom.

Desperately clinging to a handhold on the overhead, during the storm's third night, Hans asked, "Wonder how Obermeyer's taking this?"

Kurt felt compassion for the man. He was sick himself. "Go put him out of his misery."

"Aw. Tummy troubles? Don't worry about Obermeyer. He'll probably commit suicide."

Distressed though he was, Kurt still caught the seething jealousy beneath Hans's words—he probably hoped Obermeyer *would* suicide. Then von Lappus could no longer deny him a commission—Hans seemed to want that brass terribly bad.

"Would you for crissakes shut up!" someone moaned.

"Mind your helm. You don't have time to worry about your stomach," Hans growled.

There was in Hans's recent words a veiled gloating, a secret cry of victory. Kurt had heard it before, each time Weidermann got the better of him. This for Hans: it was never open or taunting, just a puffing of the chest and a heavier charge to his words.

Hans, Hans, Hans. Hans was a lifelong mystery to Kurt, more unfathomable than Karen, seldom more than half-real. Like all children, he had at times been exuberant or sulky, ambitious or lethargic, any of a hundred pairs of opposites. But in Hans there had also been an unchildlike reserve, an almost adult lack of imagination, a fondness for conformity and the established order. His father's presence, power, and person had hung over him like a cloud, molding him strangely.

Karl Wiedermann, of an authoritarian, almost monastic profession, was a stricter disciplinarian in his home than in his work. After Hans's mother died (he and Kurt had been four at the time), Karl rapidly became a tyrant of narrow limits, thunderous at home, almost too lenient with Kiel's leaders. While the High Command grip gradually eased on the Littoral, Karl's tightened on Hans (Kurt suspected the man of secretly blaming his son for his wife's death), subjecting him to growing terror.

At the age of eight, during one of their periodic spells of friendship (Otto had the measles and Kurt could find no other playmate), Kurt went with Hans to his father's shop. Karl was all smiles for a time, attentive, ready with snacks, instructive when the boys asked any of their hundred questions concerning the furnituremaker's art.

Then the Wiedermann cat came dashing through. Kurt seized its upright tail (he had been crueler then), eliciting a yowl. Hans shoved him to stop the torture. Kurt shoved back, boy words of anger were exchanged, Hans swung. Kurt countered and gave him a bloody nose. Hans retreated.

Then Karl stepped in, belt in hand. Kurt fled, pursued by Hans's howls and Karl's bellows about cowardice.

"Perhaps Hans does have good reason to dislike me," Kurt thought. "Every time we grew friendly, I eventually cost him a whipping. Maybe it's in his blood now: if we're friendly long, he'll suffer."

A groan jerked his attention from his thoughts. One of the Political Office signalmen squatted in a corner, clung desperately to the bulkhead. Eyes closed, he muttered over and over in English, "Oh, God, make it stop!"

It seemed the storm would never end. The four days of its duration were individual eternities. But the fifth day was like entering Paradise. The height of the waves dropped to six meters, the wind to thirty knots, and the rolls to reasonable angles.

The "man overboard!" cry reached the bridge that evening,

carried by Gregor, who had gone below for coffee. Beck was the victim. Kurt looked at Hans, Hans at another man, and so forth. No one believed it an accident.

Von Lappus arrived moments later, assumed the conn. "Which side?" he asked.

"Port side, sir," Lindemann replied.

The Captain ordered a turn to port. The destroyer rolled terribly as she ran parallel to the seas. They searched till dark, till even Beck's underlings were satisfied he was forever lost. As Kurt had suspected, the three now proved capable of speaking German.

The search was a grand performance. Kurt thought it a cynical sham (yet every time Beck's name crossed his mind, he felt relief because he would not now have to give the man an answer about joining High Command). He saw, in the faces of his officers during unguarded moments, that no one cared about Beck, that they hoped he would not be found.

He was not, so some were happy. Kurt was not. He knew Beck a little, knew he was real, and could not rejoice in his destruction. Nor were the three young Political Officers, who were suddenly very much on their own.

There was a three-day halt at Malta while the warships refueled. During the stay, *Jäger* suffered examinations and investigations. Political Officers from *Purpose* asked apparently endless questions, yet *Jäger* finally earned a clean bill—but, Kurt suspected, only because several ships had lost men overboard, and Beck had been none too strong.

No new Political Officer was assigned. That Kurt found curious. There must be a devious reason. Would the Political Office play *Jäger* like a fish, making certain the hook was well set before she was reeled in?

He cornered Hippke during the pause at Malta, after trying to catch him for days. Erich had been avoiding him since Beck's disappearance, speaking only when he relieved the watch, when no weighty matters could be discussed.

"Erich, did you have anything to do with Beck?" Kurt snapped, surprising himself with his own intensity.

Hippke would not meet his eyes. Nervously, he looked to see if they were watched. "I was afraid you'd think that after the way I talked. No, I didn't do it. Really. I swear. Funny thing is, though, nobody knows who did. Far as I know, it really was an accident."

Kurt had to be satisfied with that. Hippke refused to discuss it further. His apparent sincerity in denying responsibility might have been faked, but Kurt came to a similar conclusion once he had snooped around. Everyone thought Beck had been pushed, but no one knew by whom. This death was a mystery deep as Otto's.

The possibilities frightened Kurt. Was it really coincidence? Accident fulfilling threat? But it did not have the feeling of accident, no more than the attack in Norway. *Someone* had to be responsible.

Kurt suffered attacks of nervousness, compounded by inactivity. He felt compassion for Haber, whose state was now pathetic. To fight it, he began reading the forbidden book from his safe.

ELEVEN

Malta to Port Said was uneventful. Kurt spent his time puzzling out the meaning of the first chapter of *Ritual War*. After a day wrestling with words not in his vocabulary, he decided to translate the book on paper. Good for killing time, if nothing else, and time he would have, for the Suez Canal was closed, silted up since the last Meeting.

Ten days out of Malta, *Jäger* dropped anchor in Lake Manzala. Von Lappus announced that most of the crew would go ashore to help clear the canal. With some fast verbal footwork, Kurt convinced Gregor that *Jäger* could not manage without him—their being related may have helped. And there was the translation, which had become important to him. With his dictionary to explain unfamiliar and technical terms, the book soon shook the roots of his world. As the title implied, it told of the beginnings of the War.

He had not gotten far yet, but black hints had appeared like bloodstains on a neolithic altar, hints that, unless the book was one monstrous lie, everything he knew of the past two and a half centuries was purest invented history. He had to continue.

Ritual War claimed to have been written during the first two decades of the War, and had reached the public in 2008. It had become, according to the preface, an immediate international bestseller, popular throughout a savaged world. And possession soon became a crime. Production went underground. Kurt's edition was of the twenty-fourth printing of the second revision, undated, with a later supplementary pamphlet tucked in behind the last page.

Briefly, the first chapter explored the ecological-economic crisis which had set the stage for the War. The pollution problems of the seventh and eighth decades of the twentieth century had snowballed and roared into the mid-ninth decade with the fury of an avalanche as wastes, and the new microbiology evolved within them, poisoned and destroyed vast food resources. Worldwide panic and depression, ignoring ideologies, economic controls, and the efforts of man in general, followed a year of almost universal cereal-crops failures. The capitalist house of paper had fallen with a muted *crump*! The interpreters of Marx had fled Moscow a step ahead of angry workers and peasants, their carpetbags filled with yards of worthless rubles.

The book scarce mentioned human suffering, assuming the reader had endured the experiences of the time. Kurt obtained none of the misery of 1986 and 1987. He did not see the starving billions, the riots, the burning cities, the dead mounded in Western streets, the cannibalism that swept the non-Hindu east. He knew not the desperation that made men murder for a loaf or dried fish. He felt none of the frantic dismay of a man who, early on, found his entire life's savings would not buy a tin of cat food. He could not comprehend the unbalanced ecological equation initiating the collapse. The numbers, the statistics were meaningless. He could not encompass their vastness.

There is a way to channel the frustrations of a people, a way of creating work and concerted effort for a common end — though then it was certain to worsen the already disastrous ecological situation —

War.

(Like a drumbeat, its sound, like a trumpet call, like the tramp of marching men — War! War! *Krieg! Guerre!* A harsh, short word in any tongue.)

Kurt could not imagine the desperation behind the Geneva Accord of 1987. He was appalled by the author's calm, passionless picture of government heads agreeing to a vast but limited war of recovery, by economists casually establishing kill-quotas and consumption rates of mega-deaths per year.

Something had happened to upset the delicate balance of the engineering war. Something would make the war the War. The author would explain in a chapter entitled "The Nuclear Exchange."

This much Kurt learned by Lake Manzala, and, although horrified, he had to learn more. The macabre, unemotional, committee-report style of the book, dreadful in itself, drew him on — he knew the author must explode sometime. He felt like a vulture, perched and waiting for that explosion.

Kurt stood on the port wing two days after reaching Egypt, with the feelings of a condemned man as the gibbet-trap falls away beneath him. Now he knew why Fitzhugh had given him the book. The old man meant him to plunge into Gregor's movement in reaction to that disaster of the past—a disaster still in progress. And he was tempted. He had a decision to make. What to do. Drift with the tide, as he had all his life? Or join something probably as wicked as what was?

And, as he told himself he would do the latter, he knew he lied. He would always be a follower, a drifter with the flood. He did not like it. It meant he was a nothing. What had Gregor said? "You take no stands." But—what was wrong with the middle-of-the-road stand?

"Hey, Kurt. What's the matter? You really look down."

"I don't know, Hans. Just wondering why I'm here—God, the heat!—and how Karen's getting on. Thinking about the baby...."

"Suppose we change the subject?"

Kurt nodded slowly. So. Hans still had not gotten over his loss. Best humor him. Their enmity was fading. No sense tempting it.

His mind slipped off on a tangent, forgetting the present Hans in a question about Hans of the past. Why had Karen become engaged to him? It was a question he had never dared probe deeply, for fear of the answer. Karen had not had much use for Wiedermann before Kurt had gone to sea with the Danes—had, indeed, been quite cruel to him as a child. Why had she changed her mind?

These questions, long suppressed, burst upon him in full bloom, and from his subconscious—which worried such things whether he willed it or no—welled glimmerings of answers. Karen. Telemark. Brindled Saxon. Beck saying the underground had unusually good information on *Jäger*'s plans. Various other clues too subtle to label. Given the assumption that Karen was associated with the underground, Kurt could understand her engagement. She had wanted to recruit a Political Office family member for the resistance. And Hans, even without Karen for incentive, had motives for joining that movement. What better way to avenge himself on a cruel father?

Yes, that would answer several disquieting questions—but raised more, equally unsettling. Why had Karen married *him*? If for political reasons once, why not twice? All his relatives were associated with the underground—now he was lonely, solitary between tribes. Opposite Karen stood shadowed Marquis, another new question. For Kurt had gradually come to suspect Hans, because of his family background, of being that masked unknown. But, by labeling Hans Brindled Saxon, his emotions left him with a less likely suspect (assuming Marquis had killed Otto, for which he had none but emotional evidence): Haber.

It was all so confusing!

Hans was staring at him strangely. He must get back to the world, say something, anything. "How long will we be here?"

"A long time. The ships that were already here—the Greeks, Turks, and Ukrainians—have been working for months, and they haven't gotten much done. I heard about four months to reach Great Bitter Lake, and six more to Port Suez."

Kurt groaned. "Damn, Hans, I wish I'd jumped ship in Norway. Or not shown up the morning we left."

"Careful, Kurt. These Political Officers are kids, but they can still get you hung. There's too much loose talk now."

"I know. I've had to warn some of my men."

"There's one of yours I've warned myself, but he won't listen. Hippke."

"Erich? Again? I'll kick his head in. . . ." He suddenly had a strong impression that Hans was probing for something. His attitude toward what Erich had been saying? "You people made a wrong choice in picking up Hippke." He watched for a reaction, saw none.

"Oh, he hasn't done anything open. Yet. It's his attitude. He's insolent. Nothing that'll get him hung, but enough to keep them watching, hoping he *will* do something. And he will, if he thinks he can get away with it. I can't get through to him. Will you try?"

Kurt looked at Hans from the corner of his eye. He could picture the Boatswain being this concerned for someone else only if a threat to himself were involved—which supported his earlier notion about Hans being the Brindled Saxon. "I'll talk to him. Ah! There he is now, heading aft. Erich!"

Kurt walked to the rear of the wing, to the ladder leading down to the torpedo deck. Hippke was about to start up. "Stay there, Erich."

He went down. "Come over here."

They went to the port torpedo tube and sat. "Erich, you've got to be more careful."

"What? Why?" He seemed honestly mystified.

"I hear our Political Officers are watching you pretty close. So be more careful, eh?"

"What'd I do?" Defensive.

"It's the way you act toward them. You keep antagonizing them, they'll keep watching. And, sooner or later, they'll catch you making one of your organization's maneuvers. Then goodbye Erich."

Hippke popped up, shouted, "Goddammit, Kurt, am I supposed to kowtow to those zombies?"

A half-dozen sailors turned to see what was happening.

Hippke forgot himself completely. "Let's stop this idiocy here, now! We'll cut their throats and go home! You . . . Fritz! Want to see your wife again? Karl? Adolf?"

Fritz averted his eyes, afraid to show agreement. Kurt groaned, remembering Otto Kapp. "Erich, shut up!" He tried to pull Hippke back to his seat on the torpedo tube.

Erich shook him off. "Stop it, Kurt! You blind fool. Don't you give a damn about Karen? Ever wonder who she's seeing now? I care about *my* wife."

His questions struck a tender spot. Kurt jumped.

He remembered only impressions of leaping, swinging, feeling his fists connect, then arms grasping him, pinning him as he struggled. Four men pulled him to the far side of the torpedo deck while another bent over Erich, to help.

Calmness quickly returned, and with it, shame. He glanced at the bridge, thinking he had seen Hans there as he began swinging. But no, it must have been someone else, seen in a flash.

Kurt suddenly realized he might be in a great deal of trouble. "Let me go. I'll be all right."

The hand on his arms relaxed, but the sailors stayed close as he walked over to Hippke. "I'm sorry, Erich. I just went wild."

Erich, with a bloody nose and an eye he caressed gently, stared for a long moment, then smiled thinly. "I should learn to keep my mouth shut. Maybe you did me a favor. I was going after those Political Officers. . . ."

"Stop!" Kurt snapped. He waved everyone back. "Erich, be doubly careful now. A lot of people saw this."

Hippke nodded. "Will do. Only time I'll open my mouth is to shove food in."

Kurt offered a hand. They shook. "Go clean up. I'm sorry."

Kurt watched him go down a ladder and aft, to their compartment, then he turned, went forward and down, to officers' country. He knocked at the door of Gregor's stateroom. A sleepy-eyed Lindemann answered the knock. Kurt's taut expression roused him. "Trouble?"

"The biggest." He had seldom felt more alone, though his cousin was here to help him.

"Come in."

Kurt slipped inside. Gregor checked the passage behind him, then closed and locked the door. "What's happened?"

"I just had a fight with Erich Hippke."

"Oh? Why?"

Kurt explained, then, "It isn't the fight that bothers me. Just before I jumped him, he was spouting the same stuff that got Otto killed." He repeated much of what Erich had said.

"Who heard?"

"No Political Officers. But there weren't any around when Otto made *his* speech. And he was killed that same night—I think by Marquis."

"Killed?"

"I was on the torpedo deck when it happened. You know that. I never told anybody I saw someone go in a door aft."

"Who?"

"I don't know. Could've been anybody. And there was blood on Otto's jumper when we found him, like he'd been stabbed."

"You noticed, eh?"

"You did too?"

"Yes. And I've been snooping, checking on people. Otto was one of mine. . . . I've even gone through a few lockers, looking for the knife—I mean to even this."

"So do I. But I haven't found anything. I've been checking names off the muster, but I've still got over forty. Oh, you're clear."

Lindemann chuckled. "Thank you, Kurt. I've cleared you, too. Just now."

The full import did not sink in then. Later, it would, and Kurt would understand why Gregor had so long been cold. "You have a list? Could we compare?" They did so, eliminating a dozen names each.

"That's better," said Gregor. "But there're still a lot of people to watch."

"But most of them will go ashore tomorrow," Kurt replied. "If there were an attempt on Hippke, we'd narrow it considerably."

"Speaking of which, you'd better keep an eye on him. If there's anyone aboard who'd murder him for criticizing High Command—other than our three apprentice headsmen—he'll be in danger. And I need him desperately. I'll tell my Brindled Saxon."

"I'll go see him now. He's popular. Long as he sticks with a group, he'll be safe."

"Tell him it's an order from me, that it's too late to take chances. If you just warn him, he'll laugh it off. Got no sense. Keep me posted. I'll be in the wardroom."

Kurt left and went aft, hoping Erich would still be in his compartment. He wiped sweat from his forehead as he entered Operations' living spaces. It was ovenlike there. The Egyptian sun in June. . . .

Everyone was abovedecks. The compartment would be a good place to talk. "Erich?"

Hippke was not there. Kurt wandered through the compartment, climbed the ladder to the fantail. "Anyone seen Hippke?"

147

One of the loungers there rolled over, said, "He was in the head, last I saw. He was going to play chess with Bodelschwing when he was done showering."

"Thanks." Kurt went back down, walked forward through the dark, sweltering compartment, and scrambled up the ladder to the midships passage and head. A shower was running.

"Erich?" No answer. Must be someone else. "Hey! You seen Hippke?"

Still no answer. He shrugged and turned away. His eyes passed over the foot of the canvas shower curtain. He froze. Redness. Blood. He crossed the head in three quick steps and jerked the shower curtain aside.

Hippke, curled in a fetal position on the floor of the stall, dead, wrists slashed, face empty, pale, unsouled. The shower ran on, washed the last of the blood down the drain.

There was a small, almost unnoticeable bruise on the back of Hippke's neck, at the base of his skull. He had been struck before being cut. Kurt saw it only by accident, as he insanely tried to shake Erich back to life. He knew. No suicide.

He rose, stared for a long moment, taking in details with sudden calm. But the detachment was brief, the eye of an emotional storm. It passed. He kicked open the door to the weatherdeck, grabbed the nearest man, ordered, "Horst, get the Captain. Get Commander Haber. Tell them to come to the after crews' head." His words were spoken softly, but with an intensity which startled.

"What?"

"Just do it! Now!"

Eyes wide, the seaman ran forward. Von Lappus, Haber, and Gregor arrived as a group hardly a minute later.

"Secure this head!" von Lappus snapped, suddenly and startingly coming to life. Even horrified, Kurt marked again the disparity between the Captain's buffoon appearance and his hard, practical actuality.

"You men get back," Haber ordered a gathering crowd. "Everyone lay to the forecastle. Not you, Ranke." The man's nervousness was temporarily gone. Perhaps all he needed was a problem.

The three young Political Officers arrived like an officious squad of vultures. "Get forward!" von Lappus thundered.

Seamen scrambled. The Political Officers appeared uncertain. "That means you too, gentlemen!" The three joined the retreat.

"All right, Ranke, what happened?"

Quick as he could, with a stumbling tongue and the shakes, Kurt explained how he had gone looking for Hippke after telling Gregor of their fight, and had found him in the shower.

"Here, what's this?" Haber had found something beneath Hippke's toilet kit.

"Well?"

"Suicide note. 'I cannot bear the thought of my wife's infidelity any longer. . . .'" Haber read a number of thoughts which might well have been in Hippke's mind — thoughts he had certainly been discussing with the men, desperate thoughts which might cause an unstable person to take his own life.

"Well, Kurt? You said he was upset," said Lindemann. "Was he this upset?"

Gregor seemed shaken to the roots of his being, was certainly battling one of his headaches.

"He *was* worried about his wife, sir. He might've done it, except. . . ."

"Except what?"

"This, sir." He showed them the bruise. "May I see the note, Commander?"

Haber handed it over. Kurt read it all, though the first few words told him what he wanted to know. "Erich didn't kill himself."

He was certain. Then he was dismayed by the look which had entered von Lappus's eyes. He knew he was the prime suspect. "This isn't his handwriting. His was ornate, and he was a much better speller." In fact, the handwriting looked like a poor imitation of his own. "Compare this with the log entries."

"Lindemann, check it," von Lappus ordered. "Heinrich, search the ship's records and compare handwriting."

He turned to Kurt. "Ranke, we'll pretend this's suicide for now. We know it's not, but we don't want the murderer to know we know, and I don't want the crew spooked—and I want to keep you from getting the same."

"Sir?" The unexpected words were like a physical blow.

"You had a fight with him, right? So who'll be the logical suspect to the common mind? What might they do?"

Kurt looked from one officer to another, trying to read their expressions. He was certain von Lappus suspected him. Did the others? But the suspicion should lessen—unless they really thought that note was in his handwriting. He was in a bad spot, circumstantially. Twice now he had been the first man to a murder victim. He had a feeling of walls closing in, of slowly being bound in an invisible strait jacket. Was someone after him? Why this complicated method? So much easier to stab him in the back. . . .

"Kurt!"

"Sir?" He had been on the verge of something, but it now fled before other concerns.

"Come to my stateroom when you're done here," said Gregor. "Commander?"

"We'll put him over the side. Full muster. A show. A little speechmaking, or something, to divert the crew so they don't start brooding. Ranke, take a couple of men and get him ready."

The shower still ran, washing the body. The blood, except the stain on the shower curtain, was gone.

Kurt gathered several of Erich's friends for the burial detail. Two sweating, fear-filled hours passed before the ceremony — fear-filled because no one accepted the suicide story. Anger surged through the vessel, rumbled just short of volcanic explosion.

But, to his amazement, Kurt found no one questioned his innocence. All the anger was directed at the Political Officers. Something had been happening of which he was unaware — Erich's propaganda! He had seen only a little of what Hippke had been doing, cautiously developing a general antipathy toward the Political Office and *Jäger*'s mission, recruiting, organizing. Those who had become his followers automatically assumed he had been silenced because of his actions.

Kurt worked hard to prevent the outbreak of violence he expected — so near, so near, he could almost hear a fuse sputtering toward a powder keg — reminding everyone of the nearness of the High Command battleship. Perhaps because of his efforts, perhaps for some other reason, the anger crested short of combustion and gradually subsided. By funeral time the danger was past, though a lesser anger would still be there, hidden, ready to explode at any new provocation.

The ceremonies were brief, with a short prayer by the Captain and a eulogy by one of Erich's friends.

Kurt reached Gregor's stateroom five minutes after the funeral ended. "It could get ugly," he said. "The men won't buy the suicide story. They think the Captain's covering up for the Political Officers."

"Not their doing—not directly. They were in the wardroom all afternoon. Haber and I went through the records. The note doesn't match anyone's handwriting." Kurt sighed with relief as Gregor took the note from his pocket. "Here. Read it again. Don't bother with the sense, just the spelling."

Kurt read. "A lot of misspelled words. But most people just put down whatever sounds right."

"Correct. I've studied that almost since we found it. I think there's a pattern to the errors. Look. Every *sch* is spelled *ch*. And *k* where *ch* should be. Study it. You'll see others."

Kurt examined it carefully. For some reason he could not at first comprehend, Martin Fitzhugh came to mind. Then it dawned on him. "Gregor, it looks like this was written by someone who speaks, but has a hard time writing, German. Someone who thinks in another language. English, I'd guess."

"I thought so too. The errors were too regular. And I think I know the errors the Poles would make. That left the Political Officers as the other bilinguals."

"But you just said they were in the wardroom. . . . Marquis."

"Yes. One of them could've written it for him earlier. The meeting with the Captain was at their request. They needed an alibi. Kurt, they've beaten me. I couldn't win against even their most inexperienced players. It was tonight . . . tonight we'd seize the ship, at midnight when the watches change and men moving around wouldn't be suspicious. Too late. I can't do it without Hippke's help . . . and tomorrow everybody goes ashore. They knew, and they played cat with me until the last minute. . . ."

Kurt was afraid Gregor would grow hysterical—was amazed by the depth of the plot his cousin had put afoot, and how well he had been fooled. He had had no idea it had ripened, not to within hours of action. The failure, for Gregor, was shattering. "Do you want some aspirin?" he asked.

"In my desk drawer. Haber gave me a packet."

Kurt opened the desk, found the aspirin—for a moment his eyes were caught by a black leather notebook embossed with the Political Office seal, and he frowned deeply, wondering— took two to Gregor.

"I'm alone now, Kurt, and I'm frightened. You told me it wasn't a game. I couldn't believe it, deep inside. But those kids've proved there're no games being played. Kurt, you've got to help. The whole program'll collapse if they get me."

Frightened himself, Kurt shook his head, said, "No, Gregor. I'm out. No matter what, I'm out. You've got to work inside the system. That's always been true. Even the best systems strike back hard when you don't play by the rules. And here you're not only defying High Command, you're fighting your own people. You're more likely to succeed if you have Haber's and von Lappus's cooperation. . . ." Yes, his only interest in this whole mess was in finding Otto's killer.

Lindemann visibly pulled himself together. "I still have Brindled Saxon. I'm not as alone as I thought."

His expression was proud, and damned Kurt for not coming to his aid. "I'll have him start a rumor that there's an ununiformed Political Officer aboard. You find out where our suspects were when Erich died."

"There's one benefit we'll get from this," Kurt said, frowning. "The men will learn to keep their mouths shut."

He opened the stateroom door and stepped into the passageway. "Suppose the killer thought we had some evidence? He might try to recover it. . . ."

"I hope that happens, Kurt. That's why I want a rumor, why I want to push. If it's the last thing I do, I'm going to flush Marquis."

TWELVE

Marquis seemed unshakable. He remained undiscovered despite the frantic witch-hunt following Hippke's death. *Jäger's* mood gradually deteriorated from angry hunt to sedentary apathy. Two months later the mark of remembrance existed only in the careful way men thought before speaking.

Kurt's vigilance, too, relaxed as the long, boring, intensely uncomfortable Egyptian weeks passed. He spent much of his time working on his translation. Though the book was inordinately dull — the government-report style clogged and bogged the flow of a truly exciting content — each surprising bit of information drew him on.

The chapter entitled "The Nuclear Exchange" needed two translations — he could not believe it first time through. It was nothing like the history he had been taught.

The War had been started by the shadowed Australian Empire, to the satanic purpose of enslaving the world; this was the gospel he knew.

Ritual War, speaking from a different past, claimed Australia had been allied with the West. Many current allies—most of the Littoral, Bulgaria, Romania, the Ukraine—had belonged to the enemy entente. It seemed someone, sometime, had decided the alliances should be reorganized along geographical lines. So the War was a lie. Top to bottom, misty beginnings to unforeseeable end, all a carefully fabricated lie.

The book gave no indication—Kurt spent days searching for clues—of how or when the false history had been introduced. It had been written too early. High Command was undoubtedly responsible. Again Kurt resolved to stop drifting, to take a part in ending this endless insanity. And again he lied to himself. He knew he lied, was angry with himself because he lied—and would do nothing to change.

The chapter entitled "The Nuclear Exchange" outlined the first years of war, before it had become the War, told of the Western military, gradually waxing enthusiastic, breaking the planned stalemate and plunging deep into Soviet territory. Spread along a two-thousand-kilometer front, southern end anchored on, and the fighting keyed on, Volgograd (Stalingrad, where *Luftpanzer Armee II* requited the destruction of the Sixth Army forty-seven years earlier), the Battle of the Volga raged for months. Counterattacking Eastern armies were slaughtered by massed Western firepower in a tactic called "the killing pocket." An Eastern collapse appeared imminent. As fighting peaked along the Volgograd-Moscow line, Anglo-American, German, and Turkish forces descended on "impregnable" Rostov from land, sea, and air, destroyed a crack Guards Army in days. Unopposed American and German armored columns crossed the Volga and raced for Astrakhan. . . .

The Soviets, in desperation, unleashed the hounds of atomic destruction. Within a day, all nuclear arsenals were empty, cities were gone, millions were dead. But then Kurt discovered that the bombs had been less murderous then he had supposed. Very few had been delivered—wise men, foreseeing the possibility of their use, had begun dismantling those brutal weapons on agreeing to found the War. The real murderer of humanity had another and more terrible name. A chapter, "The Bio-War," calmly related details.

To ravage Asia, Western invaders used an aerially sprayed, laboratory-evolved disease of amazing properties: in its first generation, this bacteria was harmless; in its second, almost universally fatal; in its third, unable to reproduce. It did not spread, killed fast, and left human works undamaged, and troops could with impunity occupy the area of application within days.

The Chinese had had their own weapon, a virus which attacked chromosomal material—only in Caucasians—and caused widespread sterility. A weapon of longer term, but effective. Only its limited use and natural immunities had prevented the disappearance of one human race.

While dredging crews doggedly pushed toward Great Bitter Lake, Kurt slogged through a catalog of gruesome biological weapons. He was revolted by the excesses of his ancestors—yet was drawn on because the book made sense of some contemporary insanities. He finished the first half of the book, which concerned itself primarily with military events, the day the word came that the canal had been opened to Great Bitter Lake. Christmas Day, 2193, a day dedicated to peace on Earth. *Jäger* celebrated the holiday, and ignored the meaning.

That day Kurt stood on the signal bridge, watching a sandstorm over Sinai. Several men on camels, specks in the distance, were outlined against the dark rising cloud. Bedouins. They came and went, watched the ships, never interfered, never tried to communicate. Perhaps they were sane men making certain madness would not penetrate their deserts.

Kurt ignored most of this. His thoughts were northbound-winged, toward Karen and the baby. There was a good chance the child had been born. Seven lonely, terrifying months had passed.

Was she now in Telemark? Was there someone to care for her when her time came? He suffered an oppressive guilt. What would she say when he returned? Because he had a man's faith in his own immortality, he could not deep down believe that *Jäger* would be destroyed. Other ships, yes, but not his own. He feared his homecoming more.

He paced the port-side wing, staring at but not seeing those Arab riders, smashing fist into palm, smashing fist into palm, muttering.

"Kurt?"

He missed it the first time because it was softly spoken. "Kurt!"

He spun. "Oh. Hans. Sorry. I was thinking."

"You'd daydream your way through the end of the world. You all right?"

"I guess. I was worrying about Karen and the baby." He ignored Hans's frown. "It's due about now. I should be there."

"Mr. Lindemann's about to become a mother, too—I think. He's in a panic. Wants to see you."

"Why?"

"He'll explain. Commander Haber told me to send you down. That's all I know. Guess because we're supposed to move to Great Bitter Lake."

"We don't have any fuel."

"Maybe that's his problem. Why don't you go see?"

Kurt went below, knocked at Gregor's door.

"Kurt?"

"Yes sir."

"Inside! Hurry!"

He stepped through and turned as Gregor hastily re-locked the door. "What's the matter?"

"Did you hear my rumor? That I know who Hippke's killer is?"

"Yes. I didn't believe it. It's been four months. I assumed you let it out as a trap."

"I did, and somebody was touched."

"What?"

Lindemann peeled his shirt off and turned his back. Kurt gaped at bruises and abrasions. "That was one brilliant idea I wish I hadn't had." Gregor knelt and fished something from beneath his bunk. "This's what he hit me with."

"A sextant box?" A stainless-steel box taken from the wreck at Finisterre, it weighed nearly eight kilos, made a nasty weapon.

"Someone threw it off the bridge. If it'd hit me on the head, it would've brained me." Lindemann forced a bantering tone, but Kurt saw hints of the raw fear he was hiding.

"Did you see who did it?"

Gregor shook his head wearily. "No, of course not. The man's damnably cunning...."

Just then Kurt realized that he must have been on the bridge when it had happened—and he had seen not a thing! What had Hans said? "You would daydream through the end of the world." A black Christmas present for Gregor. Who, he realized, was still talking.

"All three Political Officers were conveniently on display on the fantail. Only good to come out of it is that we can scratch Kellerman off the list. He was serving the Captain in the wardroom."

Kurt scowled. "And now we're down to ten. If we've got to have someone killed or hurt for each name we cut, we'll soon be hip-deep in blood. By now, though, Marquis knows you were baiting a trap. Otherwise, you'd've had him arrested."

"I think he knew all along, Kurt. The box was a warning to mind my own business. How well did you learn English from Fitzhugh?"

"What?"

"Martin Fitzhugh taught you to read and speak English. How well?"

"Well enough. I'm translating a book. Why?"

"Just curious. Here. I want you to take care of this." He took a slim, leatherbound book from his desk, the black notebook he had seen earlier.

"What's this?" Kurt asked, turning it over in his hands.

"I don't know. It belonged to Beck. It was important to him. He never let it out of sight. Neither have I. But they're after me now. I have to trust someone else. You. Keep it hidden, and give it to Commander Haber if I get killed."

Haber, Kurt's prime suspect? He tucked the book into his waistband, fought back the flood of questions he wanted to ask. The fact that Beck had never let the book out of sight implied that he had carried it with him. Which, in turn, implied that it had been taken from him. Which implied . . .

Kurt refused to follow the chain of logic, though it explained something that had mystified everyone. Namely, who had pushed Beck overboard. He should have suspected from the beginning.

As Kurt thought, and Gregor studied him, there was a soft, stealthy sound in the passageway. Both heard. Lindemann pulled a pistol from beneath his pillow—good God, Kurt thought, where did he get that? Gregor signaled that the door be opened. Kurt unlocked it silently, opened quickly. Gregor jumped through. Kurt followed.

"Nothing," he whispered.

Lindemann signaled for silence. The stealthy sound came from the ladder leading out of officers' country. They ran, arrived too late again.

"Damn!" Gregor snarled. "There'll be trouble now, if they know we have the book."

For a moment Kurt considered the notion that Gregor was maneuvering him, trying to force him into the resistance. "Aren't you jumping to conclusions?" He scuffed the carpeted deck with his toe, listened to the sound. "For all we know, someone just walked by. You'll be in big trouble if you get paranoid."

"You're right. I'm too jumpy." He rubbed his temple with the gun butt. "But there're two men dead already—we *have* to be paranoid."

Kurt shrugged. Suddenly, he brightened. "Gregor, why don't

we send the suspects to the working parties? That might get the man out of our hair until we find something."

Still rubbing his temple, Lindemann replied, "Can't do it. Most of them *have* to stay aboard."

"No . . . no. What happens if we catch the man and he's someone we can't do without?"

"I see. We'd have to replace him anyway. All right. I'll talk to the Captain. Take care of the book."

Kurt turned and started up the ladder.

"Kurt? Would you ask Commander Haber to come to my stateroom? I'm out of aspirin."

He went to the charthouse after leaving Gregor in Haber's care, locked the black book in the safe. An obvious place, but how would anyone get to it, even knowing it was there? Then he went prowling, just walking the ship and thinking of Karen.

He noticed a Political Officer leaning on the signal-bridge rail, staring landward. The sandstorm was wandering south now, an impressive range of darkness in the east.

"What do they do up there?" Kurt realized he had spoken, looked around, saw no one had heard. It was a good question. What *did* the three do up there, other than stay out of the way? He decided to sneak up and see.

The inside route took him to the pilothouse unnoticed. Removing his shoes eliminated noise as he crept out on the wing. He reached a position where he could hear the murmur of voices, low, in English. An argument.

" —think we ought to call in!"

"So do I. If they've got his notebook, we might be in trouble."

"There's no need to worry! These dunderheads couldn't read it." Two against one?

"Wrong! That Quartermaster . . . picked up some at Gibraltar." The voices faded in and out. Kurt's imagination filled in a lot.

"How do you know?"

"Marquis told me."

"You're certain?" the dubious one asked.

"I'm sure. I'm sure. Report it."

"If you're wrong, they'll raise holy hell."

"What if we're right and don't report? You want to sweep floors the rest of your life?"

Kurt felt a sudden urge to laugh. Irrationally, he remembered characters from a Shakespeare translation in the ship's meager library. Characters on a deserted heath, over a caldron: "Double, double, toil and trouble . . ."

Kurt set a foot on the second rung of the ladder leading up and carefully lifted himself until he could see. They were in the signal shack, gathered over their caldron-substitute. A radio, Kurt assumed. One talked into it, and, at times, a muted voice replied.

He eased back down. So. He had learned something of value. The three could contact their masters at will, which meant those masters were, in all probability, getting running reports. Did it matter? Kurt wondered.

He returned to the charthouse and locked himself in. His thoughts turned to Karen again. He stretched out on his back on the chart table, stared at the overhead while daydreams ran across his mind—thoughts of home, fears for the future.

The fleeing dream again, with wolves, little change, except that Karen's face seemed clouded. Even walking he had a hard time picturing that face. Time erosion.

A pounding at the door woke him. "Kurt? You there?"

"Huh?" Growing muzzily aware, he sat up. "Gregor?" He staggered to the door. Lindemann stepped inside and seated himself on the stool. Kurt returned to the table.

"I convinced the Captain," said Gregor. Kurt saw he was rubbing his head again. "Our suspects leave tomorrow, all but Commander Haber. We'll be getting underway in an hour."

"What?"

"We're moving to Great Bitter Lake."

"At night? With no fuel?" He glanced at the clock. "Whoops!"

"Where've you been?"

"Asleep. Drifted off, I guess."

"There's a collier alongside now. We've been bringing fuel aboard for two hours. How'd you sleep through the racket?"

"Talent."

"This'll be rough. Everybody on watch all the time, here to there. Twenty hours. Know your buoys, lights, and ranges?"

"I dream about them. Red buoys on the right, black on the left. Black and white stripes mark the fairway on the lake itself. Red lights right, green left, white in the fairway. The ranges . . ."

"All right. Go clean up."

"Okay. By the way, you were right about that noise yesterday. Somebody was listening. I heard the Political Officers telling their bosses about the notebook."

"Oh? How?"

"They've got a radio up there."

"Interesting. And you've got the notebook in the safe? Too obvious. Hide it." Gregor seemed to be thinking very hard, possibly searching for some advantage to be had from this new knowledge.

Kurt did not understand, but did as he was told.

The Political Officers, though, apparently did nothing to find the notebook. Other than *Jäger* moving from Lake Manzala to Great Bitter Lake, nothing noteworthy happened the following four months. Kurt toyed with his translation, but could work up little interest in the dull political and economic chapters. He worried about Karen quite a lot.

The killer apparently had gone ashore. In any event, he did nothing to disturb vessel or crew.

THIRTEEN

The dredging crews completed their work on May 1, 2194. *Jäger* got under way on the third and moved to Port Suez, where those of her surviving crewmen returned. The privation and heat had been deadly for the working parties. *Jäger* had lost seven men and one officer — Lieutenant Obermeyer (Obermeyer's death could only be deduced — he had gone for a walk one night and never returned). Seven Littoral graves served as milestones down the borders of Sinai, poorly marked memorials to insanity.

Kurt was on the quarterdeck to greet friends as they returned. Among the last was Hans, a browned, thinned Hans. "You look rough," Kurt told him. "Lost five or six kilos, I'd say."

"That wonderful sun and exercise," Hans replied, showing his darkness and callused hands. "Just what the doctor ordered." Less lightly, "It *was* rough. I couldn't've made it the whole time. I'm surprised we only lost eight. What's happening here?"

"Nothing. Spent most of the time wishing we were with you. Let's have some lemonade."

"What's that?"

"You wouldn't know, would you? Well, we traded some stuff off that wreck to a Turkish ship anchored beside us in Great Bitter Lake. We talked our Political Officers into handling it through theirs. We got five crates of lemons—it's a little fruit, so big, and sour—three hundred kilos of real coffee, some fresh meat, and a bunch of other stuff. Lemonade's made from lemons."

They entered the mess decks. "It's cool in here!" said Hans, wonderstruck. "How? . . ."

"Oh, another trade. There was a Liberian ship with a man who knew refrigeration. He fixed our air conditioning and reefers. We fixed their fire control."

As Kurt drew two glasses of lemonade, Hans said, "I thought nothing happened. What else?"

Kurt shrugged. "Not much. What do you think?"

Hans puckered, surprised. "Not bad, after being outside."

A man came to their table as they were settling in. "Kurt, Mr. Lindemann wants you."

"Be there in a minute, Fritz." He hurriedly finished his drink. "Talk to you later, Hans. I want to hear all about digging the grand canal."

He went down to officers' country. Gregor waited at the door of his stateroom. "Come in. I thought we'd better talk before things get too hectic." Kurt settled himself on the edge of Gregor's bunk.

"Business first. We sail for Bab el Mandeb tomorrow, about seventeen hundred kilometers. We'll anchor off Perim while the stores ships return to Cyprus and Turkey to load up. We'll have to stack wood on in piles like we did in Norway. There're no forests between Perim and India, almost four thousand kilometers. We'll refuel underway. Get with Mr. Czyzewski and Wiedermann on that. I suppose he'll get Mr. Obermeyer's job. Get the refueling points figured as soon as possible."

"Got them already. We haven't had much else to do."

"Good. They should've given you a commission, Kurt. But I suppose you're too young." He rubbed his right temple with his fingers, rolled his head.

Kurt, stimulated by the statement, wondered just how Gregor *had* managed to win the navigator's appointment. He, Kurt, certainly had the edge in experience, though his cousin was older. He began to wonder just how much influence the underground had in the Littoral's *Bundestag*. He wondered if Hans would have been First Lieutenant if Obermeyer's father had not been president of that assembly.

"About our killer," Lindemann continued. "Two suspects didn't return. That leaves eight names — we need evidence. They all seem unlikely."

He used both hands to rub his temples. His headache had been almost constant since the day he had been attacked, and grew stronger whenever he and Kurt discussed the murderer. Aspirin helped, but never drove the pain completely away.

Kurt shrugged. "Every one of those men is a friend. That pains me."

As he spoke, he considered the cruise's effect on *Jäger's* officers. Gregor had the constant headache. Obermeyer was dead.

Haber, though fighting it gamely, was on his way to a break-down. He now shook so much he dared not touch anything breakable. Von Lappus's suffering was apparent only in the rapidity with which his little hair was graying, and in his loss of weight. He was at least twenty-five kilos lighter than a year earlier. The others suffered in ways uniquely their own.

"One's no friend," said Lindemann. "But we've got another problem. We're getting a new Political Officer—I imagine because of that notebook."

"Oh?"

"Well, I'm not sure. The English you've been teaching me wasn't up to the job. . . . I've been listening in on those kids. Yesterday they ran Brecht off the signal bridge. I wondered why, so I went up and listened while they were talking on their radio."

"And?"

"The battleship will, if I understood right, send a man over when we get to Bab el Mandeb. They want someone here who can overawe us. We're on their list of unreliables—probably thanks to Marquis. Those three kids are easy to fool."

"I don't know. They seemed pretty sharp when we were trading with the Turks. . . ."

"Maybe. Point is, we've got to be even more careful if our killer survived—and we've got to assume he did."

"Right." Kurt raised the hem of his jumper, exposed the sheath knife he had begun carrying. It had been a gift from Karl Wiedermann for excelling in Boy Volunteer activities.

"Good. There's something else. You've been reading the book you got from Fitzhugh, haven't you?"

Suddenly wary, Kurt replied, "Just some dull novels."

"I'm talking about the one in the safe, the one you've been

translating. *Ritual War*. It's like a Bible to the resistance. I've never read it because I've been unable to locate a German edition. I'd like to."

"It's a pretty rough translation, and I'm not finished." He wondered if Fitzhugh had meant that he do so, and see others read it.

"How much left?"

"Two chapters, a summary, and a supplementary pamphlet that was added later."

"Finish it. Don't worry about polish. Oh, just a cautionary note. The Political Office imposes the death penalty for possession."

"Martin told me."

"We'll talk about him sometime. Bring the book when you're done."

"Okay." Kurt rose and started for the door.

"Oh, I almost forgot. We're rotating watches. We'll have the midwatch."

Inwardly, Kurt groaned. Midnight to four in the morning. Bad.

"And you'll stand with Brecht part time, too, until he knows what he's doing." Brecht, the signalman, otherwise out of a job, was taking Hippke's place.

Kurt returned to the mess decks.

"You look glum," said Hans, chuckling. "What'd Mr. Lindemann say?"

"Work. Piles and mountains of work. And we're rotating watches. We now have the midwatch. And, on top of it all, I've got to stand watches with Brecht, who's taking Hippke's place. How'd you like to be a Quartermaster? Why don't you throw one of your Boatswains overboard and let me have his job? There's never been a Boatswain, since they invented ships, who's ever done any work."

"Bitch and gripe. This lemonade's good stuff." Hans held his glass high and stared into it.

"You tried the coffee yet? Better, before it's gone. No comparison with ersatz. Look, I've got to get to work. Maybe we can talk later, at supper."

"Sure. Got work of my own. Have to straighten out the mess Adam made while I was gone."

"What mess?" Kurt asked. "He didn't do anything."

"That's what I mean. Have you seen the rust on the forecastle?"

Kurt went to the charthouse, labored over his translation the rest of that day, and during the few free moments he obtained during the passage to Bab el Mandeb.

The summary chapter was incredibly dull. It took all his will to keep plowing through the rehash. All the way through the book, Kurt had expected the momentary collapse of the author's reserve, a sudden explosion of emotion and outrage. That, as much as content, had kept him going. Now, at the end, he was left disappointed and wondering if he who had written had been truly human. But the supplementary pamphlet, written much later by a more excitable author, proved highly interesting, once he started. It sketched the founding of High Command.

High Command, in concept, was a clandestine military United Nations, a joint council of general staffs. The foundations of such an organization had been laid the day the War began, but it did not become reality until the post-Bio-War era—the War could be divided into two major phases; the first, that undertaken to solve the economic problems of the pollution-initiated

famines and depression; the second, the war undertaken to recover from the ravages of the first phase gone mad: the latter
was the only phase truly deserving the name "the War." The
council was meant to determine and negotiate the levels of violence needed to keep national economies expanding, and was
to act as an umpire in the fighting. Insanity. As far as Kurt could
see, a better effect could have been achieved with a planned program of reconstruction (thinking back to the Bio-War, he wondered if the West now fought itself because the East had been so
effectively destroyed).

Yet the establishment of a ritualized war for economic reasons seemed a logical step forward from the earlier situation,
moving from a stopgap to a permanent measure. Typically bu-
reaucratic. But God! The blood and misery!

And it seemed two logical steps forward from the situation
extant prior to the great depression—the endless attention-get-
ting, uniting, balance-of-power-maintaining, economy-stimu-
lating, contrived wars of the sixth, seventh, and eighth decades
of the twentieth century.

Perhaps the planners of the past had been unable to see another way out. Or, another perhaps, warfare had been the easy
way.

What had gone wrong? The fighting was no stimulus. The
world was too exhausted, was slipping back toward barba-
rism—albeit slowly. Had the violence been maintained at a level
too high for success? Did High Command keep stepping it up
as they saw their program failing? Certainly, Kurt thought, too
much energy was being spent on the War in the present, right or
wrong. There was little left for rebuilding.

He slammed a fist against the chart table. Why? he asked

himself. Why was there always violence to prevent progress? He wished, for perhaps the thousandth time, that he had gone to Norway with Karen.

He also realized that he had gotten something valuable by coming. Knowledge. Not necessarily truth, but another viewpoint on history. But how to use that knowledge?

He penned the last line of his translation a short time before *Jäger* anchored off Perim. Arabia lay on one hand, Ethiopia and Somalia on the other, legendary lands.

When the hook dropped and the hecticness of Sea Detail faded, Kurt left the bridge. He collated his translation and notes, took the book from his safe, and gave the lot to Gregor. Lindemann immediately took the material to his stateroom.

Kurt joined Hans on the port wing. They stared toward the Arabian Coast.

"How long do we stay here, Kurt?"

"I don't know. Until they bring enough fuel from Turkey. Maybe a month."

"The middle of June?"

"About. Why?"

"I'm getting nervous. We're awful close to the Meeting."

"Sometimes I wonder if we'll ever get there," said Kurt, a faraway look on his face. Past, present, future melted and mixed in his mind, and he was all at sea, without time. This journey seemed timeless, endless, like Earth itself, its beginnings lost in mist, its end hidden in unreachable shadows beyond the rising sun.

"Why?"

"We've been at it a year already, and we're not halfway there, not if we're going to Australia."

"I guess. It doesn't seem like a year to me, though. Yet, if it keeps going this way, we'll be old men before it's done." Hans chuckled. "Maybe we'll meet the last Gathering coming home."

Entirely serious, Kurt replied, "No. The last Gathering returned years back. That Turkish ship we traded with . . . it went to the last Meeting too. I couldn't learn much because the Political Officers wouldn't let me ask, but our side lost."

"Find out anything about *U-793*?"

"Not much. The Turks had heard about it, but knew only that it didn't come back. They fought two battles, one off India that they won, where *U-793* was last seen, and another at Malacca that they lost."

"Sad, your father not coming home," said Hans. "He was a lot of fun. A good father."

Kurt sensed unspoken envy. His father had been more interested in his children than had Hans's. Karl Wiedermann's usual reaction to Hans had been to tell him to go away, he was too busy—or he had brought out the belt. But he had had a great concern for outsiders.

"I don't know, Hans. Your father was a bit heavy-handed, but not vicious. Blind, maybe, setting standards adults couldn't attain. He was good to me. I learned a lot from him." Strangely, Karl Wiedermann had been Loremaster of Kiel's Boy Volunteers, a Scout-like organization to which most boys belonged. He had been an excellent leader, had taught many youths many things—much of Kurt's early sea lore had originated with Karl.

As Kurt finished his comments, he saw a wicked expression flicker across Hans's face. Jealousy? And he suddenly felt, without any evidence to anchor his feeling, that he had intuited much of the cause of Hans's old dislike—and the reason for their getting on well aboard *Jäger*. Memories returned, of Boy Volunteer activities. Karl, in view of other boys, had often upbraided or beaten Hans for trifles, had more often and cruelly demanded he be like Kurt, well-behaved and attentive. Indeed, though he had not paid much heed, nor had really cared at the time, Kurt now realized that Karl had treated him far better than his own son. Perhaps the older Wiedermann just had not realized what he was doing, slashing Hans's soul with dull razors. Hans had been terribly shortchanged.

But not here. Here Hans was an equal, under no pressures, able to compete on his own, to be his own man. Here, out of the shadow of his father's person and power, he was a true individual for the first time. He now had friends, was increasingly popular. Sad that one man could so beat another down.

"He might've been easier to please," Hans said distantly, "if he hadn't been a Political Officer. . . . Hey, speaking of Political Officers . . ."

He pointed to a boat approaching *Jäger*. It flew the High Command ensign. An old man in Political Office black sat in the stern, wiping sweat from his face with a rag.

"Looks like our new man," Kurt mumbled. "Let's hope he's less trouble than Beck."

"Why? He never hurt anybody."

"Only because he never got the chance. Anyway, just having him aboard was bad. You could smell fear wherever he went."

They watched as the old man was helped from the boat to the quarterdeck. There he was greeted by von Lappus, Haber, and the three young Political Officers, and immediately hustled off to the wardroom.

"Now there's an idea," said Hans.

"What?"

"Let's go somewhere where it's cool. Mess decks."

"All right. I'll see if Brecht's got everything secured."

FOURTEEN

The new Political Officer was no Beck. He had the coldness and penetrating stare, but was an old man, primarily interested in his own comfort. He spent most of his time in his stateroom, with the air conditioning. His name was de l'Isle-Adam. The Germans called him Deal Adam.

The heat and humidity at the mouth of the Red Sea might have been borrowed from Hell itself. *Jäger*'s men endured it as little as possible. The ship's air-conditioned spaces were often so crowded the machinery did little good.

Refueling, a daylong high-lining of bundles of wood, was pure torture. Once it was completed, however, there was nothing to do but wait for the supply ships to return from Turkey (those ships had been hauling all along, but warships burn fuel even while at anchor, to provide steam to power generators and to make fresh water), and try to keep cool.

A week after refueling, in the heat of the afternoon, Kurt was summoned to the wardroom. He hastily examined his memory as he went, wondering what he had done—for it was the day and time for Captain's Mast.

Surprises awaited him. The first came when he stepped through the wardroom door and found the entire officer complement, with the exceptions of the Political Officers, awaiting him. General court-martial?

"Sit down, Ranke," said Gregor, indicating a chair at one end of the long table there. The seat faced von Lappus, which made Kurt even more nervous—and the Captain's stare did nothing to calm him, the more so when he noticed his translation beneath the man's heavy hands. General court-martial indeed. He glared accusingly at Gregor, seated on his right.

Haber spoke first. "You translated this *Ritual War* thing, Ranke?"

Kurt thought a moment. What had he gotten himself into? He had better tell the truth, since they had him anyway—yet it was hard. These men were authority, the powers with death in their hands. That some were old friends and relatives might be a weight in the balance against him. "Yes sir." Weakly.

"Take it easy, son," von Lappus rumbled. "There's nothing to worry about. We're not Political Officers, this isn't a tribunal, and we're not going to hang anyone."

"Now then," said Haber, "is your translation accurate?"

"It could be better, sir. I'm unfamiliar with English idioms."

"What do you think of the validity of the work?"

Kurt struggled with fear of answering. When his pause grew

uncomfortably long, he forced, "I'd say it's the truth as the author saw it, sir. I felt it was sincere."

"Commendably cautious. Well, for the sake of argument, let's assume the thing's valid. Where'd you get it?"

"Gibraltar, sir."

"Yes, I know. How? Where?"

Kurt bit his lower lip, stared down at the table top, tried to decide how much he dared tell. "From an old man who ran an antique shop, sir."

"The man who taught you English?"

Again Kurt gave Gregor an accusing look. "Yes sir."

Haber leaned back in his chair, folded his hands before his mouth. Thoughtful, he looked like a giant squirrel. "Tell us something about him." A nervous squirrel. His shakiness had lessened, but was still there.

Kurt told them a little about the cripple.

"His name?"

"Martin Fitzhugh, sir."

"You spent twenty-two afternoons with this man. I'm sure you learned more about him than that he liked history, was crippled, and was a kindly old crackpot."

"Excuse me, Commander," said Gregor, interrupting. "Kurt, you're not on trial here. They're after information which could be important to *Jäger*'s future. Your future. Fact is, they're trying to decide whether or not to leave the fleet." His words were intense, commanding. His gaze was heavy, yet, surely, he was trying to be reassuring.

"You could've told them," Kurt mumbled. "You knew Fitzhugh."

He pondered the situation. He had already earned a death

sentence by accepting *Ritual War*. The officers would too, if they did not report him. He shrugged fatalistically. Talking might do some good. "Fitzhugh opposed High Command — quite cautiously, of course."

He told of his last day with Martin, when the Spanish and Portuguese ships had made their breakout. "He was somehow involved, perhaps the organizer," he finished.

"That's damned obvious," von Lappus grumbled. "Otherwise, would he have known of the breakout beforehand?"

Haber shook his head, mystified. "But that would, it seems to me, imply the existence of an organization opposing High Command."

"The organization exists," Kurt said. "During our talks, Beck told me a lot about it. It's a growing movement, especially strong on Gibraltar and in the Littoral."

He ignored Gregor's warning frown. They would see who would expose whose secrets. "It's headquartered in Telemark . . ." He paused to savor their surprise. ". . . and was once well represented on this ship. Kapp and Hippke were agents."

"I don't believe it," said Haber.

"Beg your pardon, Heinrich," said von Lappus. "He's right. Consider the situation at home. My brother's been witch-hunting for years — for such I thought his search for an underground behind the kids running away to Telemark. And Karl Wiedermann was certain there was an underground. He's been after it for a decade. Maybe we shouldn't've laughed."

"An organization like that couldn't exist without making itself known," Haber protested.

"Pardon me, sir," said Lindemann, "but I'm sure there's no such organization — unless it's something like early Christianity, people giving other people the message, without being organized."

"No," von Lappus grunted.

Ha! Kurt thought. Trying to smokescreen.

"All right, picture Kurt's friend at Gibraltar. He can't be the old kind of revolutionary, can he? He's more the passive sort. Just passes the word on to a few selected people, hoping they drop out, hoping they pass it on to a few more. That's revolution too, but slow, until everyone's stopped obeying. . . ."

"I think I like Ranke's theory," said von Lappus, chuckling. "Really, Lindemann, I'm not blind. Your efforts have, at times, been anything but subtle. Nor do I think you really want to hide. You *want* attention. Else, why bring me this?"

He slapped Kurt's translation. "This's the real underground, Lindemann. An idea, not people with guns, not espionage, not secret plots of mutiny. Ignoring High Command would be tantamount to overthrowing it—because it's an idea, too. It has little real physical power."

"Which raises a good question," said Haber. "What motivates High Command? The book tells us what did two hundred years ago. What does today? We'll probably never know, but consider: institutions change, forget their original purposes. Look at the Church. . . . Say, I think there's an analogy. Aren't Political Officers priests of a fashion?"

"Comments, Ranke?" the Captain asked.

Kurt avoided his eyes. "I've been thinking something similar. High Command's dedicated to the perpetuation of the War—my opinion. What was once a means is now an end in itself. The level of violence, though decreasing with time, has risen above our social and technological capacity. What I mean is, while the Meetings get smaller, each requires a bigger portion of our manpower and machinery. It's gotten to the point where the Littoral has little time for anything but training men and fixing ships. Everything else's maintained at a subsistence level. Look at what happened after *Grossdeutschland* sailed . . ."

Here Lindemann interjected, "Wrong, Kurt. This's the biggest Gathering ever. *All* the ships left in the West." But everyone ignored him.

"A point," said Haber. "I was a child at the time. Putting the cruiser in service took so many men, and so much material, out of Kiel, that we almost went under."

"Maybe High Command *is* a religion," said the Supply Officer. "Like religions, it seems to ignore the problems of the present because of an overwhelming concern for the future."

"I'd rather compare it to a machine with a broken Off-switch," von Lappus growled.

"Excuse me," said Haber, "but I seem to've led us off the subject. We're here to discuss the book, and to find out if Ranke knows anything about an organization opposing High Command. We have his statement. I suggest we proceed. Ranke, you can go. Thank you."

Kurt rose hastily, excused himself, and slipped out. His immediate reaction was relief at being free. He went up to the charthouse, to do a little reading in the novel *The Anger Men*, and to be alone, to think.

He pushed his key into the padlock — it would not go. He looked down, frowning. He had the right key. The lock? He looked, snorted. He was trying to push it in wrong side up. Curious, though. He always closed the lock with the open side of the catch toward the door, but it was closed the other way, contrary to habit. He frowned again, trying to remember the last time he had closed it. It seemed he had done so according to custom. He shrugged and opened the lock.

Something was indefinably wrong in the charthouse. Without being conscious how, he knew someone had been there. How? Why?

The *how* he recognized quickly enough. The padlock on the door was a standard Navy lock. There were a dozen others aboard which took the same key. Anyone who wanted to examine the pattern numbers on enough keys could find one to fit.

He knelt before the safe and ran through the combination quickly. Despite the fact that the charthouse was now air-conditioned, sweat dribbled down his temples. He swung the door open. Yes, someone had been inside. The navigator's copy of the signal book was on the wrong shelf.

He chuckled nervously. Luck had saved him some tall explanation. He had given Gregor the damning *Ritual War* material just in time, and he had long ago hidden Beck's notebook.

But a threat existed. Someone was snooping. Sooner or later they were bound to find something. He was being pushed, perhaps unconsciously, into the underground camp. If Gregor wasn't his cousin—damn him! This had to be countered.

He locked the door, went to the communications box, called the wardroom. "Wardroom, charthouse. Mr. Lindemann, please."

A momentary pause, then, "Mr. Lindemann. What is it?"

"Someone went through the safe this morning."

"Was it locked?"

"Yes sir."

"Anything missing?"

"No sir."

"Good." Muttered talk, incomprehensible, Lindemann presumably asking advice. "Still there, Ranke?"

"Yes sir."

"I'll be right up. Get the classified material out so we can check it."

"Yes sir." He switched off, then rechecked the classified charts and publications. He did not need the custody log to tell him they were all present.

Gregor knocked shortly. Kurt let him in.

"Anything missing?"

"No. There wasn't anything worth taking. They were after the notebook."

"Notebook?"

"The one that belonged to Beck."

"Oh, damn! Forgot about it. Meant you should find out what was in it. What'd you do with it?"

Kurt started to tell him, then had an unpleasant thought. He glanced toward the door, opened a drawer, and took out memo pad and pen. He wrote: "Combat. Air search repeater. Inside access panel." Meaning he had hidden it inside a radar repeater in the Combat Information Center, as safe a place as he could imagine. The repeaters, because they were dead, were furniture everyone ignored. No one had bothered them since a vain effort at repairs made following the salvaging at Finisterre.

"Good," said Gregor. He took the pad and pen and wrote: "Get it. Translate it." Aloud, he added, "And be careful."

Kurt nodded. Gregor slipped out. After shredding the note and making certain everything was locked up, Kurt followed. Once he was sure no one watched, he slipped through the door to Combat.

No one was there. No one would be on such a day. The sun made it an oven. Moreover, there was no point in anyone's presence. Half the gear did not work, and the other half need not be operated while the ship was anchored.

Kurt locked the door, then hurried to the repeater containing the notebook. He loosened wing nuts and slipped the access panel off the back of the blockish gadget. "Ah," he murmured. Right where he had left it, hanging in a tangle of dusty wiring. He slapped the dust off and tucked it inside his waistband.

He was replacing the last nut when someone tried the door. Finding it locked, the person knocked. Kurt rose and quietly passed through the heavy curtains screening the sonar room from the remainder of Combat. A key turned in the lock behind him. Taking care to make no sound, he undogged a watertight door opening on the torpedo deck.

Someone crossed the room beyond the curtain. Kurt peeped through, saw one of the young Political Officers. While he watched, the youth went through books lying atop the dead-reckoning tracer. Grinning, Kurt slipped into the bright sun beating down on the torpedo deck. He took the long way back to the charthouse, and immediately set to work translating.

FIFTEEN

The fleet departed Bab el Mandeb on the fifteenth day of June.

"Where are we now?" Hans asked days later, as he and Kurt leaned on the rail of the port wing, staring landward.

"Ras al Hadd. We'll begin crossing the Gulf of Oman soon."

"It's like living a fairy tale. Ever since we left Perim, I've been expecting magic carpets, or something. Aden, Oman, Hadhramaut ... it's a downright black-sad world that's too serious for magic."

"Uhm," Kurt agreed. The past ten days had been a bit like living an episode of the Arabian Nights—two hundred ships full of Sinbads sailing for an Eastern Doom, bound to fail Serendip's mystic shore—though there was no real reason for his feeling, other than a wish to believe.

"Quartermaster!" Magic carpets unbraided.

"Got work to do, Hans." He turned. "Sir?"

"I need an anticipated course."

"Zero three eight." He turned back to Hans. "I was wrong. He irritates me sometimes. He could've looked at the damned chart."

"He wants everybody to feel part of the team. You could've had Obermeyer, instead."

"Speaking of Obermeyer, have they made up their minds yet?"

"About my commission? No." The sudden anger and bitterness in Hans's voice was frightening. He wanted that brass terribly. "Never will, I guess. Tomorrow, if the seas are right and you're ready, I want to refuel."

"It'll have to be soon. We're low. I was talking to Zlotopolski this morning, and we could be in trouble. There might not be enough wood to get us to where we can cut more."

"Zlotopolski worries too much. Anyone can look at the chart and see it's only sixteen hundred miles from Gwadar."

"Kurt?"

He turned. Brecht, his relief, had come to the bridge, "That time already?" He went to the log, signed it over. "Seems time's rushing past, now we're getting close."

Brecht nodded, a little pale. The crew were growing increasingly tense.

Kurt went down to the charthouse and returned to translating the notebook taken from Beck.

For days he had plodded through the pages of a dull life, from Beck's initiation into the Political Office through fifteen gray years to his assignment as agent for bringing a Littoral vessel to the Gathering. Here and there there were comments concerning the growing underground, or an occasional bland word about Office policy (Beck, strangely, would not editorialize), but little to indicate the author was other than a human zero. His first fifteen years were covered in a mere fifty pages of crabbed handwriting.

Later, as he touched the high points of his Littoral assignment, Kurt found him more interesting. He examined Karl Wiedermann briefly, stating the man could do a better job. Then Beck mentioned meeting High Command's chief agent in Telemark. He recruited a new agent, designated Marquis, but gave neither name nor description. Here and there Kurt encountered names of shipmates—and his own—always accompanied by cryptic little comments concerning loyalty.

The pages of Beck's life turned, *Jäger* sailed, the Norwegian event took place. There were empty weeks between entries. Beck's handwriting changed, grew shakier, fear seeped oilily up through the earth of his words.

Kurt turned a page and found his name suddenly prominent. He proceeded with renewed interest. "Ranke is a gullible, apathetic, romantic daydreamer," Beck noted at one point, "easily maneuvered through manipulation of a stableful of overly human ideals he is too lazy to defend."

Kurt frowned at this, but was little bothered. He had heard it from other sources. However, a bit later, when Beck, with a delight Kurt imagined as fairly reeking from the page, described him as an unwitting, unwilling Office agent, useful because he revealed all he knew through his evasions, he became righteously indignant, and, as he read on, saw that Beck had repeatedly played him for a pawn. He grew increasingly angered and hurt—this was a rapier-thrust to his ego. That Beck often expressed a strong regard for him, and several times mentioned he might be a candidate for Political Office employment, ameliorated the pain not at all. Each reference to his having been used plunged him deeper into despair until, at last, they birthed hatred—not so much of Beck as of himself, for being what he was, for allowing himself to be so easily played for a fool.

And hatred's child was a foolish decision, as when he had joined *Jäger* to spite Karen. He would commit himself to the underground, tear down this wicked system that had used him so. Later, when he had to rationalize an explanation for others, he claimed his decision had been spurred by his readings in *Ritual War*. Eventually, he believed the lie himself.

He knocked at Gregor's door when done, entered, announced, "I'm ready to join. Just tell me what to do."

Lindemann's eyebrows rose, but he asked no questions. Such might have reversed his good fortune. "What'd you learn from the notebook?"

"Very little." Kurt gave the highlights.

"So he did know us, all but Brindled Saxon. That's it?"

"No." Kurt had saved the best. "Some about Marquis. No name, but a way to find him."

For one of the final pages told of Marquis going into High Command's underground fortress to be formally indoctrinated, quickly trained, and given an identification code. This latter was the means by which Kurt expected they would catch him, for the code was described as a tattoo on the left arm, death's head and serial number, invisible except under ultraviolet light.

"But *Jäger* hasn't any such light!" Gregor protested.

Kurt explained. Beck had gone into detail because fate had provided High Command's enemies with a means of identifying their man. Marquis's tattoo had become infected shortly after application, festered, and left a scar in the death's-head shape, the size of a small coin, on the man's left arm. Beck felt he should not be assigned anywhere that the mark was known.

"We've got him!" said Lindemann.

"I've seen the mark on somebody." Who? Kurt felt close, so close, to the killer he had been hunting so long. But, damned! Though he could picture the scar, the face of the man wearing it refused to focus. Did he not want to know?

By lurking around the showers — strange behavior, duly noted by others — he managed to eliminate four of his eight suspects by the time *Jäger* reached Gwadar. But the other four he could not catch bathing.

The midwatch, two nights after refueling in the Gulf of Oman, and the night after passing the ruins of the Pakistani city, Gwardar: Kurt and Gregor were on the port wing, ostensibly taking star sights.

"We'll get Deneb, Kurt." Gregor sighted on the star, adjusted the sextant, said, "Mark!"

Kurt noted the time on his stopwatch, quickly wrote it down. Then he jotted down the star's altitude as Lindemann held the sextant before him.

While Kurt wrote, Gregor whispered, "We had an officers' meeting tonight. Von Lappus decided to leave the fleet."

Kurt glanced up, surprised.

"Trouble is, we can't do anything while we've got Political Officers aboard. And we don't dare do anything to them. Marquis would radio the battleship and . . . boom! No more *Jäger*!"

Someone approached the nearby door to the closed bridge, looked out.

"Now Capella."

They took the sight and dithered over it until no one was near.

"We could throw both the Political Officers *and* their radio overboard. . . ." Kurt stopped, aghast. He had been seriously suggesting murder. What had this mad voyage done to him?

"Wouldn't do any good," said Gregor. "Suppose we did? As soon as we left station, the battleship would radio. And they'd open fire when they got no answer. Where does that leave us?"

"We can run faster."

"Faster than a shell? But assume we got away. What then? We'd run out of fuel somewhere off the coast of Arabia. We're too late, Kurt. We should've left a long time ago. We're past the point of no return. The only fuel source inside our steaming range is India."

"That we've been told of." He felt too late also, though in a different way. It had been too late for him since the day he agreed to join the crew.

"Yes, that High Command let us know about. We might find something on the Persian Gulf coast, but we don't know. The Captain's working on it, anyway. You told me to operate inside the system. I tried, and the results have been amazing. . . ."

"Can you get Dubhe, sir?"

Lindemann glanced at the sky. "Not now. There's a cloud. I've a good shot at Alphecca, though it's low." He lifted the sextant to his eye. The breeze whispered, the seas whispered around *Jäger* while they waited.

Kurt glanced at the door. Clear again. "What'll we do?"

"We'll try to smoke Marquis out. I'm pretty sure who he is now. Here, let's get one more shot, then you go figure our posit. Bring the notebook when you come back."

"What?"

"Just do it. Then keep a close watch." Lindemann rubbed his temples, a sure sign his headache haunted him with redoubled savagery.

Kurt did not like it. Flashing the notebook was certain to cause trouble. But that seemed what Gregor wanted.

"Regulus?"

"Good enough." Gregor shot it. Kurt noted the time and altitude, then went to the charthouse. He spent a while working the fix, a while dithering, and finally forced himself to take the notebook from hiding inside the inoperative loran receiver. He returned to the bridge, was surprised to find Haber there, observing the watch.

Kurt flourished the book as he handed it to Gregor, who slipped it into a hip pocket, left a third plainly visible. Haber frowned.

"Sir, did you notice which sextant you used?"

"No, why?" Lindemann asked.

"Near as I could narrow it down, we're in the Arabian Sea. You must've used the one with the wiggly mirror."

Gregor retrieved the sextant. "So I did. Well, it doesn't matter. We'll get a sun shot tomorrow. Why don't you get this thing off the bridge? Take it down to the charthouse."

A bit later, with a hint of false dawn coloring the horizon to the east, the watch reliefs came up. Kurt, exhausted as always after the midwatch, signed the watch over to Brecht and started for his compartment.

He walked aft along the starboard weatherdeck, watching the phosphorescent waters whisper past. He paused near a door, before going below, to look out at the galaxy of running lights marking the presence of the fleet. Water murmured along the hull, the engines muttered like dwarfs hammering in caves beneath his feet. An aircraft carrier was a shadowy leviathan a half kilometer away. Flying fish darted from *Jäger's* side like fluttery green sparks.

The world was always so peaceful early in the morning. A man could forget he was living on and in a killing machine, moving inexorably toward an appointment in Samarra. On a ship running down the quiet seas of the night, he could forget he was the blood and soul of that machine, an acolyte of destruction. He could feel one with creation, a part of God; and could understand the emotions which made some flee to Telemark. Telemark. Karen . . .

A light flashed on the carrier's signal bridge. Idly, Kurt read the message, sent in English. An escort was being berated for moving too close.

There was a sharp sound from up forward. Frowning, Kurt turned. He listened. It was repeated—the choking cry of a man in pain.

He ran, for the moment forgetting he was on a ship. The deck sank away beneath him. He lost his balance, fell, rolled into the lifelines. One hand thrust through and hung over the side, getting splashed as a swell rolled along *Jäger's* flank. Shaking because of the nearness of personal disaster, Kurt scrambled to his feet. Moving more carefully, he hurried forward.

A groan came from the darkness just inside the open door of the 'thwartships passage. Kurt stopped, crouched, felt the cool tingling of hair rising on the back of his neck. His hand stole to the hilt of his knife.

Nothing stirred in the dark passageway, though he waited a

full minute. Just a low moaning. Crouching lower, he felt inside the bottom of the door for the battery-powered emergency light. He flipped the switch with shaking fingers. A weak fan of light illuminated the passage and the man at the foot of the ladder to the bridge. Gregor, in a fetal position, the back of his shirt glistening wetly, scarletly—just where Otto Kapp had suffered his wound.

Kurt visualized: a man waiting at the foot of the ladder, hidden by darkness, moving in from behind, clapping one hand over Gregor's mouth, stabbing with the other.

The light reached Gregor's mind. He lifted himself slightly and turned a pain-contorted face toward Kurt, then fell back to the bloodied deck. Kurt glanced around. No one in sight. Shaking, heart constricting as though in the grasp of a strongman, he sheathed his knife and knelt beside his cousin. "Gregor?" softly.

Lindemann's eyes opened, fluttering, as if this were a major effort. "Kurt?" Blood-foam from his punctured lung dribbled from the corner of his mouth. He forced a sickly grin. "Looks . . . like . . . he moved . . . too fast . . . for us."

"Who?" Kurt clenched his hands, to control his shaking.

Gregor's mouth opened and closed several times before he was able to say, "Don't know. . . . Couldn't see. . . . Came from . . . behind. . . . Got the book . . . Kurt . . . you have to . . . take over."

"Take it easy. I'll get Commander Haber." Futility. Haber's skills certainly were not up to repairing a punctured lung—if he had not been the one to puncture it originally.

Kurt's shakes grew worse. He had trouble controlling himself as he went down the ladder to officers' country, slammed through the door closing off the passageway leading between staterooms, and ran to Haber's door.

He lost all control, began pounding and shouting, unaware he was doing so. Several doors opened. Von Lappus came from his cabin, antique in a nightshirt—Kurt missed it.

Haber opened his door. "What the hell's going on?" He was still dressed from having been to the bridge. The anger in his voice was icewater to Kurt's emotions, calmed him till he could speak coherently. He managed, "Gregor's been stabbed!"

"Stabbed? How?"

"With a knife, dammit! He's dying!"

"All right. Let me get the bag." Haber ducked back into his stateroom, pulled the medical kit from beneath his bunk. "Where to?"

Kurt led the way back. He pointed. Haber dropped to his knees, felt Lindemann's wrist, bent and placed his ear against the man's back. Kurt dropped down beside him. Other officers crowded around, waiting expectantly. "He's dead."

Silence. For minutes, perhaps.

Kurt slowly raised his eyes until his gaze crossed that of de l'Isle-Adam, standing behind the others. His hand stole toward the hilt of his knife.

Von Lappus's fingers settled on his shoulder, lightly but sobering. Kurt glared a moment, then let his hand fall. The anger went the way of his panic. His motions became mechanical, his verbal responses zombie-like. His eyes locked on a small pool of blood a half meter from the corpse, shifting back and forth with the roll of the ship. Von Lappus's grip on his shoulder tightened painfully, lifted. Kurt rose, but his eyes did not leave the blood.

"Mr. Heiden, take care of this," von Lappus ordered. His voice was a monotone as he carefully controlled his emotions. "Ranke, Heinrich, go to my cabin."

De l'Isle-Adam asked something plaintive, speaking in a tongue no one understood.

Von Lappus glared at the Political Officer. "I have nothing to say to you, sir." Again the hard, carefully controlled tone. He followed Kurt and Haber down the ladder to officers' country.

The Captain became less unimpassioned once they entered his cabin. Kurt grew more zombie-like.

"What happened?" von Lappus demanded, his sagging face reddening with anger. With much of his bulk now gone to worry, his loose skin made him appear half empty.

"I don't know," Kurt replied dully.

"Tell what you know."

"I was on my way to my compartment. I heard a cry. When I arrived, he was on the deck, bleeding."

"Did he say anything?"

"Just that Marquis had moved quicker than expected."

"Why?"

"Sir?"

"I want to know why he expected the attack."

"He was carrying a notebook that belonged to Beck. A diary. The other Political Officers have been trying to get a hold of it."

"I know. Why was he carrying it? To force things?"

"Yes."

"Heinrich?"

"He did it on his own authority." Haber was now pale, shaking worse than usual. He was trying to take notes, but could not keep a grip on his pencil. "In fact, I specifically forbade it when he asked earlier."

"I wonder. Why is it that Ranke's always first to these murders?"

Kurt, mind dulled, did not catch the implication.

"Ranke, give me the knife!"

Numbly, he handed it over. Von Lappus examined it close-ly. "Ah, well. I didn't think so. Too logical. Or illogical. If they wanted the book and Kurt was their man, there'd've been no need for the killing. All right, Ranke, why was the notebook important? What was in it?"

"You don't know, sir?"

"No, I don't." He sounded exasperated.

"He has the translation in his stateroom, sir. But there wasn't much to it." He was too numb to feel the pain that notebook had cost him. "He thought they wanted it back because they weren't sure what it said."

"Nothing at all?"

"Just a diary." He was coming to life, the shock receding. "The only thing important was a description of an identification tattoo they wear, here on the left arm. A skull and a number, but they only show in a special light. Marquis's mark is supposed to be scarred."

"That would be important to someone looking for him."

"If I were Marquis," said Haber, "I might kill to keep that secret."

"Yes sir," Kurt replied, "except how could he have known what was in the notebook?"

"Does anyone have this scar?" von Lappus demanded.

"Not that we could find, but we didn't get a chance to check everybody. Gregor was afraid to be too open. Said we'd have a whole battleship load of Political Officers here before we could get started. . . ."

"He knew more than you. We've more trouble with the Polit-ical Office than you think. They know damned well Beck's death was no accident. This Deal Adam told us in so many words that if we so much as raise a hand against another Political Officer, we'll be blown out of the water. I expect that includes their undercover man."

"We can't do anything, even if we find out who killed Gregor?"

"Right. From the Political Office viewpoint, he's not a murderer. He's a man doing his duty. Duty's always been a shield for abominations."

Kurt had been caressing a coffee cup sitting on the Captain's desk. He hurled it across the cabin.

"Ranke."

"Sorry, sir. It's just . . . well, like . . . like being in a cage with an open door, but you get shot if you step out."

"An apt description. We have to divert the gunman's attention. You and Lindemann kept lists of suspects?"

"Yes sir." Nervously, he took the list from the pocket of his jumper, handed it to von Lappus. He wondered what the Captain would think on seeing Haber's name underlined. Kurt noted that, as von Lappus examined the four names, sweat ran down his sagging jowls. He finally realized the man was as angry as he, but better controlled. Much better controlled.

"Explain what you two were doing tonight. Everything."

Kurt talked for fifteen minutes, telling all he could remember. Speaking made him feel better, as if all rage and sorrow departed via his mouth. He finished. Von Lappus extended the list to Haber. Kurt, staring into nothingness, missed a bit of silent byplay. Von Lappus indicated a name with his thumbnail. Haber nodded.

The Captain turned back to Kurt. "Ranke, move your gear into Lindemann's quarters. This Marquis, once he discovers what's in the book, may assume you know too much. You'll be safer in officers' country. Heinrich, stay with him when he goes above. We'll commission him Ensign, Navigator."

"Sir. . . ." Haber was to protect him? He felt the first light caress of the high terror Gregor must have endured for months.

"Be quiet. Heinrich, help him all you can. Between you, you should get Lindemann's work done. You should be capable, anyway, Ranke. You've had the experience. Who'll replace you?"

"Horst Diehn? He doesn't write well, but he knows the simpler things, log keeping and weather reports."

"Fine."

"Wiedermann won't like this," Haber said softly. "He's wanted Obermeyer's commission for two years, and we haven't promoted him. . . ."

"To hell with Wiedermann's ambitions," von Lappus rumbled.

"A thought, Sepp," said Haber, looking thoughtful. "Suppose we release the word that the killer has this scar. There'd no longer be a secret for him to save. Kurt'd be safe."

"That'll start a witch-hunt. . . . Uhm, do it. Might flush the man. But take care the men don't get carried away. No more trouble with Political Officers. That'll be all for now. Help Ranke move."

Later. The sun was well up. Time to be up and about ship's work, Kurt thought. The ship was abuzz with talk about Lindemann's death and his promotion. Still somewhat dazed, he ignored the questions and congratulations and Hans's bitter stare as he moved.

Once the move was finished, he stretched out on his new bunk and stared at the overhead, wrestling with himself. Illogically, based on little evidence, he had decided that Haber was the killer—only two suspects had known Gregor had the notebook in time to move so swiftly. But he had no proof beyond emotional certainty. He fought an urge to vengeance.

To divert himself he sorted Gregor's effects, put the intimately personal aside, the useful out to be distributed where they could be used—such was custom in a world where once common items were so difficult to obtain.

Gregor's uniforms he passed over, certain they were to be given to him. His cousin's footlocker contained little: mementos, the most noteworthy being a pine cone—from Telemark, Kurt thought. The desk held only what one would expect, things a navigator would need. Only when he began on Gregor's safe— which had been left open—did he receive a surprise.

In prominent view was a sheaf of papers, punched, tied into a volume with twine. A letter was straight-pinned to the first page.

Kurt, it said, if you read this, I will be speaking from the grave. I am frightened. Marquis is getting close, as I am getting close to him. Our courses will converge, and only one will survive. If he kills me, you have to take over. Trust the Captain. He is on our side. He has promised to take Jäger out of the fleet when he can. Attached are notes I have kept. They will tell you something about the resistance. Do not let the Political Officers get them.

I am sorry we have not gotten along better. I knew when I left Norway that there would be a Marquis aboard. For too long I thought you were he, trying to take advantage of our relationship. I apologize. Be careful.

Your cousin, Gregor

Kurt went on to read Gregor's notes. They were not unlike Beck's; rather personalized accounts of the activities of a small human cog in a large, impersonal human machine. He got very little from them except the names of some underground leaders, the names of trustworthy men aboard ship, and confirmation of his theory that Hans was Brindled Saxon.

He did not know what to make of that. If Hans was angry that he had not gotten a commission first, how would he feel when he learned he was still second-best in the ship's underground?

Gradually, Kurt sank to the depths of a great despair, mourning Gregor, Otto, and Erich. Again he fought himself on a battlefield of pain, wanting revenge so badly, not certain who should suffer the arrows of his hatred. Haber, he thought, but Heinrich was so hard to hate. Too many childhood happinesses stood as a shield before him. . . .

Time passed, the seconds, minutes, hours. Each second was a bitter assassin, thrusting cruel knives into his guts and twisting. The minutes were great angry birds, and he Prometheus bound, feeling their beaks and talons ripping the flesh from his soul. The hours had the mocking humor of the universe, black and eternal. . . .

He was so engrossed in himself he did not hear the knocking till the knocker shouted, "Kurt!"

Haber, he realized. He opened the door. "Sir?"

"Chow. Have you tried the uniforms yet?"

Kurt shook his head slowly. "Makes me feel like a vulture."

"He doesn't need them. You do." He leaned closer, searching Kurt's face. "Snap out of it. We haven't time for self-pity."

Ensign Heiden passed. "Hold it!" Haber growled.

"Commander?"

"Have you spare insignia to loan Ranke?"

"Yes sir."

"Bring them around, will you?" Haber turned back to the stateroom.

Kurt had disrobed and was about to step into a pair of Gregor's trousers. "It seems like someone's trying to cut me off from the world." He buttoned the trousers. "Loose around the waist, but the length's right."

"Use the belt. What do you mean, trying to cut you off?"

"Oh, nothing. Just a wild notion. The three people killed were about the closest to me, here on the ship. Which made me think you or Hans may be next."

"The shirt fits well enough. Try the cap. I don't know if I should feel that's a compliment. Anyway, the dead were all underground. I'm not." Haber's shakes increased visibly while he spoke.

"Not a serious theory. All three gave reason for Political Office action." He pulled Gregor's battered hat down on his head. "Too tight."

"Loosen the band." *Sotto voce*, he added, "I pray your theory's stardust."

After fumbling a moment, Kurt got the hatband loosened. "There. How do I look?"

"Like a sloppy edition of Lindemann. Ah. Heiden. Thank you. Kurt, put these on, then come to the wardroom."

"I'm not hungry," Kurt said as he turned to the mirror.

"I don't care. You'll eat anyway. Get a move on. We go on watch soon."

Kurt frowned thoughtfully as the door closed behind Haber. They were not going to let him ease out of *Jäger*'s affairs. And there was nothing he wanted more than to drop out of everything, to escape — especially Haber.

202

Then he realized how much better he felt because of Haber's visit. In fact, he was ready to plunge back in. He decided, as he was pinning the last piece of insignia in place, that he was hungry after all.

Dinner in the wardroom was singularly quiet. Kurt had no familiarity with wardroom procedure, but was certain the stillness was not the normal state. The point of the rapier-silence seemed directed at de l'Isle-Adam. And the quiet accusation bothered the old man. Kurt could see his agitation, suspected he was as shocked by the murder as anyone else.

Kurt wondered how it would feel to be completely surrounded by hating men. He tried to picture himself aboard the High Command battleship, in a position comparable to de l'Isle-Adam's. A bad vision. He considered himself a loner, but that much alienation would soon have driven him mad. Perhaps such had helped make Beck the cold man he had been.

Kurt's first watch as an officer, understudying Haber, proved socially awkward. His old watchmates were uncertain how to treat him, were more than cautiously respectful. The bridge remained silent, with none of the soft joking and easy reminiscing which had characterized Gregor's watches. Kurt, still somewhat withdrawn, did not notice. He tried to teach his replacement, and to pay attention to Haber's advice. Hans he let be as much as possible. The Boatswain seemed extremely sullen about the promotion.

Jäger moved steadily eastward, never increasing speed, never slowing, each minute closer to that point where her course intersected the path of Fate.

SIXTEEN

Indian coastline lay off the port beam. Kurt stared at it, in a mood for contemplation. He had recovered from his depression, had almost forgotten Gregor's death—in the way evil memories are hastily abandoned, dread lumber to be shed—and had temporarily laid his suspicions to rest. Now, though, he sometimes shook like Haber. The Meeting . . . it could not be far in the future.

The watch had recovered too. Kurt was an officer much like his cousin. As long as the men did their jobs, he paid them no heed. That is all he felt he could expect.

India had been on the left hand for three days. Behind *Jäger* lay the Rann of Cutch, the Gulf of Cutch, the Gulf of Cambay. The ruins of Bombay could not be far ahead. Kurt's eyes continually sought the dark line where land met sea, searching—for what he did not know. Perhaps some of the wonder gone the way of the tales of innocent childhood. Somewhere behind that coast lay the northern end of the Western Ghats, but he never could find their purple breasts.

"Quartermaster," he called into the pilothouse, "have you got that fuel estimate yet?"

"Yes sir," the new Quartermaster replied. "Mr. Czyzewski estimates thirty hours minimum. Should last longer. He's steaming maximum economy."

"Very well. Boatswain."

"Sir?"

Kurt felt warm inside each time Hans called him "sir." Their feud was a thing almost forgotten, yet he still got a wonderful feeling of power. . . . Hans was very polite, though his jealous anger was never entirely concealed. He avoided speaking of Karen more carefully than ever. "Send the messenger to the wardroom. Ask Commander Haber when he'll be up."

"Yes sir."

Karen. Kurt felt guilty when his mind turned to Karen, because he thought of her so little. No matter that he had little time for thought. His mind should be on her often.

Yet he knew others had the same problem. Wives, home, children, childhood, were things no longer real, had gradually become dulled silver images of memory. Faces were rose nebulosities, memories with the fuzzy quality of dream. The bad times had been forgotten and the good romanticized into more than they had ever been.

In the early days, with memories fresh and the battle distant, men had talked of home and plans for the future. No one had looked beyond the horizon to that grim reckoning called the Meeting. But now the days, weeks, and months of waiting were gone. The Meeting loomed tall, a few days, a week, surely no more than a month away. Each man, from Captain to lowest seaman, grimly knew. No longer did they speak of the future, nor often did they speak. When they did, they talked of the present, as ship's work demanded, and of the past. Rosy, rosy pasts, with childlike dreams and fantasies, half-forgotten adult hopes, haunted the ship, phantoms from fairyland minds.

And yet, poised on the borders of battle, each man insisted there was no time for dreams — no time for the dreams of others. The ship must be made ready. A specter stalked the metal passageways, invisible, but known by all: Fear.

Kurt hit the rail with his fist, hard enough to hurt. He turned, hitched his trousers, strode into the pilothouse. He glanced at the log and charts of his replacement, complimented the man, recrossed the bridge, climbed into the Captain's chair. He leaned forward, chin on fists, rocked as the ship rocked, watched the green seawaters part around the bow, and thought.

The messenger returned. "Commander Haber will be up shortly," he said.

"Very well," Kurt replied. He turned back to his problem.

Nothing was happening. As had been the case after the first two murders, Marquis bode his time, waiting for the anger, indignation, and caution to die. Or, perhaps, there was nothing more he needed do.

Why should the man do anything? Kurt asked himself. The notebook had been recovered. Its only secret was common knowledge. If Marquis had half the brains Kurt believed, he would now do nothing unless directly threatened.

The watch ended, with Bombay still below the horizon, and the Indian forests farther. *Jäger* could exhaust her fuel in as little as twenty-eight hours. The situation, he knew, was as bad on other ships.

Next noon fuel estimates were more optimistic, but the bunkers were emptier than ever. Twelve hours' steaming. Other ships were paired for highlining, sharing the remaining fuel. The carrier *Victoria* had launched a recon flight an hour earlier, looking for a forest. Signals between ships told of desperation.

Imagine, Kurt thought, an entire fleet dead in the water in the middle of nowhere, able to do nothing but drift like so many wood chips, at the mercy of wind and sea — and of their crews. Life depended on fuel, fuel to heat the boilers providing steam to the turbines driving the ships, fuel to make steam to drive the generators of electric power so necessary aboard *Jäger* and her like, fuel to heat the water in the fresh-water evaporators. Kurt pictured two hundred derelicts, two hundred *Flying Dutchmen*, patrolling the Malabar Coast.

He grew aware of sudden tension on the bridge, looked up, found all the men staring to starboard. *Victoria* was recovering aircraft. The *clunk-clunk* of feet overhead told him the Political Officers were preparing to receive messages.

A half hour passed before anything came in. One of the young men brought it down. Kurt read it quickly, surveyed the intensely inquisitive faces of his watch, smiled. "They found a forest. Not far." Only fifteen kilometers south of the leading elements of the fleet. Five hours' steaming for *Jäger*, she being kilometers back in the formation. She would make it with fuel to spare.

Kurt called the Captain's cabin. "Officer of the Deck. Signals from the flag, sir. Stop for refueling off Rotnagiri. Five hours, sir."

A pause. "Yes sir."

Kurt turned to Hans. "The Captain said to have all boats and tools prepared before securing ship's work."

"Yes sir."

Kurt again felt that little twinge of pleasure at having power over Hans, though it stirred some of the old enmity.

Although he objected strenuously, Kurt had to remain aboard while the bulk of the crew went ashore. He was willing to endure the tiresome work for the feel of earth beneath his feet—it had been a year—but von Lappus denied him on grounds of safety. He would not be allowed to risk the assassin's knife.

Two of the three days spent at anchor were hell. The third proved both amusing and informative. Early that morning one of the boats came out with an odd, skinny little brown man perched atop a small mountain of wood. An Indian.

Kurt had the quarterdeck watch at the time, looking officious and trying to stay out of the way of ship's work. Then came the native.

"What've you got there, Deckinger?" Kurt shouted as the boat came alongside.

The native jumped up, saluted in magnificent parody, and, with an abominable accent, shouted, *"Hallo, Unterleutnant!"* There followed a flood of speech, of which Kurt caught perhaps a third, mangled German mixed with the dregs of a half-dozen tongues. Kurt recognized some Polish and English.

"Deckinger! Can't you turn him off?" The Indian shut up. "What's going on? Who's this?"

The coxswain shrugged as his boat nudged the accommodation ladder. His oarsmen chuckled. "Near as we can figure, he ran into survivors from the last Meeting. Must've been a rare mixture. German and Polish I speak, English I recognize. He mixes all three with as many others. Name's Boroba Thring. Be good to him. We fought a French corvette to get him."

The Indian galloped up the ladder, grinning, snapped another remarkable salute, promptly disappeared through the nearest door.

Kurt's mind ran like a dog chasing its tail. He knew there had been but one ship at the last Meeting carrying men who spoke German and Polish. He hurried after the Indian, found him below, in the after crew's quarters, cheerfully poking through everything loose.

Hours later, after questioning by the team of von Lappus, Czyzewski, de l'Isle-Adam, and Kurt—because he spoke Danish, though the Indian did not—the man's story became clear. A party of survivors of the last Meeting had camped near Rotnagiri while recovering from an epidemic fever, passing several months there before continuing their march to Europe. How long ago? Close to ten years.

And that was all they had from him, hopes raised and crushed. Germans and Poles had survived the Meeting, but, almost certainly, not the march home—or they would have arrived. Kurt spent the remainder of the day in depression. It had been a long time since his father had weighed so heavily on his mind.

The Indian announced he was there to trade. He offered fresh food for tools and medicines. Von Lappus turned him down. No time. High Command wanted the fleet moving before nightfall. They let the Indian stay aboard until the last boat departed.

Jäger recovered that last boat on the run. The leading elements of the fleet had been underway for an hour. Sun setting, boat being hoisted out of the water, the ancient lady began the last leg of her journey to her date with Fate.

Six eventless days passed. Signals flew increasingly thick during that time, until *Jäger*'s Political Officers were almost continually busy. Flags festooned the vessels by day, flashing lights winked like hundreds of low, twinkling stars by night. In her wardroom, *Jäger*'s officers spent long hours over the messages, and battle assignments which had been delivered during the refueling pause — von Lappus still had not broached his plan for escape.

Jäger's battle assignment was minimal. When the fleet divided into fighting and support groups, she would be left to convoy the auxiliaries. Kurt suspected this was because High Command did not trust her in the battle line. He was pleased, as was von Lappus. This seemed to fit well with something building in the Captain's mind. Late on the afternoon of the sixth day, signals went up directing all ships to the second degree of battle readiness. Watertight doors were secured, hatches were battened, life preservers and helmets were hauled from their racks and lockers and checked. Ammunition was prepared, nervous gunners labored over their weapons, making certain they were in perfect order. The cooks prepared cold foods for when men would be unable to leave battle stations. The tension built, soon became overwhelming.

It redoubled when, on the morning of the seventh day, off Trivandrum, the signal came for general quarters, the first degree of readiness. The flag expected contact soon. Kurt wondered, briefly, how anyone could know, but was too busy for deep speculation.

When there was sufficient light, one of the carriers launched a recon flight. Grumbling like tired old men disturbed, the aircraft staggered into the sky and chugged away across the southern tip of India.

An hour later, *Jäger*'s men were startled by the sound of guns kilometers ahead. Black puffs spotted the sky. Soon four air-craft—jets by their speed and racket—came darting down the length of the fleet, trailing a rolling barrage of anti-aircraft fire. They were come and gone so quickly *Jäger* managed but a single salvo. The tension was a violin string twice too tight scraped with an unrosined bow. . . .

Kurt, watching the silver darts climb and turn behind the fleet, overheard a muttered, "This's it! This's really it. After all this time . . ."

And, "They're real! I never thought . . ."

And, "Christ, we're in for it if all their planes are like those. . . ."

The wing markings of the planes burned in Kurt's mind. Australian. The Enemy. He, too, had never completely believed . . . but there they were, trailing thin white as they raced eastward.

The bridge was ahum with subdued, frightened talk. Jets. The hope was that those were all the Australians could put in the air. The hope was that the Australian carriers would be sunk before planes like those could strike. . . . They hoped.

Hours of nothing followed, until the recon planes returned. Then signals soon flew.

Twenty-eight enemy ships, cruisers, destroyers, and two car-riers, had been found in the Gulf of Mannar, steaming south-ward at fifteen knots. The division of the fleet, which had begun at dawn, hastened.

As evening drew near, powerboats raced through the fleet, collecting Political Officers. They were carried to the battleship.

"This looks strange," Haber observed as the bridge gang watched *Jäger*'s four clamber into a boat.

"Wouldn't be surprised if they didn't come back," Kurt growled. "They're rats deserting a dead ship."

"How're we supposed to get battle signals?" a seaman asked plaintively.

"Oh, they've given us a very good battle plan," Haber replied sarcastically. "We don't have to communicate." Signals could, though, be made via the signal books.

The man missed the mockery, Kurt saw. He simply nodded and returned to work, reassured. Kurt wished he felt the same — sure of anything.

"Not all the rats have left the ship," the Commander said in a lower voice. Kurt searched his face. He had been waiting for some comment on this, wondering how Haber felt about being left behind.

"Why didn't they take him with them?" Kurt asked, not really expecting an answer from the man.

Haber shrugged. "Maybe *they* don't want him either." Was that a bit sour? "More likely, though, they feel there's still work for him here. Every ship probably has an undercover man who's being left behind."

"A gruesome thought." But he got no rise from Haber.

More wearying hours passed. The battle group formed and pulled ahead of the auxiliaries. Both forces were well into the turn around the tip of the Indian subcontinent.

By twilight the fighting force was beyond the horizon, position marked by a pall of black smoke. All was quiet.

Near midnight, when most of the men were asleep at their stations, there were light flashes far ahead, in the clouds. Not a surface engagement. A night attack from the air. Kurt worried. The Australian technology appeared more and more formidable. A night attack would have been impossible with the rickety Western aircraft.

The flashes and subdued, thunderlike mutterings continued for almost two hours.

Morning came. The cooks served sandwiches on station, with vast quantities of coffee. Soon the auxiliaries reached the scene of night-battle. Wreckage. Floating corpses. Men in liferafts who were rescued by the larger support ships. A few prisoners, downed flyers.

The sun, following some retarded timetable, took eons to reach the zenith. *Jäger* and her convoy entered the Gulf of Mannar. The sun, after an eternal pause, started down its path to the west. Tension mounted, though that seemed impossible.

The first attack came from the south, low, so swiftly that bombs were falling by the time *Jäger*'s gun started around. There were less than forty planes, all—thank God!—prop jobs as sickly as their Western opponents. Aircraft cannon shells were racketing off the forecastle when *Jäger*'s guns first spoke.

Inside the death machine, men scrambled here and there, to little purpose, doing themselves and the ship little good.

Steel, fire-tipped fingers tracked aircraft across an angry sky, hurling fifty-five-pound packets of death as fast as men could load.

Kurt dove for cover as aircraft cannon shells hit the bridge. Supposedly bulletproof windows exploded inward. One shell screamed through, exploded in the Captain's Sea Cabin. The mattress there smoldered. Kurt, in a daze, unaware of risk, staggered out the portside door.

The sky was speckled black with the puffs of exploding shells. A bomber scored a hit a thousand meters away. An ammunition ship became a tremendous fireball, exploding and re-exploding. Off the port quarter a destroyer took a torpedo at the waterline amidships and became two. One half sank in seconds. Kurt leaned on the rail and pitched his breakfast over the side.

A scream. "Get in here, you idiot!" Hans Wiedermann. Kurt half turned, saw the little Boatswain charging, was seized, hurled into the pilothouse. Hans leaped in after him, centimeters ahead of the deadly debris of an exploding bomber.

A dull roar ran through the ship, *Jäger*'s gunners cheering their kill.

Another aircraft, unseen but felt and heard, dying, screamed over on a kamikaze run. A wingtip brushed the maintruck, ripped away useless radar antennae. It hit water three hundred meters on, skipped like a flat stone, spinning, sailed another hundred meters, and broke up in midair.

Then came a strange quiet. The enemy fled, leaving a quarter of his strength behind, his planes low silhouettes on the southeastern horizon. *Jäger*'s bridge gang got to their feet and stared at the tortured sea, at the flames rolling from the corpses of ancient ships. Overhead, imagined Valkyries wailed in a black mackerel sky of past explosions, and black oil smoke veiled the watching faces of the disturbed gods of the deep.

Faces pale, guts taut, men studied sea and sky, the mad waterfield of their first sea battle—so quickly come and gone. . . .

SEVENTEEN

It got easier, the shooting and killing. Less panic, more professionalism, if thus it may be said. The threat of death spurred men to faster, more efficient reactions— though weariness sapped some of the improvement. More kills, fewer casualties, except for the Australian aircraft, whose numbers rapidly dwindled.

During the long night after the first attack, and in the interims between the two attacks the following day, Haber kept busy. The mess tables became operating tables; engineers' quarters, the best protected, became a convalescent hospital. Deaths were gratifyingly few, fewer than the thirteen paid for passage to the Meeting.

During the interlude separating attacks three and four, *Jäger* heard the big guns muttering in the north, a surface engagement in Palk Strait. Those ships with operable radios received progress reports, passed the news by signal flag. Both sides had expended their aircraft. The Australians, outnumbered, were losing, but were tenaciously holding the strait. The fighting was a hundred kilometers distant, but scores of five- and eight-inch trolls' mouths were bellowing in chorus there. Their cruel song rippled down the ocean, serenaded the auxiliaries with atonal sounds of mortality.

The fourth raid came during the night.

Psychedelia: orange flashes with yellow, the green sea sparkle suddenly exposed by gun-light, and phosphorescence in the waves; poor tiny confused fishes jumping; the gun barrels with their flames talons tearing at the night; brief dots of light which crackled in the sky; screaming aircraft engines, screaming shells, screaming bombs, continual explosions, screaming men; a burning ship, a burning plane. Kurt grew dizzy trying to follow it all.

A plane hit water a hundred meters before *Jäger* and escaped being overrun only because she was in a high-speed turn. The pilot, inexplicably surviving the crash, scrambled from his cockpit and dove into the sea. Someone, with unusual presence of mind and even more unusual compassion, dashed out onto the maindeck and snagged the man with a boathook as *Jäger* drove past.

Kurt saw the man being hauled aboard. He studied the sky, looking for aircraft betrayed by moonlight. Nothing coming in. He ran along the starboard wing, down two ladders, and reached the pilot just as he rose with the help of two sailors.

Snarl of an aircraft engine, climbing in pitch and volume. "Get him inside!" Kurt ordered. "Mess decks." The sailors supported the pilot, half carried him to the mess decks door. Kurt pulled it open.

The roar came in low, amidst bursting shells, blazing a trail with tracers. Kurt threw himself inside, as did the others. A swarm of shells accompanied them. There were screams. . . .

Kurt rose, jerked the watertight door shut. "You all right?" he asked.

Stupid question. The sailors were broken, ruined, chopped meat. The Australian, whom they had pushed ahead of them and thus shielded with their bodies, groaned weakly. Kurt, with the reluctance of one touching a poisonous snake — the pilot was that mythical Enemy he had his life long been conditioned to fear and hate — placed his fingers against the man's cheek. The Australian's eyelids fluttered. Kurt looked at him closely, surprised. This was an old man, at least sixty, from his brass almost certainly a high-ranking officer. Such an ancient flying combat?

"Got by my own mates." He coughed. A rough smile tugged the corners of his mouth. "Three Meetings now, thirty-four missions, shot down three times. And finally scragged by my own wing man." He laughed weakly. Kurt sat silently over him — said nothing because he felt the man would not want him to — stared as blood trickled over his fingers — Australian blood, yet warm, red, human.

"Ah, but it's the Enemy's fault, isn't it?" the pilot murmured. "Oh, Billy, my Admiral brother Bill, you'll play avenger for me, won't you?"

He coughed gurglingly, spit up red foam. "Neatly tucked them in, didn't we? Bottled them up. . . . Maybe this's the true Last Meeting. . . . Molly!" Suddenly he was frightened, terribly frightened. Though he was as suddenly no longer an enemy, Kurt jerked his hand away, frightened himself. This could not be far in his own future. . . .

"Molly!" the Australian gasped again—then seemed deflated when his soul departed.

Kurt rose slowly, suffering overpowering sadness. He had so wanted to talk to this man, even if only in anger, to make contact with a fragment of the other side. But the fellow had evaded him, died without saying anything.

Or had he? Halfway to the bridge, in midstride, he jerked to a halt, finally grasping the sense of those dying words. Bottle? A picture of Ceylon, India, and the sea between flashed across his mind, and he considered the odd fact that air attacks always came from the south. And he knew.

What seemed an easy victory at Palk Strait was but a small gambit in a huge defeat a-making. Almost certainly, another Australian force had hidden east of Ceylon and was now closing the Gulf of Mannar behind the Western armada. It had to be. . . . The northern force would hold while the southern took the auxiliaries from the rear, wolves into sheep poorly shepherded, destroying, and the Western fighting units would be without supplies. They would be easy killing once their ammunition was gone. He ran on to the bridge, reported his suspicions to von Lappus and Haber.

While he talked, he watched Haber patch a deathly pale Hans's arm. A shell fragment had taken a chunk from it. Shock, plus the depression he had been suffering of late, had raped away the last of Wiedermann's cockiness. His expression was that worn when his father was about to descend on him with a belt. But the punishment, this time, would be final.

The night marched slowly on. Enemy aircraft—less than a dozen now—came and went, concentrating on the escorts. Kurt wondered if this was the prelude to a surface engagement. Made sense, if his theory were correct.

Jäger received her share of attention, but, by zigzagging, changing speed, and luck, she remained relatively unscathed. Plenty of holes from strafing; nothing interfering with ship's operations.

Von Lappus paced. Any plan he may have had had to be scrapped, now *Jäger* was in a trap. His face was pale and tired, his weight seemed to pull him down. "How far to the Indian coast?" he asked.

Kurt went to the chart table. "Excuse me, Paul." He studied the charts. "Fifty kilometers, sir."

"And Ceylon?"

"The same. We're right in the middle."

"We'll head for the mainland. If we can't hide, we'll beach her and walk."

Kurt's mind rushed back to the visitor of a week earlier. Others had tried walking home.

"Left full rudder. All ahead standard. Tell the engine room to stand by for emergency maneuvers. I want all boilers on the line, burning coal. Ask how long they'll need to get full steam."

The helmsman, lee helmsman, and telephone talker did as they were directed. All eyes were on the Captain, expectant.

"Captain," said the phone talker, "they say they'll need a half hour to get superheat on the standby boilers. . . ."

"Tell them to get those fires burning, and to call as soon as they can put the boilers on the line." Von Lappus resumed pacing. "How long till sunrise?"

"About two hours, sir," said Kurt. "But we'll have light before then."

"Lookout reports flashing light from the screen commander, sir," a phone talker announced.

Kurt grabbed a memo pad and stepped out on the starboard wing. "Brecht, get up to the signal bridge and tell them we're ready to receive. Take your time."

Haber grabbed the signal book as Brecht scrambled up the ladder to the signal bridge. The commodore's message soon arrived. Kurt noted the groups. Haber, looking over his shoulder, searched the signal book for their meanings.

"Should've known," Haber said shortly. "He wants to know where we're going. Captain?"

Von Lappus shrugged. "Send some nonsense. 'Proceeding independently to air bedding, run a degaussing range, and attack with missiles and depth charges.' By the time he figures that out, we'll be clear. I don't think he'd shoot, anyway."

Haber encoded the message, taking his time. Kurt handed it up to Brecht. Brecht sent it slowly, as if unfamiliar with the light. All the while, the range between ships opened at a relative twelve knots.

That range opened to four kilometers. The commodore requested a repeat. Brecht sent the message again, with minor changes. Before more was heard, *Jäger* could no longer read the incoming.

She ran a point off parallel with the seas. The rolls were bad. Her bows rose high, she yawed, her bows fell, and the phosphorescent waters rushed past to make a sparkling silver trail behind. A tinge of false dawn smeared the horizon line east.

"The seas are running high," von Lappus observed. "Is a storm too much to hope?"

Kurt looked around. A deeper darkness loomed to the south. "Looks like a squall there, sir, but we'd be steaming right into the Australians."

"Forget it."

There were flashes behind them, and a few ships silhouetted, as the fleet's guns opened up on a new wave of aircraft. *Jäger* hurried on, ignoring the fighting. Kurt suffered a moment of guilt and regret for thus abandoning others to their fates.

"Engine room reports all boilers on the line, sir," a phone talker announced.

"Very well. Tell them to give me every possible turn."

Soon *Jäger* was shuddering. She surged forward. Kurt watched the indicator on the pitometer as it crept past twenty, toward twenty-five knots. The destroyer had not run this fast in decades — perhaps centuries.

"Oh-oh," someone muttered, "they've found us."

Aircraft noises approached. Half a dozen planes gathered like vultures gleeful at finding a lone and staggering man in a desert, happy to have a target outside the anti-aircraft umbrella of the fleet.

Jäger corkscrewed across the waters, dodging the bombs. Her guns tore the dawn with flaming orange claws. Her frame shuddered time and again as salvos left her main battery. Kurt and others held hands over their ears, trying to keep out the deafening *crack* of the five-inchers. The sound jarred the teeth and rattled the bones. It could be felt with the skin. Beside the main battery, the three-inchers and 40mm mounts were chattering children.

"Tell the engine room to give us more speed!" von Lappus bellowed. A bomb hit water just fifty meters off the starboard bow, drowning the threats with which he punctuated the command.

While the waterspout from the bomb burst was still falling, the phone talker replied, "Mr. Czyzewski says he doesn't dare put on any more turns, sir. She's shaking too much now."

Jäger rattled like a skeleton in a windstorm. Her frame groaned. The old lady was too tired to sprint as when she was young.

"If he can make another turn, tell him to make it!" von Lappus thundered. "Down!"

Shells rang against the pilothouse. A man groaned, hit by a fragment. *Jäger* shuddered even more. Kurt watched the pit log climb slowly, so slowly, toward thirty knots.

"Sir," the phone talker cried, "we're taking water around the patch where we lost the sonar dome."

"Very well."

A plane burned across the lightening sky, right to left, like a comet, exploded like a holiday rocket half a kilometer ahead. The gunners cheered, but weakly. Their fourth kill was much less exciting than the first, and they were too tired to waste the energy.

A small bomb from a plane unseen tumbled from the sky and hit the number one gunmount. Kurt saw the result, as in slow motion, while throwing himself under the chart table.

The bomb hit. The turret rose on a small ball of fire and, intact, arced into the sea to port. Then concussion from the explosion shattered glass, bounced men around, and everything loose became a vicious missile. A cloud of acrid TNT smoke swept past the bridge, filled the pilothouse with its stench. The warship heaved and groaned and, for a moment, Kurt thought the explosion had reached the magazines. But no, the firestops had held.

He looked down to the forecastle again as he rose, then turned away fighting his last meal. The mount was gone. In its place was a hole surrounded by burned-metal flower petals. The upper handling room, ammunition miraculously unexploded, lay open to the air. Men and parts of men were scattered about its walls. Streamers of smoke drifted out.

"Get Damage Control!" the Captain bellowed. "Get the men out of that lower handling room! We've got to flood that magazine." And all the while the surviving guns thundered their defiance.

The helmsman, frozen to the wheel, followed his zigzag course with zombie-like precision. No one else moved. A mountain of water hurled up by a near miss drenched the bridge through broken windows. Haber tended the wounded amidst blood and seawater sloshing on the deck.

The phone talker spoke up. "Captain, forward fireroom reports they're taking water around a buckled hull plate."

"How much?"

"Just a little. The pumps are handling it. Damage Control's putting a patch on now."

"Very well."

Kurt looked back to the forecastle, saw water filling the hole where the mount had been. The liquid was scarlet in the morning light. Human carrion mingled with pieces of ship.

The guns spoke on, and the bombs replied. "How far to the coast?" von Lappus demanded.

Kurt tried to estimate. "Twenty kilometers."

"What speed are we making, helmsman?"

"Twenty-four knots, sir."

Kurt glanced at the pit log. *Jäger* was losing speed. Too much for the boilers?

Haber looked up from the man he was tending. "Got to keep her going for a half hour. Can we?"

The guns never slowed, nor did the bombs.

A napalm canister hit water portside amidships, spraying *Jäger* with flaming jellied gasoline. One of the 40mm mounts was in its path. Screaming men died before the washdown system could save them.

Von Lappus risked looking out a door. The washdown system was unable to flush the napalm. He whirled. "Wiedermann! Man some hoses. Get rid of the torpedo in that port tube! If the fire reaches it. . . ." He did not need to describe what a ton of TNT could do.

Hans took several men and ran down to the torpedo deck. While some brought hoses into action, two stripped the canvas covers from the tube, and Hans readied the firing box. He hit the fire button. The torpedo left the tube with a *whoosh*, dove through fire, hit the sea—and did not go anywhere. The propellers were dead. Bullet holes along the tube told why. As *Jäger* hurried away, the torpedo's nose sank. Its aft portion stood out of the water like a milepost along a doom-time road.

Another plane came in, cannon fire sweeping the hose crews and Hans's two helpers off the torpedo deck. A three-inch mount evened things as the plane pulled up, going away.

Hans crawled from beneath the torpedo tube and sprinted forward, up the ladder to the bridge. Kurt hauled him through the door. His wound was bleeding again.

"Damn! You were lucky!" Kurt said, patting him on the back. His mind slipped right off thoughts of the unlucky ones.

"Not finished yet," Hans replied as Haber replaced his bandage. "Fire's still burning."

"Ranke, get some men from Combat and reman those hoses!" the Captain ordered.

Swallowing his adam's apple, Kurt said, "Yes sir." He hurried down the inside ladder, into Combat, and selected a half-dozen men whose jobs were least important. They went out the so-nar-room door, caught the flopping hoses, turned streams of water and foam on the napalm.

They killed most of the fire during a lull. There was just one small pool in the maindeck, a ways aft. Kurt ordered the hoses moved that way.

Something spanged off the deck near him as he watched the work. A second something whined by, then a third ricocheted off his helmet, spinning him around and down. On hands and knees, he took cover behind a ruined potato locker and looked for the plane. He saw none.

The nearest was just banking in for an attack. He searched the ship around him, saw nothing. His heart suddenly doubled its pace as full terror struck. Marquis was in action once again, for what reason he could not imagine. It was madness to shoot at a man here where Death was already establishing his throne.

The last of the napalm washed over the side. "Get those hoses secured!" Kurt shouted. "Down!"

The attacking plane roared over, strafing the bridge. "Get back to Combat!" Once they were gone, he sprinted to the lad-der leading to the wings.

He reached the bridge level panting and started forward, but something caught his eye. Scattered on the deck aft the closed bridge, where the mainmast and a small locker for keeping cleaning gear provided a good hiding place, were several brass cartridge cases. He knelt and touched one of the casings. Still warm. He glanced toward where he had been standing on the torpedo deck. Yes, Marquis had crouched here to do his sniping.

He heard the scream of air over wings, the gossip of cannons, hit the deck. Shells played tattoo on the bulkhead nearby. One shattered the wooden box housing the psychrometer. A pistol hit the deck near Kurt's head. He glanced up. Hidden inside the psychrometer box? He sniffed the muzzle. It had been fired recently. He rose, tucked it inside his waistband.

And almost instantly threw himself down again. Another plane coming in. But it passed over aft, leaving a horrendous roar and the scream of metal torn like paper. A ball of fire boiled up from the fantail.

Kurt scrambled to and through the door of the closed bridge. "A hit aft!" he gasped as Hans pulled him in.

Across the bridge, in the Captain's chair, Haber was patching a wound in his own left leg. "I'll have to go to the mess decks then," he gasped.

At the same moment the helmsman shouted, "Rudder doesn't respond, sir."

Von Lappus growled, "Shift your engine and cable."

"Aye, sir. Shifting to port steering engine and port cable." A few seconds passed. "Rudder still doesn't answer, sir."

"Shift control to after steering."

"Sir," a phone talker said, "Engineering reports after steering heavily damaged. Damage Control is there now. Some flooding, and a small fire."

Von Lappus swore vitriolically, asked, "What's your rudder angle, helm?"

"Ten degrees starboard, sir."

Glancing out the door, Kurt could see *Jäger* was running a large circle. Smoke poured from the hole in the fantail. "We could steer with our engines," he said.

Van Lappus nodded. He let *Jäger* finish her circle, gave the orders. The vessel shuddered, slowed as her engines fought to balance the frozen rudder. "How far to the coast now?"

"Fifteen kilometers!" Kurt shouted. But his words were lost as a stick of bombs exploded before the bow. *Jäger* staggered into falling spray. "Fifteen kilometers!" he shouted again.

Beside Kurt, Hans muttered, "Don't they ever run out of bombs?" He stared at a plane coming in low from starboard. A five-inch shell scored a direct hit, shattered the aircraft five hundred meters out. There was a tremendous fireball as aviation fuel exploded. A tongue of hurtling fire almost reached the ship.

"Maybe that was the last one," Kurt said. "I don't see any more."

He was correct. Air and sea soon grew quiet. Fighting her rudder, *Jäger* staggered landward.

"Boatswain, pass the word that the men can leave their stations to go to the head, or get sandwiches — after battle reports reach the bridge."

A half hour passed. The sun rose. Kurt walked the wings, looking at the ship. She appeared wrecked, yet damage reports were optimistic. The rudder was almost clear. Most all flooding had been stopped. Men were clearing the topside wreckage. A miracle — *Jäger* was still afloat. Not a man aboard had expected her to survive the concerted attack of a half-dozen Australian planes.

Kurt returned to the pilothouse and slumped against the chart table, exhausted. He had had, finally, time to think.

Haber, after finishing his work in the mess decks, with a covey of Boatswains and junior officers, limped off to inspect the worst damage. Once his party cleared the bridge, Kurt turned to von Lappus and whispered, "I'm sure I know who Marquis is now." He began shaking. "He took a couple shots at me while I was getting the napalm off the torpedo deck."

The Captain's eyebrows rose. Kurt gave him the shell casings and pistol. He considered them a moment, frowned, asked, "Who? And what do you think we should do?"

Kurt rubbed his temples, thought, finally replied, "I don't know. . . . I always thought Heinrich was my friend. . . ." His eyes caught something, his shoulders slumped forward in despair. "It doesn't matter now." He pointed.

Far away, on the horizon, was a line of silhouetted masts, and dark smoke hanging low. The trapping force he expected, coming from the south.

"How far?" von Lappus asked, pointing to the Indian coastline ahead.

"Maybe two kilometers." Estimating was difficult. It was a jungled coast, ragged, indefinite in its meeting with the sea.

"Can't make it." Von Lappus grabbed a phone. "Engine room!" he shouted. "Secure your boilers!"

A pause. "I don't care if you'll have trouble firing them again! I don't want any smoke." The stacks were soon clear. *Jäger* quickly lost way.

Von Lappus returned to the phone. "Engine room? Get Mr. Czyzewski." A pause while the Chief Engineer was located, then, "Ski? Trouble coming up. Give me a twenty-degree list to starboard. Yes, you heard right. Flood the voids, the bunkers, whatever you have to do. No! Just do it. You got that fire out in after steering? Good. Forget the repairs. This's more important. I want this ship to look dead."

He slammed the phone down. "Boatswain, I want every man

below the maindeck, hidden. Hoepner! Where's Lieutenant Hoepner?"

"Here, sir."

"Break out the small arms. Issue them to the landing party."

"Sir?"

"You heard me. Do it." He turned to Kurt. "Ranke, you stick with me. How long till those ships get here?"

Kurt looked toward the Australians. He shrugged. "Half an hour, I suppose. They're probably running all out."

"Thank you. You men, clear the bridge. Get below the maindeck. We'll organize later." He paused, thinking. "Wiedermann, launch the boats. Drag the liferafts below. We may need them later. Dress the dead in lifejackets and put them over with the boats. Anything we can afford to throw away, do it."

"Sir?"

"Why does everyone ask questions? Do it."

Hans hurried away. Within minutes he had men scurrying here and there, working. Soon *Jäger* was surrounded by boats, corpses, and debris. With help from Engineering, she had taken on a pronounced list to starboard. She soon appeared a badly wounded ship whose crew had abandoned her for the nearby coast.

"Good!" the Captain rumbled, surveying her from the bridge. "Now, if we get the 'if's' working our way, we may get out of this."

"Sir?" Kurt asked.

"*If* they're interested in capturing salvageable ships, and *if* they're not willing to waste a warship to do the work, we may get home yet." He would add nothing more.

EIGHTEEN

The enemy cruisers came within firing range. One lobbed a tentative shell which fell half a kilometer short. Kurt, half asleep against a bulkhead, awakened. Von Lappus studied the Australians through binoculars. Minutes passed. Another shell fell, again at a distance. "Ah," said the Captain. "They're interested. A destroyer's turning out to look us over."

Kurt studied her, was dismayed. Even unharmed, *Jäger* would have been outgunned.

Far to the east, beyond the horizon, a rambling commenced. Little guns and big made their forceful arguments, cried, *Männerdammerung!*

In the north, defying High Command orders, the Admiral of the Western fleet withheld the final blow of an easy victory, turned his ships and raced to the aid of his beleaguered auxiliaries.

"They've caught the fleet," the Captain muttered. "Come on." He went to the inside ladder and down.

Kurt collected his machine-pistol and followed, tired, fighting the urge to drop and fall asleep. He stumbled, caught himself. The ladder was difficult because of the list.

Von Lappus led Kurt to the ship's laundry, puzzling him until he saw the shell holes in the outside bulkhead, just above the deck, facing the approaching destroyer. They lay on their bellies and watched the Australian rush closer.

"What if we drift inshore while we're waiting?"

"A chance we have to take. We're gambling big." Von Lappus smiled thinly. "We can always walk home. Might do me good, help me lose a little weight."

Shortly, one of the destroyer's guns belched fire. The shell fell two hundred meters short, woke Kurt.

"Stay awake, boy," von Lappus growled.

Kurt rubbed his eyes. "I'm so tired I don't really care any more," he mumbled. "I want to hurt them because they're keeping me awake. But I never wanted to hurt anybody."

Von Lappus looked at him narrowly. "Take it easy, or you'll earn yourself the big sleep."

The destroyer came on. Three kilometers. Two. One. She wasted no more ammunition, but did keep her guns fixed on *Jäger*. She slackened pace as she drew nearer, until, at a distance of a few hundred meters, she was just making steerage way. She stole past her wounded relative mere meters away, increased speed, turned, came back for another pass. This time, as she drew abeam, the doors of her bridge opened and a half-dozen men with rifles stepped out.

"What? . . ."

"Get down!" von Lappus snapped.

Kurt dropped and buried his head in his arms. The chatter of small arms and the whine of ricochets lasted perhaps a minute.

"Hope the men keep control," the Captain muttered.

The destroyer turned again and made a third pass. The small arms again, worse, then water foamed under her stern and she sped after her fellows, by this time well on their ways north. The sound of distant firing had become a constant grumble.

"What now?" Kurt asked.

"We wait, and hope the salvage ship's unarmed. You can sleep now."

Kurt made a pillow of his arms and weapon, slept. Others prepared, were given their parts in detail. *Jäger* was ready when the salvage ship appeared three hours later.

She was not unarmed, being a tanker with a three-inch mount on her forecastle deck.

Von Lappus woke Kurt and gave him his instructions — he was to lead the operation about to begin. He felt no better for his sleep, nor for the charge placed on him. The latter depressed him. He hoped he would not fail. His own survival would depend on his betraying his ideals. . . .

The oiler approached as cautiously as had the destroyer, but wasted no time making passes. She stopped alongside. Her deck force put fenders over to keep the vessels from injuring each other. She eased closer.

"She must have a full load," Kurt whispered to von Lappus. "Look how low she's riding."

"This's more than I'd hoped for," the Captain replied. "She'll have enough fuel to get us home — assuming we take her and get away clean. She'll be slow."

"They're ready." A dozen Australians jumped to *Jäger*'s maindeck, immediately set about making the two vessels fast. "Now?" Kurt asked.

Von Lappus shook his head. "A couple minutes yet. Let them tie up first. Don't want them to be able to pull away. Oh, hell!" A wish for tears was in his voice. Someone had opened up with a machinegun. "Too soon," von Lappus moaned. "Too goddam soon!" Firing broke out all along *Jäger*'s starboard side. Men were failing and fleeing aboard the Australian. "Go!" the Captain thundered. "Try anyway. Get the wireless room first."

Kurt studied the tall superstructure built over the tanker's stern, spotted what he thought was the wireless room, nodded. Then he was on his feet and running. He burst through a door, sprinted to the side, and, exhilarated, leaped aboard the Australian. Others rushed with him. Small arms chattered, clearing the enemy decks. *Jäger*'s main battery swung around, but remained silent.

"Wieslaw! Fritz! Adolf!" Kurt shouted at three men nearby. "Stick with me!"

He sprayed a ladder with his machine-pistol, climbed it, did the same with another and another. Then he stopped, jerked a door open, plunged through.

Terrified sailors inside were desperately preparing a radio message. Kurt shot the man at the transmitter. Someone shot back, missed Kurt, hit Adolf. Kurt threw himself back out, to one side. Wieslaw chucked a grenade in. A moment later, the wireless and several operators had been silenced forever.

Then up another ladder, to the bridge level.

Someone there had had time to react. Several shots whined past Kurt and his two men. They ducked behind a ventilator.

More shots. Kurt fired back, emptying his weapon. He slipped a new clip in. "Cover me, Wes," he told the nearer of the two.

Wieslaw fired at the door. Kurt crawled toward it, beneath the bullets.

Whang! Something hit the bulkhead a foot above him. He scrambled for the ventilator.

"Over there!" said Wieslaw, pointing. He and Fritz fired several wild shots. Kurt looked. A figure in Littoral white leaned around the signal shack and snapped off a shot. The bullet narrowly missed Kurt's hand.

"Damn! Wes, give me a grenade!" Strangely, he felt none of his earlier fear. He pulled the pin, stood, hurled the grenade across the space between ships. It arced down, wide of its mark by a half dozen meters, plunged into a flag bag. A cloud of torn fabric exploded upward, drifted like holiday confetti.

The gunman quit before Kurt could throw again, a white flash as he slipped over the far side of *Jäger's* signal bridge.

"All right, let's try these people again."

The Pole resumed shooting, with Fritz doing his loading. Kurt crawled forward until he was beside the door of the Australian pilothouse. "Captain?" he called in English. "To surrender this ship you had best."

No answer.

Jäger spoke. Kurt jumped to his feet, startled, saw that the remaining forward five-inch mount had fired on sailors trying to man the oiler's anti-aircraft guns. The mass of smoking wreckage on the tanker's forecastle deck seemed convincing proof of who had whom. . . .

But no. The Australian, still shuddering from the explosion, jerked underfoot, rolled, yawed swiftly. Mooring lines parted with loud reports. Water boiling behind her, the tanker began to pull away.

"Mr. Ranke," Wieslaw called, "they're free. We've got to get off!"

Kurt considered hastily, decided he could not take the ship with the few men already aboard. "Jump!" he shouted.

Wieslaw and Fritz hesitated. "What about Adolf?" one asked.

"Jump!" He fired at the bridge door, turned, hurried to the lower level, where they had left the wounded man. "Adolf, we've got to jump for it. How's your arm?"

"I'll make it—with a little help."

Kurt helped him to his feet. "A long way down," he said, looking over the rail. "Scary."

Shots from above whined past them. Adolf jumped. Kurt leaped behind him, weapon held high.

It seemed an eternity before green water smacked his feet. Below, bullets sent white splashes reaching toward him. . . . He hit poorly, lost the machine-pistol. The wind exploded from him. He nearly drowned as he fought taking a breath, surfaced sputtering, coughed up bitter seawater, struggled in panic—until he remembered Adolf.

Treading water, he looked around. Bullets fell like raindrops, it seemed, though in reality they were few. Others jumped from the tanker. *Jäger* covered them with her lighter weapons. A 40mm mount systematically wrecked the Australian's bridge. The oiler strained desperately at the hopeless task of escape. She was dead, and probably knew it. Surely, when she opened to a range where fires and explosions would no longer endanger *Jäger*, she would receive a fatal shelling.

Blood stained the water in places. As Kurt located Adolf, trying to swim one-armed, he realized sharks would soon gather. Lent strength by sudden fear, he seized Adolf's hair, quickly towed him to *Jäger*'s side. Risking Australian fire, sailors tossed them a line. Kurt looped it beneath Adolf's arms, treaded water while awaiting his own turn to be hoisted up. Above, riflemen already stood by, watching for the first gray, dark-finned torpedo shapes to come gliding in for the feast.

40mm mounts and machineguns nagged the Australian endlessly. Return fire died — the tanker was beyond the range of her small arms. Then, as Kurt drippingly approached the man to explain his failure, von Lappus ordered, "Main battery, fire!" The five-inchers interrupted lighter natter with fiery exclamations. The oiler had managed almost a kilometer, her last. The big shells ripped her open, fired her cargo. Kurt, suddenly ashamed, watched mites of men leap into the sea, only to be received by floating, burning oil. He turned away, forced his mind to business — so much death, so many at his own hand, and he the man who always insisted he would hurt no one. . . .

"Ski, get steam as fast as you can." The Captain's voice betrayed none of his disappointment. Kurt glanced around. The officers had gathered while he brooded. Von Lappus was planning a new move already — in the light of the burning ship he appeared demonic. "Heinrich, see to the wounded. Hoepner, clean and check the guns. Inventory the small arms, see how many we lost."

Far, scarcely audible over the noise of the dying tanker, the Meeting's rumble suddenly redoubled. The Western fighting units had come to rescue the auxiliaries, though for most it was too late. "Ranke, you and I will take us to shore. Heiden, inventory stores. Separate the essentials, especially salt. It'll be a long trek through hot country. . . ." This last was weary, more to himself than his listeners.

As they reached the bridge, Kurt said, "I'm sorry I couldn't manage." Emotionally numbed by what he had done—the shooting, the killing—he had not as yet recognized the full depth of *Jäger*'s plight. The walk home was a matter of theory no longer. The destroyer was too gravely wounded to hazard the sea journey—even providing she evaded Australian capture.

"No matter," said von Lappus, now a sad old man. "You did your best. If only I could find the man who fired that first burst. . . ."

Kurt had a sudden grim suspicion that Marquis was responsible, then decided the man could have no motive. Yet the notion was less insane than High Command operations as a whole. Even after *Ritual War*, he had no idea of the true, modern end toward which that organization worked.

Two hundred quiet, gloomy men labored listlessly to bring *Jäger* inshore, into a cove where she anchored and hoped to be invisible against the jungled background. The guns yet rumbled on the sea, and smoke made a cloud in the north. Dawn's slow-moving rain arrived. In the wet, weary sailors filled the liferafts with stores. Some, unenthusiastic about the long walk ahead, insisted the ship was hale enough to make it home.

On the watery battlefield, Western ships expended their last shells. They had fought bravely in an uncommonly long and savage engagement, and still had numbers in their favor, but could do nothing with empty magazines. One revived the ancient practice of striking colors. Others followed suit, for all escape routes were closed. Gradually, the Australians bunched them up, forced them southward.

Steaming independently, out of sight, *Purpose* and a smaller sister waited for the end. When the battleship's radar repeaters portrayed the disposition of forces directed and desired, she would turn toward the waning battle.

Unaccountably, to Kurt, the sun set that dying day. He had not expected to see its rising, let alone outlive its passage west. Should he thank the Fates for his survival? In those few free moments he obtained during the day, when he was not too busy to think, he dwelt upon what he had done, on faces which had abandoned life before him. All he could do to soothe his conscience, at first, was repeat a silent formula that he had had to do it for his own survival. Yet a small monster with a Karen-voice gleefully mocked in the dungeons of his mind, down in the deep darkness where the evil was imprisoned, loudly reminded him he need not have been here at all. As a consequence, he worked harder than necessary, drowned his conscience in a dizzy wine of fatigue.

And, as men have shown a nearly universal knack for doing, he soon managed a transference of guilt. The true culprit, he convinced himself, was High Command. Without High Command, none need have died, none need have spilled blood to the pleasure of Ares. Thus he reinforced his developed hatred, grew increasingly determined to see the spiders of Gibraltar fall prey in their own web—no matter that he was fifteen thousand kilometers distant and a lone man unequipped to drag them down. As, on leaving Kiel, he had not believed in *Jäger*'s mortality, neither could he accept his own death as a possibility of the journey home.

In weariness, with his conscience temporarily appeased, he slept soundly that night. Not even the threat of Marquis bothered him. Because he feared so much and this interfered with his blithe advance into the future, he had tried to ignore the dangers of the day. By nightfall he had almost forgotten. The wardens of his subconscious kept him in van Lappus's company, or in a crowd, always armed, but at levels of awareness he abandoned the matter to Fate.

In fact, when Marquis did cross his mind, he welcomed the possibility of confrontation. He had things to say to the man, things which had brewed and boiled within him since Otto's death.

Day dawned fair, and Kurt had hopes he might soon set foot on land. As at Rotnagiri, von Lappus had kept him aboard for his own safety. Darkness ashore was too much Marquis's ally, the beachhead too widely dispersed and confused. . . . His hope was stillborn.

Just six kilometers distant, a vast mass of battered ships milled. Through *Jäger's* telescope, Kurt saw they were of both sides, Western ships shepherded by a handful of Australians. Almost every vessel was terribly wounded.

"What's happening?" Hans asked breathlessly, climbing onto the signal bridge.

Kurt turned from the telescope, saw that most of the dozen men aboard had gathered. "I don't know. Strange business. Hope they don't spot us." He did not think they would. Lying parallel to the coast, *Jäger* blended well with her background.

"Look, Kurt!" Hans pointed.

Kurt looked, was too startled to note Hans's renewed familiarity. The High Command battleship, with a smaller cruiser in company, had appeared in the north, perhaps twelve kilometers from the formation. "What now?" Kurt mumbled, turning to Hans.

Wiedermann was pale beneath his tan. He stumbled over his tongue several times, fighting some fierce internal battle, before managing, "Get down from here! Everybody get inside the ship. Engineers' quarters."

His reward was questioning looks, then slow compliance as sailors heeded his urgency. Kurt bent to the telescope again, turned it toward *Purpose*. That vessel's guns swung slowly toward the ships. . . .

"Kurt, come on! Let's get out of here!" Hans seized his arm, pulled him toward the ladder.

Bemused, Kurt wondered why the excitement, supposed Hans had his reasons. He did not like those that came to mind.

As they reached the maindeck, smoke belched from one of the battleship's guns. Hans ran. Kurt followed, ducked inside, went down the ladder to engineers' quarters. . . .

Color faded from the passageway above. It was flooded with raw, overwhelming light. Even several times reflected as it was, it hurt Kurt's eyes. When, after a few seconds, it faded, he found the afterimages almost as blinding. And it was hot, so hot.

"Grab something!" Hans shouted. He threw himself to the deck, braced his body between partitions. Kurt and the others followed his lead, though all faces wore questioning frowns. . . .

There was a roar like all the guns of time firing in salvo, a thunderclap followed by the grumble of a cosmic waterfall. *Jäger* leaped, heeled over, groaned. Air pressure changed radically. Kurt's ears were pits of agony.

"Hang on!" Hans cried. "Tidal wave . . ." It hit, lifted the destroyer, bounced her like a cork, passed on. Kurt started to rise.

"Not yet!" said Hans. "Back blast." That came shortly, a fierce wind from the direction opposite the earlier shocks, though not nearly as bad.

Then Kurt climbed to his feet. He had a dozen bruises and

abrasions; a trickle of blood ran from his nose. "This's where it started," he mumbled. Memories came back. "But natural weather. A bird's cry. A cool north wind. And Man, who would be a god, what hath he wrought?" He suspected, oh, he suspected the worst of evils. He rushed up the ladder, out onto the maindeck.

His worst suspicions were confirmed. A mighty, wicked tower it was, standing where a hundred ships had died, a tombstone tickling the clouds, a huge, phallic mushroom, the thing not seen these past two centuries of War. . . .

"Atomic bomb!" he gasped. The ultimate horror, the bleak black wicked thing of such hated history, such conditioned dread, that even the hardest, most uncaring man watching was permanently turned against High Command.

"Oh, no!" someone cried in a voice of angry tears. Kurt turned, glad someone shared his outrage and dismay. But, he immediately saw, the cry was not for the bomb. It was the eulogy of the crew, the two hundred men who had been camped on the beach—flash, heat, wind, wave had done what the Australians had failed to do, destroyed them utterly. A dozen blinded, dazed, burned men wandered the wrack- and corpse-strewn beach, the holocaust's few survivors. Smoke from seared trees drifted on now still air, a veil for ruin. Kurt noticed how all *Jäger*'s paint, facing the blast, had been blackened and blistered. . . .

He checked his men. Of the dozen who had been aboard, all but two stood with him, staring at the dying mushroom. "Where's the Captain?" he asked. Drawing no response, he shouted, "Captain!"

"Up here." Looking up, Kurt saw von Lappus leaning against the bridge rail. "Mueller's here, too."

"Shall I send the raft ashore, sir?"

"What raft?"

Kurt looked aft. Not only the liferaft, but the accommodation ladder as well had been lost to the wave. They would have to swim.

"Look!" Hans gasped. Kurt turned again. The atomic cloud had begun to disperse, but another event had claimed Wiedermann's breath. Limned by the cloud, a ship staggered landward. She was many times more damaged than *Jäger*. Her masts and stacks were gone, much of her superstructure was destroyed. Her pace was terribly slow, barely steerage way. Though she was little more than three kilometers offshore, it might take her an hour to reach the beach—if she made it at all.

In her grim, determined try for life, Kurt saw an allegory of the struggling race. Mankind was, these days, a ruined, dying vessel in its last desperate hour, grasping for anything to save it from following the dinosaurs into oblivion.

There was little allegorical significance, for Kurt, in the High Command battleship's getting up steam and charging toward the mortally wounded ship. He had, though unconsciously, been expecting something of the sort. From all he had learned since departing Kiel, this was High Command's function: destruction. Once again, the mystery of that organization's purpose plagued him.

The game was hare and hounds—with the hare already half dead. Or cat and mouse, for *Purpose* ignored the quick kill of which her guns were capable. Rather, with her smaller sister tagging kilometers behind, she raced to cut the vessel off. Though this seemed cruelest torture, Kurt suspected there was good reason—perhaps to make certain there were absolutely no escapees. Which bode ill for *Jäger*.

The events of the past few days, of the whole cruise, were

coming to a head in Kurt's soul, he hated, and needed to cause pain. His "How?" in response to Hans's "We've got to help them" was cold, deadly serious. His whole existence, briefly, was bound toward one object, destruction of that battleship.

Hans thought. Obviously, the guns were useless. They would be mosquito bites to that steel leviathan. "The other torpedo!" he declared.

"It's all shot up."

"How do you know? Let's look, at least." Hans grew excited, much as Kurt remembered him when he had gotten a chance to lead in their childhood games — so long ago, that age of innocence, so happy even in gray times. So much he had lost by coming: wife, child, youth . . . He caught Hans's enthusiasm, raced with him to the torpedo deck. Both ignored von Lappus's shouted orders to abandon ship and get far inland before *Jäger* was discovered.

Purpose came implacably onward, would intercept the wounded vessel little more than a half kilometer offshore, would do so in less than fifteen minutes.

"No holes," said Hans, after a quick check of the tube. "You pull the covers. I'll check the firing circuits."

Kurt bent to his task ferociously. The minutes hurtled past. A small, sane part of his mind screamed that this was madness, that he was risking his life on an impossible venture, that he should swim for safety as fast as he could. He ignored that voice. For once he would stand and fight. He tried to forget how he had played the tool in previous stands, ignored the fact that he fought only for anger and hatred — twin heads of a dragon, the same that had gotten this War rolling in the first place.

Hans shouted angrily, inarticulately. Kurt yanked the last of the canvas free, went to his side, discovered the cause of his rage. An aircraft cannon shell had punched a neat hole through the firing box. The test circuits said it was dead. "Kurt, I've got to sink that ship!" said Hans. His intensity was tremendous. "I *have* to. . . ."

As a symbol of his father, like his secret rebellion, his joining Gregor's movement? Or something else? A kaleidoscope of notions swirled through Kurt's mind. From odds and ends came shape, at first fuzzy, then solid certainty: atonement. And Kurt, who had seen Hans suffer so much, for the moment forgave. He had no time, then, to weigh in the balance and see how it tipped. "Open it," he suggested.

Hans did so. The damage was instantly apparent. Two thin wires, color-coded, had been cut by the passing bullet.

"Twist the ends together," said Kurt. He glanced at the battleship, looming huge now. "Hurry. We haven't long." Maybe five minutes if they meant to save the cripple. That vessel continued landward unswervingly.

"I've got the blue ones," said Hans, "but there isn't enough slack in the red."

"Oh, damn!" Scarcely thinking, Kurt dashed to the other tube, ripped its firing box open, yanked out a handful of wire.

"Hurry up!" Hans demanded.

"I'm coming, I'm coming!" As he crossed the deck, he used his knife to pare away insulation. "Here."

Hans snatched the wire, quickly bridged the gap in the circuit. He closed the box. "How deep does her armor run?"

Kurt shrugged. "I don't remember. Try six meters."

"She draws about eleven. I'll go for eight. Contact detonation?"

"Best hope, old as the torpedo is. I'd guess she's doing fifteen knots."

"The circuits are clear. Air pressure up . . ."

"Shoot!" Kurt cried. Something told him the battleship was about to open fire. Worse, he had just seen sudden activity on this side of the warship. *Jäger* had been discovered.

"Go!" Hans shouted. Compressed air *whooshed* the torpedo from the tube. It hit the sea with a great splash and vanished. For a long moment nothing happened, Kurt and Hans felt their hopes toppling—then a trail of bubbles boiling surged toward *Purpose*. The two danced, howled, hugged one another. This was the first time they had done something together and carried it to fruitful conclusion.

The battleship spoke. On her far side, at no more than two hundred meters, the flying dutchman abandoned her unnatural life, disintegrated.

"Hans, we've got to get off!" said Kurt. *Purpose*'s secondary mounts were turning toward them.

The torpedo struck. An immense veil of water rose and momentarily concealed the forward half of the battleship. Water-born concussion and sound hit *Jäger* with almost the fury of the atomic blast. The destroyer groaned. . . . *Purpose*'s bow lifted clear of the sea, fell ponderously back.

Kurt waited to see no more. He ran, leaped from the torpedo deck on the landward side, fell, fell. He was still struggling upward when Hans hit nearby. They surfaced, swam hard.

Something roared, something hit them with a million fists. Agony. A moment later, gasping for breath, Hans said, "Must've been her magazines."

"Swim!" Kurt gasped in reply. He remembered *Purpose*'s smaller sister, now surely dashing in for revenge. They reached land, lay panting on the beach, listened to the ongoing explosions. Kurt rolled onto his back, saw, though *Jäger* blocked part of the view, *Purpose* slowly turn belly upward like some monstrous, dying fish. Her entire bow section had been torn free, stood nose out of the water a short distance off. She was surrounded by swimming men, some of whom tried to climb onto her corpse, some of whom started for the beach. "Hans, we've got to run. . . ."

Something roared overhead and fell into the blasted jungle, exploded. To the north, *Purpose*'s Eastern sister bore down like a fiery dragon, trailing smoke of muzzle blasts. Kurt and Hans staggered to their feet.

"Where're the others?" Hans demanded.

After a thunder of exploding shells, Kurt replied, "Already gone. Grab something to take. Anything."

Without real thought to future needs, they chased about the beachhead, seizing anything portable. Kurt took an abandoned pistol, a rifle, an ammunition box, some loose clothing, his soggy seabag—found lying beneath a decapitated tree. Staggering under the unwieldy load, he hurried into the jungle. Hans was close behind with an equally difficult and inappropriate burden.

Behind them, a salvo fell squarely astraddle *Jäger*. With only a sigh, which might have been for her long-delayed release, she settled to the bottom. Only her mastheads, stacks, and signal bridge remained visible.

The High Command cruiser, which had directed the Australian Gathering, eased to a stop nearby. Some of her men set about rescuing *Purpose*'s crew. Others armed themselves to go ashore. High Command wanted no single lay survivor of this Meeting.

In the jungle, Kurt and Hans, both in pain, hurried along the trail left by *Jäger*'s fleeing survivors. "It's finally over," Kurt gasped. "We're free." But, inside, he knew it was not. There were still a few last moves in the game.

NINETEEN

They lay close, behind a fallen tree, as the High Command landing party passed. Kurt shivered, his teeth chattered, as he peered down the moonlit barrel of his rifle. He tried to convince himself he was cold, but the lie would not stick. The jungle was sweltering. At least fifty men were out there, and he was afraid. He and Hans would have no chance against those numbers.

All day they had vainly sought von Lappus and his party, all day they had listened to the hunters moving close behind them. Finally, unable to continue, they had hidden. Kurt hurt inside. He had wanted to warn the others of the pursuit. His body had failed him. Hans, though wounded, had been able to go on, but had refused to leave him.

As the noise of the High Command rear guard faded, Kurt noticed Hans's breathing was deep and regular.

Moving closer, he saw Wiedermann sleeping, cheek against rifle stock. He should keep watch, but he was just too tired. . . . Yet sleep would not come, once he surrendered—because now he had an opportunity to think, and bleak, sad thoughts kept him awake.

He thought mostly of Hans Wiedermann, this strange little man beside him, who had shared so much of his life, who was such a great unknown. Hans, who had saved his life more than once, and who had tried to take it as often. Hans, he had sadly decided, was Marquis, the killer he had sought so long, Marquis and Brindled Saxon, part of two worlds. And, Kurt suspected, he had played both parts to the hilt, for Hans was that way—yet how had he managed two loyalties?

Though the evidence had been before him for months, Kurt had refused to surrender his suspicions of Haber—he wanted Hans to be innocent, wanted Hans as his friend, wanted for Hans the human things so long denied him—till this morning. Proof of Haber's innocence had come during the assault on the tanker. The sniper, then, had worn enlisted white, not officer's khaki. Then the atomic shell. Only a Political Officer could have expected it, had been intended to survive it.

After fleeing his thoughts through mind-jungles for an hour, he could resist no longer. He shook Hans.

Wiedermann was instantly alert. "What? They spot us?"

"No, they're gone." There was a period of deep silence between them. Hans knew his thoughts. Kurt asked, "Why?"

Hans accepted the question without emotion. Kurt thought he had been misunderstood. Then Hans said, "I really don't know, Kurt. I seem to be two people. What's the word? Schizophrenia? I don't always know what I'm doing, but I know what I've done—though I don't always know why."

His words were soft, neither contrite nor defiant. "I don't understand me. If this were the Middle Ages, I'd call it possession. This morning, for instance. Something hit me, I fired the burst that warned the tanker. Why, I can't explain. I just *had* to. I could've killed myself once I did. I went to the signal bridge, then, to cover you. You were my friend. I didn't want you hurt. And, as I lay there shooting through their pilothouse door, I thought about Karen. I wondered if she'd have me back if you didn't make it. Next thing I knew, you were throwing a grenade at me. Kurt, I don't know why I did it! I must be sick." He tapped his temple.

Kurt found he could not be angry—Hans's flat tone somehow made his explanation acceptable—nor could he hate. Perhaps the emotion and killing that day had burned him out—yet there were scores of long standing to be settled. "What about the others? Otto, Erich, Gregor?"

"And Obermeyer. Can't forget Obermeyer. He hurts the most. The others, at least, I can justify to myself."

"Justify? Go ahead."

"Should I start with Otto? Otto was an accident. He was drunk, wouldn't stay down in the compartment. He woke up after we took him down—several times, in fact. He'd start toward Operations' quarters, to get Hippke—those two hotheads could've ruined the whole resistance program that night— would pass out, and I'd carry him back to bed. The last time, though, he wouldn't pass out. We argued. He called me traitor, pulled a knife, we wrestled around. Then something took control of me. Next thing I knew, Otto was hanging on the lifelines, I had his bloody knife in my hand, and someone was running on the torpedo deck. You. I panicked, ran. I didn't think anyone would believe it was an accident, not with my father a Political Officer and Otto talking like he did at dinner."

Uncertain whether or not to believe, Kurt made no comment. It sounded logical, plausible, and Hans appeared to be making no excuses. On the other hand, he had had more than a year to put together a good story.

"Erich was planned. I didn't go crazy killing him, not till afterward. I didn't want to do it, but they made me."

"Who?"

"The Political Office. They took me to the signal bridge the day before, told me they knew I was in the underground, and, if I wanted to stay alive, I would do what they said. I doubt they cared if I got caught—so long as Erich died. They knew the mutiny was due, wanted it stopped. Erich was the weak spot in the plan. It couldn't work without him. They put every pressure on me possible, even fixed up a radio link, through the battleship and Gibraltar, to Kiel. They made me listen to my father telling me what a disappointment I was. Finally, I gave in. They gave me the note, which was supposed to look like you had written it—they thought the crew would jump you 'cause some men thought you killed Otto, and they wanted you out of the way because, knowing English, you were a threat—and told me to set you up for an argument with Erich. That was easy. Erich was jumpy because the mutiny was so close—he was a coward, never mind all his lies about the freecorps—and you were both short-tempered because of the heat. We all were. But I really wished you no harm. Even though I once hated you for taking Karen, you're the best friend I've got."

Kurt doubted. Now Hans's story did not fit what Beck's notebook said of Marquis. Yet, surely, Hans must know that. He could have prepared something better. So much uncertainty. . .

"Obermeyer . . . that was another mad fit. He went walking one night. I followed him, like a fool asked if he'd resign his commission. He said no. A few minutes later, I came around with a strangled man at my feet. It was just like with Otto, and I panicked again. I covered him with sand and stones, sneaked back into camp, and tried to forget. I don't think anyone ever suspected—but his death's the hardest for me to live with. So pointless . . ."

"And Gregor?" Kurt caressed the trigger of his rifle, mildly tempted, though he suspected he could never use it.

"And Gregor. His was the only death I *wanted*. I was compelled. You see, he was pretty sure I'd killed Otto and Erich—I could sense it by the way he acted whenever we discussed resistance problems. He was very distant, very careful not to tell me anything he didn't want the Political Office to know. At the same time, *they* were putting on the pressure to get me to betray the underground. I knew they were terribly interested in finding a notebook that had belonged to Beck. They were afraid of what was in it, that you might read it. When I saw you give it to Gregor that night, I saw a way out of both my predicaments. I could kill Gregor, saving myself from him, and the notebook would buy me peace from the Political Office.

"There was trouble, especially with Deal Adam, but it worked out. Everything went fine till this morning, when I thought about Karen and shot at you. They'd even accepted me as a trainee, of sorts, which was how I heard about the atomic shell—though I wasn't supposed to know. They spoke English the day they discussed it. You're surprised? It was always my secretest secret, the one thing I had that you didn't, something I had that you couldn't win away. It was one of the few things my father ever gave me, back when he thought I'd follow him into the Office."

Kurt sadly listened. He did not know what to do. For more than a year, now, his hatred, his search for Otto's murderer, had sustained him through trials and boredom. Without it, *Ritual War*, and the futile search for meaning in High Command, he might have sunk into the semicomatose, total apathy characterizing many of the journey's-end crew.

He had found his killer and discovered he did not care as he thought he should. Only feelings of duty, and debt to Otto and Gregor, kept him from that fall. They, at least, deserved avenging in payment for the days of their lives laid waste.

Yet logic and emotion bid him let Hans be. Logic: he would need help and companionship traveling home from this weary night — dawn now, for wan gray light filtered through the leaves above. A gray sky sometimes could be seen, when the branches moved in the growing breeze. Emotional: he wished Hans no harm because he owed the man something in return for taking from him. Curious, he wondered at the bond laid upon them. Never had they been friends, not in the deep way he and Otto had been friendly, yet, in lucid moments, when not trying to hurt each other, they were close as men could be.

He pondered it. Hans sat silently, waiting. Finally Kurt abandoned the problem. Put it off. Maybe it would resolve itself. Always, this was his way. . . . Nothing made sense. He returned to the inconsistencies in Hans's story. He was about to ask a question. . . .

Heavy firing broke the jungle stillness, far, small arms and grenades . . . like, Kurt thought, one of the mighty battles of old. It was scarcely a skirmish by ancient standards, though.

"Come on," said Hans, "let's follow the noise."

Kurt was no less tired than when they had stopped, yet the pause had refreshed his will. He shouldered the pack he had made of his seabag, followed Hans.

Nearly an hour passed. The firing died. Only voices heard kept them from walking into the midst of High Command sailors gathered in a clearing.

"Get rid of your pack," Hans whispered. Both did so, checked their weapons. Then, as learned in games of Boy Volunteer days, they crept toward the voices. But this was no game of steal the flag, and if you're caught, you go to jail. Nor were there any bases. Life was the prize, and all the jungle the playing field. They stopped near the edge of the clearing. There were a dozen High Command sailors in a knot there, and perhaps half as many of *Jäger's* men, seated, hands atop heads. Those were the living. The dead, mostly in black, were everywhere, much more numerous.

From all appearances, von Lappus—who was nowhere to be seen—had pulled a desperate maneuver, had turned on and ambushed his pursuers, and had failed, though three-quarters of the hunters were dead or badly wounded. Kurt did not know how many of *Jäger's* men there had been, though he doubted there were many more than those visible from his hiding place. Von Lappus was the only man he knew to be missing. Most likely, the Captain and others lay dead in the surrounding jungle.

"How should we hit them?" Hans asked.

"What if they're not all here?" Kurt realized he had no question as to the rightness of attack. Strange. Here, violence seemed somehow appropriate. Perhaps because it was a dying place.

"We've got to do something. . . ."

Indeed. The High Command sailors were discussing execution. Kurt shrugged. "Just shoot, I guess." The group, standing separate for their planned bloody purpose, left shipmates out of the line of fire.

"All right. Make sure you're on full automatic," said Hans. "You go from right to left. I'll go the other way."

Shivering as if a sudden coldness had come into the breeze, Kurt glanced right for reassurance—great towering black doubts assailed his mind with burning power. Hans was shooting left-handed, favoring his wounded right arm. . . .

"Hans, take your jumper off."

"Why?"

"Please?"

"Kurt, there's no time for games." Nevertheless, he rose carefully and did as he was asked.

Kurt stared at his unmarked left arm. All these hours he had thought Hans's wound intentional, to destroy the Political Office ID mark. . . . The wrong arm. At sea, suddenly smitten by the fact that Hans was not Marquis—uncertain even if he had committed the murders confessed—Kurt tried to banish his confusion in the press of business at hand. Down deep, the wish to believe innocence, the need for Hans, and motives he could never understand, mixed, swirled like pinwheel colors, and from them came, unrecognized then, forgiveness.

They fired, emptying magazines in long, dread bursts. High Command sailors jerked, danced, fell like marionettes with tangled and broken strings. They reloaded, paused, saw they had done their murderous task well. The enemy was fallen, some groaning—stunned shipmates came to belated life, seized dropped weapons.

Too late.

Fire came from the far side of the clearing, doing unto as had been done. Littoral sailors fell among their captors. Kurt and Hans shot back, lacing the jungle with death. One man in black appeared briefly, staggering. But three live weapons remained.

They exchanged fire for several minutes, to no effect. Bullets tore the vegetation above Kurt, showered him with twigs and leaves. His rifle jammed. Cursing softly, he fought it. No matter what he tried, he could not eject the bent cartridge. He pushed the weapon aside, drew his pistol.

As he did, a submachinegun came to violent life near the enemy position—friendly fire, apparently, for two High Command rifles were quickly silenced. Sounds of a man fleeing followed. Soon, from the far side of the clearing, von Lappus stepped into the open, smoking weapon in the crook of his arm.

Kurt and Hans crossed that graveyard field to meet him. Small it seemed—just large enough to contain the dead and dying. Of the latter there were few, mostly High Command sailors. With a dreamlike feeling of slow motion, of floating, Kurt stepped over blank, familiar faces, shipmates who were strangers now, gone to distant lands. . . .

The day had never been more than gray. Now a drizzle began falling. They stood there, the three, just looking down at the dead and soon-to-die, silent. Surprisingly, von Lappus made the sign of the cross.

"And this's where it ends?" said Hans. It was barely perceptible as a question, purely rhetorical.

The jungle was very still. Only the raindrops made any sound, pitter-pattering on earth and leaves. Kurt watched drops trickle down the cheeks of a seaman named Karl Adolf Eichhorn, like Nature's given tears for the folly of man. Somewhere a jungle bird called tentatively, perhaps seeking a mate lost in the flight from the fighting.

"Well," said Hans, "one long journey done. Must we try another?" The gloom behind his words was as gray as the morning. "Why not end it here?"

Kurt understood. Why prolong their misery by a futile effort to reach home? "No," gesturing with his pistol. "Nothing else matters, but I do have to try to get back to Karen." He turned to fetch his pack.

"Kurt!" von Lappus bellowed, falling into a sudden crouch, lifting his weapon....

Something hit Kurt from behind. He staggered forward, fell, rolled as von Lappus's weapon fired. He aimed, pulled his trigger three times, wildly. Hans had time for a single shrieked "No!" before a bullet smashed his skull.

"You idiot!" von Lappus thundered through tears, "you goddam rock-headed beetle-brained idiot!" He hurled his weapon to the earth. "Not Wiedermann." He fell to his knees beside Hans....

Kurt finished rolling—and there, at the edge of the clearing, trying vainly to push entrails back inside a ruined abdominal wall, was Heinrich Haber, shirtless. Slowly, he toppled forward—and Kurt spied the scar on his left arm.... Here was the source whence Hans's killing orders had come.

Killing. He'd killed Hans. He'd killed Hans. It ran through his mind in an endless chain, and suddenly he knew what Hans had been living since Otto's death. Torment. Mad wanderings through the Dantesque hells of his mind. He wanted death himself. "Hans!" he moaned. "I'm sorry. I thought it was you...."

But Hans was not listening. How do you explain to the dead? How do you tell them, how do you make them understand? He threw himself on Hans as though the corpse were a lover. "No, no, no . . ."

Von Lappus turned away, to see if any of the wounded could be saved, though he knew the search was futile.

Kurt wept a bit, then looked north through rain and tears. Small hope that way, but Karen, and at least a chance for a future.

ALSO FROM GLEN COOK
AND NIGHT SHADE BOOKS

The Starfishers Trilogy

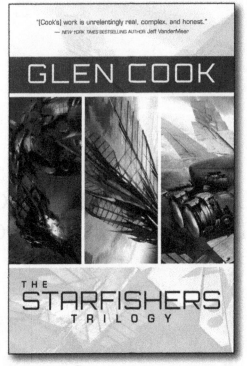

"[Cook's] work is unrelentingly real, complex, and honest."
— NEW YORK TIMES BESTSELLING AUTHOR Jeff VanderMeer

GLEN COOK

THE
STARFISHERS
TRILOGY

978-1-59780-900-9 / Trade Paperback / $24.99

Centuries ago, a private army's deadly strike freed human slaves from their cruel Sangaree masters. A single Sangaree alien survived—and swore vengeance on the Storm family and their soldiers. Generations later, his carefully mapped revenge scheme explodes as the armies of the galaxies collide.

From Glen Cook comes an omnibus edition of his landmark space opera, trilogy, collecting the novels *Shadowline*, *Starfishers*, and *Stars' End* in a seamless blend of ancient myth, political intrigue, and scintillating space combat.

Passage at Arms

978-1-59780-0679 / Trade Paperback / $14.95

The ongoing war between Humanity and the Ulant is a battle of attrition that Humanity is losing. Humans do, however, have one technological advantage—trans-hyperdrive technology. Using this technology, specially designed and outfitted spaceships—Humanity's Climber Fleet—can, under very narrow and strenuous conditions, pass through space undetected.

Passage at Arms tells the intimate, detailed, and harrowing story of a Climber crew and its captain during a critical juncture of the war. Glen Cook combines speculative technology with a canny and realistic portrait of men at war and the stresses they face in combat. *Passage at Arms* is one of the classic novels of military SF.

Find this Night Shade title and many others online at http://www.nightshadebooks.com or wherever books are sold.

The Dragon Never Sleeps

978-1-59780-1485 / Mass Market / $7.99

In *The Dragon Never Sleeps*, Glen Cook delivers a masterpiece of galaxy-spanning space opera. For four thousand years, the Guardships ruled Canon Space with an iron first. Immortal ships with an immortal crew roamed the galaxy, dealing swiftly and harshly with any mercantile houses or alien races that threatened the status quo. But now the House Tregesser believes they have an edge; a force from outside Canon Space offers them the resources to throw off Guardship rule. Their initial gambits precipitate an avalanche of unexpected outcomes, the most unpredicted of which is the emergence of Kez Maefele, one of the few remaining generals of the Ku warrior race—the only race to ever seriously threaten Guardship hegemony.

A Matter of Time

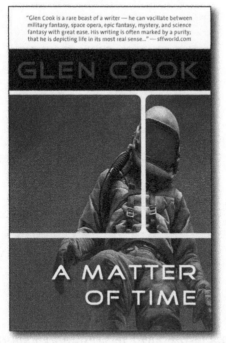

"Glen Cook is a rare beast of a writer — he can vacillate between
military fantasy, space opera, epic fantasy, mystery, and science
fantasy with great ease. His writing is often marked by a purity;
that he is depicting life in its most real sense..." — sffworld.com

GLEN COOK

A MATTER OF TIME

978-1-59780-279-6 / Trade Paperback / $14.99

Originally published in 1985, this classic science fiction novel is
equal parts spy thriller, murder mystery, and time-travel mind-
bender.

May 1975. St. Louis. In a snow-swept street, a cop finds the body
of a man who died fifty years ago. It's still warm. July 1866, Lidice,
Bohemia: A teenage girl calmly watches her parents die as another
being takes control of her body. August 2058, Prague: Three political
rebels flee in to the past, taking with them a terrible secret. As past,
present, and future collide, one man holds the key to the puzzle.
And if he doesn't fit it together, the world he knows will fall to
pieces. It's just *A Matter of Time*!

**Find this Night Shade title and many others online
at http://www.nightshadebooks.com
or wherever books are sold.**

Darkwar

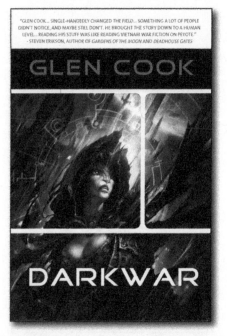

978-1-59780-2017 / Trade Paperback / $16.99

As the world grows colder with each passing year, the longer winters and deepening snows awaken ancient fears within the Degnan Packstead: fears of invasion by desperate nomads, of attack by the witchlike Silth, who kill with their minds, and of the Grauken, a desperate time when intellect gives way to cannibalistic instinct.

For Marika, a loyal young pup, times are dark indeed, for the Packstead cannot prevail against these foes. But stirring within Marika is a power unmatched in all the world, one that may not just save her world, but allow her to grasp the stars themselves . . .

Darkwar collects the epic science fantasy novels that originally appeared as *Doomstalker*, *Warlock*, and *Ceremony*.

A Cruel Wind

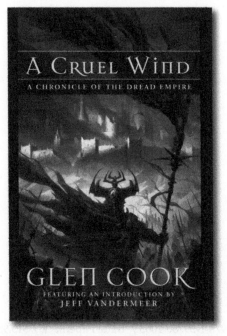

978-1-59780-1041 / Trade Paperback / $16.95

Across the Dragon's Teeth mountains, beyond the reach of the Werewind and the fires of the world's beginning, above the walls of Fangdred castle, stands Wind Tower, from which the Star Rider summons the war that even wizards dread—one fought for the love of Nepanthe, princess to the Storm Kings . . .

Before the Black Company . . . there was the Dread Empire, Glen Cook's enormously influential first foray in fantasy worldbuilding. *A Cruel Wind: A Chronicle of the Dread Empire* is an omnibus collection of the first three Dread Empire novels: *A Shadow of All Night's Falling*, *October's Baby*, and *All Darkness Met*, and features an introduction by Jeff VanderMeer.

A Fortress in Shadow

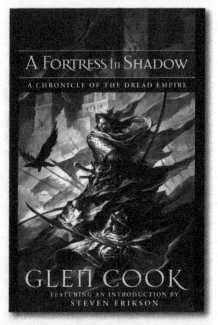

978-1-59780-1003 / Trade Paperback / $15.95

In the vast desert, a young heretic escapes death and embarks on a mission of madness and glory. He is El Murid—the Disciple— the savior destined to build a new empire from the blood of his enemies, who vows to bring order, prosperity, and righteousness to the desert people.

But all is not as it seems, and the sinister forces pulling the strings of empire come into the light. Who or what lies behind El Murid's vision of a desert empire?

A Fortress in Shadow collects *The Fire in His Hands* and *With Mercy Toward None*, which together make up the prequel series to the Dread Empire, and features an introduction by Steven Erikson.

Wrath of Kings

978-1-59780-938-2 / Hardback / $34.99

The Dread Empire spans a continent: from the highest peaks of the Dragon's Teeth to the endless desert lands of Hammad al Nakir; from besieged Kavelin to mighty Shinsan . . .

The time of the wrath of kings is close at hand. Bragi Ragnarson, now the king of Kavelin, has decided to join forces with Chatelain Mist, the exiled princess of Shinshan looking to usurp her throne. But in the deserts on the outskirts of the empire, a young victim of the Great Eastern Wars becomes the Deliverer of an eons-forgotten god, chosen to lead the legions of the dead.

Wrath of Kings collects the final Dread Empire trilogy (*Reap the East Wind, An Ill Fate Marshalling,* and *A Path to Coldness of Heart*) into a single volume.

An Empire Unacquainted with Defeat

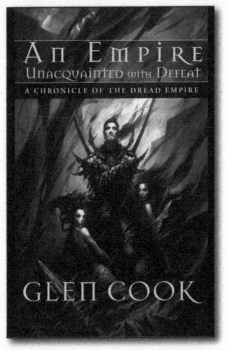

978-1-59780-1881 / Trade Paperback / $14.95

The Swordbearer

978-1-59780-1508 / Trade Paperback / $14.95

A young boy's dreams of glory and war turn into a bitter nightmare as his father's kingdom is overrun by an invading army, led by the Dark Champion Nevenka Nieroda and his twelve Dead Captains, the Toal.

Lost and alone in the woods, with his family slaughtered—or worse—Gathrid finds Daubendiek, the Great Sword of Suchara, a restless and thirsty ancient weapon that promises him the ability to claim his vengeance. But as Gathrid begins to take that vengeance, he comes to realize the terrible price that the sword will demand of him. Enemies soon become allies and strange bedfellows abound as the prophesies of an age swirl into chaos.

Find this Night Shade title and many others online at http://www.nightshadebooks.com or wherever books are sold.

Sung in Blood

978-1-59780-5056 / Trade Paperback / $14.99

For three centuries the city of Shasesserrehas has been kept safe from harm, shielded by the wizardry of its legendary Protector, Jehrke Victorious. Those many generations of calm, however, have just come to a calamitous end: the Protector has been murdered.

Immediately, it falls to Rider, Jehrke's son, to take on his father's responsibilities as Protector of the City and to avenge his death. Rider and his cohorts must utilize their every resource—wits, swords, and magic—against the vile minions of the devious dwarf Kralj Odehnal and his terrifying and merciless master, the wicked eastern sorcerer Shai Khe, who conspires to conquer Shasesserre and rule the world with an iron fist.

Glen Cook is the author of dozens of novels of fantasy and science fiction, including the Black Company series, the Garrett Files, Instrumentalities of the Night, and the Dread Empire series. Cook was born in 1944 in New York City. He attended the Clarion Writers Workshop in 1970, where he met his wife, Carol. "Unlike most writers, I have not had strange jobs like chicken plucking and swamping out health bars. Only full-time employer I've ever had is General Motors." He currently makes his home in St. Louis, Missouri. *The Heirs of Babylon* was Cook's debut novel, first published in 1972.